Time of Our Lilac Love

Norma Jean Lutz

NUWS Link, Inc. Publishing

ISBN: 978-1-947397-12-5 - print

ISBN: 978-1-947397-13-2 - digital

NUWS Link, Inc. Publishing

8703-R North Owasso Expressway

Ste. 143

Owasso, OK 74055

You can connect with Norma Jean here:

https://njnotations.myshopify.com/

normajean@beanovelist.com

http://www.beanovelist.com/

Contents

Chapter 1

Helen's task of pulling out basting threads proved to be the easiest task in the Briggs Tailor Shop. The more difficult tasks were the dresses and men's suits that required neat, even, tiny stitches. Her shoulders ached after just one single hour of the detail work.

That morning, the lively melody of the calliope came blasting over the still March air as she pulled basting threads from a heavy wool coat Irma Briggs had pieced together the day before. While Irma's attitude as an employer was ever fair, still she permitted no dilly-dallying. Even though Helen longed to go outside, run down the main street of Chancey's Bend to the crude landing and watch the fancy showboat dock, she must remain seated and continue pulling threads.

This particular showboat, *Pleasures A-Plenty,* announced their pending arrival with posters pasted on buildings and flyers handed out around town. A stack of those flyers now lay on the front counter of the tailor shop. Only a few remained as the stack had shrunk throughout the previous weeks. Except for a few hardline Baptists who held that all forms of theater entertainment were of the devil, the arrival of the showboat excited everyone in Chancey's Bend.

Helen had once heard someone say that the calliope's throaty sounds carried for over six or seven miles. That bit of information had to have come to her sometime in the past year since she and her mother, along with her younger sister and brother, had moved to town. Before that, her knowledge of showboats, and even that of the calliope, had been vague. Only bits of hearsay from their farmer neighbors.

Sunshine poured in through the window of the back room, warming Helen's shoulders as she worked. Signs of spring showed in the soft green budding of the trees and the daffodils peeking their slender stems up from the cold Kentucky soil. Winter had come hard that year and many a day Helen resorted to stuffing scraps of fabric into the window casing to stop the frigid air from seeping in. She was never sure whether it was better to sit by the window for the advantage of the light, or move her chair and work table closer to where Sid might be working with the mangle-iron in the presser room, trading off light for the warmth. But today, she had both—light and warmth.

From the sounds of talk and laughter in the street she was sure the boat had docked. People were headed to the landing to get a good look. At midday there would be a parade starring their brass band all decked out in spiffy red and gold uniforms. At least she'd be able to see them through the window. Even though she was in the back room of the shop, the view from her window was of the street between their shop and the café.

It was still early morning when Helen caught sight of a tall figure of a man, carrying a large bundle in his arms, stepping briskly down the street toward the tailor shop. His starched white shirt, red bow tie, red suspenders, and captain's hat gave away his identity—Captain Milton Coopwood, known as Coop.

Helen remembered him from the previous summer as the *Pleasures A-Plenty* traveled north to their winter quarters in Henderson. Mostly she remembered his booming voice, which she now heard again as the bells on the front door jingled.

"Anybody home?" he called out. "I'ma looking for the best tailors this side of the Alleghenies. Wouldn't trust nobody else."

Chuckling to herself, Helen knew full well that Sid and Irma were right there and there was no need for the loud greeting. When she first met Coop, he'd told her, "On the river we speak in volumes because it's a noisy place."

She knew however, that his sweet soft-spoken wife, Opal, held to no such views.

The bundle under Coop's arm was work, for which they were all thankful. Business in a small-town tailor shop can be mighty slow in winter. Showboat costumes get hard use and are in constant need of repair.

"Opal can do some," Coop explained, "but she can get kinda stubborn if I stack too much work onto her shoulders. I sure don't know why you folks moved all the way out here from Cincy. You was closer to me there."

Helen heard Sid laugh. She knew the answer. Same one he always gave when people asked why they moved to Chancey's Bend. "Winter comes later and leaves sooner."

Helen knew Sid Briggs hated winter.

Almost holding her breath, Helen waited, praying she'd be called up to the front. And in a few minutes the magic happened. At the sound of her name, she carefully folded the wool coat to where she could easily see where she left off, then stood up and stretched. Even at mid-morning, she was stiff from sitting.

"Helen, come look," Irma said as Helen pushed through the crimson velvet curtains that cordoned off the back room. "This is your specialty."

Irma held up a flaming red dress, decked with a voluminous tulle overskirt, each layer trimmed in delicate lace. The lace had come loose and tears appeared in the tulle. Another dress sparkled from an array of spangles from top to bottom—also in need of loving attention.

The sleeve of a men's suitcoat had pulled loose. "Happened as the hero snatched the heroine from the arms of the villain," Coop explained as he poked his fingers through the hole to show them. "I heard it rip from the wings as I was waiting to go on. I knew it meant safety pins till we got to Chancey's Bend."

Helen could never be sure if Coop was sincere, or simply a lot of bluster when he bragged about their shop. But Sid did say they seemed to hold all the needed repairs until they arrived there. It didn't really matter. The joy of extra income said it all.

After the contents of the bundle had been spread out on the counter, the work estimated, and the bill tallied, Coop reached in his pocket and drew out a handful of tickets.

"Do I rightly remember, you got family who'll want to come?" he asked, looking straight at Helen.

How could he remember such details after all these months? Embarrassed, she could only nod. She was embarrassed to say she needed nine. In her kindly fashion, Irma spoke up for her. "She'll be needing nine tickets, Coop."

Counting them out, Coop handed them to her. "Enjoy the show, Sweetie. All the troupe thanks you for your work."

Before Coop took his leave, Sid ask him about war news. The newspapers that arrived in Chancey's Bend were often a week or more behind the times. Coop, on the other hand, would have the most updated facts. "Do you believe President Wilson that he can keep us out of the war?"

Thoughtfully smoothing his mustache, Coop said, "I know he meant it. But that was before those Huns started sinking every vessel afloat. That's just heartless cruelty. How could anyone commit such atrocities?"

"When they torpedoed the Lusitania in fifteen," said Sid, "we all thought that was the moment of reckoning. It's been almost two full years, but here we are still letting them get away with it."

"You saying you want war, Sid?" Coop asked.

Sid pulled off his glasses and pinched the bridge of his nose. After a long pause, he said, "I don't know, Coop. I sure enough don't know. No one wants to send their boys off to die. But how else we gonna stop those murderous monsters?"

"I know you're right, but I keep praying that we can let the Huns and the Brits fight their own fights without sucking us in."

Now Irma spoke up. "That's exactly how we're praying as well. We know it's not the German people doing all this killing. It's mean-hearted leaders. God willing those perky Brits will crush Germany and it'll all be over."

"I like that reasoning. And I heartily agree." Coop tipped his hat. "I'll be seeing you all tonight. Enjoy our fabulous show. It's better than ever. Good talent just seems to be drawn to *Pleasures A-Plenty.*"

Once Coop was gone, Irma dealt out the tasks. The one who finished first would lend a hand to the others. Helen felt almost giddy when the red tulle was handed off to her. Stepping over to the trays holding an array of spools of thread, she found the matching red and returned to the back room. Soon, the bigger table was brought out and Sid and Irma joined her.

Helen enjoyed these times. It meant she'd hear more stories about the days when the Briggses owned their larger shop in Cincinnati. That was before their children grew up, married, and moved away.

"That place became more headache than we needed," Irma explained. "And the city just kept getting bigger and bigger."

"Swallowing us up, it was," Sid agreed.

Helen worked as they talked, fingering the fine lace and creating hidden stitches to reattach where it had come loose, and wondering what it would feel like to wear such finery. Before Pa died, before they moved to town, she and Ma worked with coarse wool fabric and inexpensive cotton prints. She'd never seen or touched tulle before starting work at the shop. Nor silk either. And very little lace.

While she never for a moment welcomed Pa's horrible death from typhoid, still and yet, she couldn't help but wonder what her life would have been like had they never left the farm. Of course, Pa loved her. He had loved all of his family, but he was a stern, quiet, unemotional man of few words. Never in her life did she have an actual conversation with him. Nothing like what she enjoyed with Sid and Irma. She could never imagine Peter Heise striding down the street like Captain Coop wearing a red bow tie and red suspenders. And bellowing words as opposed to simply talking in a normal voice.

As Pa lay dying, surrounded by his family, he confessed to them that the rent on the farm was delinquent. Even in his agony, it was as though he needed to clear his conscience. But Ma, through her tears, told him to quiet his fears. She kept assuring him that God would watch over them. And that she had no plans to work the farm after he was gone. That seemed to bring the peace he needed and within a few hours of that confession, he was gone.

Chapter 2

To Helen's everlasting delight, as soon as the sounds of the brass band filled the air, Sid jumped up and declared, "We need to take a breather. What say you? Mother? Helen?" Cocking his head and making a silly quizzical expression, he added, "Me thinks a parade might be on the way. Let's go see."

Pulling on wraps against the chilly March wind, they stood on the board walk in front of the shop and watched the band pass by. The entire town turned out. And of course, school let out early. It was quite clearly, a holiday. The lively music brightened their spirits. At the tail end of the parade were two acrobats, a man and a woman. He effortlessly lifted her and held her upright as she stood on his palm with one foot, then flipped high in the air. He caught her as she came down, and the crowd gasped and then cheered and clapped.

Alongside them came a man dressed in a clown costume, leading his trained donkey. As they walked along, the donkey abruptly stopped and plopped down. The clown cavorted around with wild gestures and much yelling. Then he stepped behind to push the donkey's rump in an effort to get him to get up and move. As he pushed, seemingly with great effort, the donkey suddenly jumped up and the clown sprawled face-first in the dirt.

All the way up River Road they marched until they reached the point where the railroad tracks intersected, then turning around and returning. At the main intersection in the middle of town, they stopped and Coop, carrying a red-tasseled baton, shouted, "This is just a small taste of what our show will offer tonight, folks. Doors open at six-thirty; show starts at seven. Don't be late. Hurry to get a seat before we're all sold out. You think *Pleasures A-Plenty* is just a name? No siree. Not on your life. It's our promise to you. And we never go back on our promise."

Twirling the baton with the golden globe head, he directed the band to resume playing and back down to the dock they marched. Looking backward up the street toward the railroad tracks, Helen saw her mother, her younger siblings, along with her aunt and cousins standing on the board walk. She wanted to give a big, wild wave, but thought it not ladylike to do so. Nevertheless, she was quite pleased that the little ones were allowed to be included in the festivities.

By four-thirty, Sid, Irma, and Helen were tearing off large sheets of brown wrapping paper from the roll, and spreading it across the front counter. As they wrapped and tied up each garment in neat bundles, they felt quite proud of their day's work.

"Think you can handle these and take them down to the showboat?" Sid asked Helen as he snipped a length of string, securing the last parcel.

The question surprised her. Of course, she could handle them. Just the thought of stepping onto that boat again, thrilled her to no end.

When *Pleasures A-Plenty* came through last fall, she remembered the excitement of walking across the stageplank at the landing to enter and watch the show. But back then she was entering in along with the crowd. Now she would be stepping on board all by herself. A shiver of delight ran all through her.

Donning hat, gloves, and shawl, she let Sid pile the bundles into her arms and hold the door open for her. She could barely see around them, but she didn't care.

"Watch your step at the landing," he warned. "Best you wait till someone sees you and comes to your rescue."

Nearing the second block of River Road, she could see the showboat sitting proudly ahead of her. Glittering from top to bottom, all in bright white, trimmed in delicate grillwork, the name, *Pleasures-A-Plenty* painted in green lettering nearly two feet high on the upper deck. The site nearly took her breath away. A more beautiful thing, she believed she'd never seen.

The sound of voices and laugher rang out as she approached the beer hall. Old geezers habitually sat on the benches outside like a row of gossiping windbags. And some people would say women were the primary gossipers. Helen had her own opinions about that. She heard enough, not only in the shop, but in Jarrett's Mercantile. The menfolk were always jawing about something.

What caught her attention, wasn't the customary grouping of old men, but the young man conversing with them. His tan fedora and smartly-fitted, camel-colored overcoat marked him as what Pa would have called a *city slicker*. But Helen knew exactly who he was. It was Brett Lochlann, son of Conway Lochlann, owner of Lochlann's Hardware Store.

From what she'd heard, the younger Lochlann had just arrived home from two years of studies at some kind of music conservatory in Cincinnati. She knew he was a pianist because he played in church just last Sunday. His playing put Mrs. Bechtel's in the shade. Mrs. Bechtel played ordinary chords. Brett's fingers were all over the keys, from one end of the piano to the other. The entire congregation sat up and took notice.

As Helen drew nearer, she could hear the conversation.

"That steam-driven pushback be too much for those little lily fingers of your'n," one of the older men was saying. "They ain't made for a light touch."

Helen wasn't sure what was going on, but she had to pass right by them. It couldn't be avoided. Quickening her step, she made as though she were in a rush, which actually she was.

"Here now," Brett said as she approached, "we have an objective observer." Stepping right in front of her, he blocked her way.

"Miss, we need your input. These men are casting wagers that I am unable to play that calliope down there." As he waved his hand toward the showboat, he accidentally jostled the top parcel from her grip. It landed at his feet.

"Oh, clumsy me." Stooping to fetch it, he said, "Here, let me take those. I take it you're headed to the boat?"

He took the load from her which was quite a relief. It'd been tricky holding them and navigating the uneven board walk.

"You're from the tailor shop and these are costumes. Am I correct?"

Helen could only nod. How did he know she was coming from the tailor shop?

"This is perfect timing, Miss. Please give us your unbiased opinion. Your objective viewpoint. Do you believe I can play the calliope on *Pleasures A-Plenty*?"

In an attempt to find her voice, she cleared her throat a bit. "I would have no way of knowing if you can or cannot," she ventured. "All I know is that Coop's wife, Opal, plays the calliope and seems to do quite well."

At that, Brett Lochlann let out a peal of laughter that seemed to fill the entire street. Tipping his hat with his free hand, he said to the beer-hall jury, "There you have it, gentlemen. If a lady can handle those steam-driven keys, I guess I can as well." Replacing his hat, he added, "Hope you didn't squander too much of your hard-earned cash."

Offering his arm to Helen, he said, "Come now, we mustn't keep the showboat crew waiting."

Opal Coopwood intercepted Helen and Brett as they came across the muddy landing bridged by the stageplank. Hailing them with warm greetings she took the parcels from Brett and directed him to the stairs at the hinder part of the boat.

"Up that way, Brett. I'll be with you in a minute. You're gonna have a gay old time with that noise maker."

With a nod, he thanked her. "I'm ready to give it a turn. I conquered a pipe organ in Cincinnati. Can't be that different." To Helen, he said, "Your positive input back there was appreciated." He jabbed a thumb toward the beer hall.

She managed to give him a quiet "You're welcome," though she still found it almost impossible to speak to him.

"And your name is?"

"I'm Helen. Helen Heise."

"Well, Helen. I'll be seeing you another time then." And he was gone.

I'm not sure when, where, or why that could ever happen, Helen thought.

Adjusting the packages in her arms, Opal said, "Helen, do you have a few minutes to spare? There's someone I want you to meet."

Now that was a surprise. Helen had no idea who on the showboat Opal would want her to meet. She really didn't have minutes to spare. The family was expecting her at the house.

"I should be getting on home. Mother will be looking for me."

"What if we send the cabin boy with a message that you're being delayed? That should settle her mind."

Helen nodded. Still mystified.

"This way, then."

Helen followed Opal into the boat's interior, through the resplendent, but now empty, auditorium. With no distractions, Helen was free to soak in the beauty of the velvet crimson seats, and the decorative ceiling complete with brilliant golden overlay. Yes, she was gawking, but no one was around to notice.

Midway down the sloping auditorium, Opal turned right, through the rows of seats to the far side. She opened a door that Helen had never noticed was there. Through the door they went up a flight of stairs and out another door which led to the upper deck. Rather like a back porch, the deck was set about with wicker chairs and tables along with large potted palms. Several white bird cages hung from the ceiling of the deck roof, where yellow canaries greeted them with cheerful songs.

Opal waved to one of the chairs. "Have a seat. I'll just be a minute. These need to be deposited in the state rooms." Disappearing around the far side of the deck, she left Helen alone to take in the view.

From this upper deck she could see all the way across Chancey's Bend, past the town to the wooded hills beyond. The hills where she and her sister, thirteen-year-old Alice, loved to wander and explore. From this point, she was almost as high as when she climbed Watson's Bluff.

Chancey's Bend's early settlers chose a perfect spot at the bend in the Chancey River where the river widened and the current slowed. Tucked into a valley, the town was surrounded by rounded, wooded hills. When she was a small girl, and the family ventured into town to purchase supplies, the town seemed huge and a little overwhelming with all the traffic and activities. Now that she was nineteen, and lived and worked here, that overwhelming feeling had dissipated. Now the town seemed small and ordinary. She longed to see cities like St. Louis and Cincinnati.

Rather than sitting down, Helen walked over to the guard rail which ran the length of the deck. Leaning back a bit, and looking upward, she could see the third deck and the texas from which the captain steered the boat. Though she was unable to see it, she knew the calliope was up there as well.

Behind the *Pleasures A-Plenty* was docked the steamboat, *Odyssey*. Helen knew this provided the steam power that pushed the showboat up and down the river. She'd not had a good look at it last summer when they docked, but here it was in all its glory. Not as glamorous as the showboat, but a hardworking vessel.

After a few moments, Opal reappeared with Ralphie, the cabin boy in tow. Helen didn't think she'd ever seen a skinnier boy in all her life. Pa would have called him a *beanpole*. His overalls were too short and his wrists hung past the sleeves of his red-plaid flannel shirt. While the clothes were too small, the work shoes were too big, giving him a clown appearance.

Following introductions, and after Helen had given Ralphie the exact directions to Aunt Linnie's house, he was on his way with a written message of why Helen was detained.

Once again, Opal waved Helen toward two chairs that were situated on either side of a small table decorated with a Mason jar filled with red and yellow wild flowers. Helen found every detail to be more charming than she'd ever imagined. Who would have believed the other part of showboat would be so homey?

Once they were seated, Opal said, "Thank you for staying, Helen. I think you know we all appreciate your talents as a seamstress."

Helen was sure Opal referred to Sid and Irma. "We strive to please our customers. The Briggs have a long history of..."

"I know they're talented as well," Opal interrupted, "but I've noticed your style. I can pretty much tell your work over the others."

Helen felt her face go hot and flushed. No one had ever complimented her in quite this forward a manner. She had no reply.

Opal continued as though a reply was unnecessary. "We have a new addition to our lineup this season. You may have read about her in our circulars. Her name is Cat Callahan. She's starred on the Broadway stage and she's decided to take a break this summer."

Helen had seen the woman's picture on the flyer, but had paid little attention to it.

"You may know that oftentimes stage stars come to work on the showboat because it's an easier life than traveling from one city to another on the summer theater circuit."

Helen didn't know. She had no idea.

"Cat has an idea for a new costume," Opal was saying. "I want her to tell you about it. To describe it. And you can then let her know if you think you can create it."

Back on the farm, it had been Helen's job to sew the family's clothing. From shirts for Pa and Seth, to dresses, aprons, and even the undergarments for her and Ma and Alice. Once Ma realized Helen had the knack, she left off sewing entirely, except for the mending, and let Helen take over.

"Are you willing to give it a try?"

Helen nodded. She seemed unable to carry on a clear conversation. This was too bewildering. But she did manage to say yes, she was willing to try.

At that moment, the door to the deck opened and in walked the most beautiful human being Helen had ever seen. Tall and willowy, she moved with grace and poise. The picture on the advance posters and flyers did her very little justice.

Chapter 3

H elen made a move to stand up, but the lady said, "Oh please, don't get up. Here. I'll just draw another chair over. Make this a cozy little threesome. Right, Opal?"

"Of course. Helen, this is Cat Callahan. Cat, this is Helen, the highly talented seamstress I told you about."

After pulling a chair close to the other side of the small table, Cat extended her hand and Helen returned the handshake. The hand was soft as a suede glove.

"Please to meet you, Helen. I'm in a real pickle being so far from New York and my regular tailors. But I've come up with this marvelous idea for a costume and I don't want to wait till the end of the season."

"Cat here is our soubrette between scenes," Opal explained, "in addition to being our star ingenue."

Helen saw no similarity to a cat. This Broadway star's face, painted with arching eyebrows, black-rimmed eyes, cheeks flushed with rouge, and red cupid-bow lips, was framed in soft curls that shone like spun gold. Her sheer, pale-blue fitted bodice was tucked into a navy pencil-skirt, which worked to define her tiny waist. Helena was quite certain Cat had never milked a cow, walked behind a plow pulled by a team of horses, weeded a garden, or gathered eggs while fighting off setting hens who loved to peck bare skin.

It took all Helen's will power not to gawk.

"The needed costume will be for my solo numbers," Cat was saying in a voice sweet as honey. "I have a sketch right here. I'm not much of an artist, but I believe you can get the idea."

From her skirt pocket, she drew out a paper. Unfolding it, and laying it on the table in front of them, she said, "This is my idea. Great puffed lace sleeves, snug bodice with a satin sash tying in the back with a large bow. The full skirt will be shorter in front swooping down into a ruffled train. Each tier edged in lace. What do you think?"

Helen's face felt hot. The ladies' eyes were on her, studying her. Waiting for her response. What was she supposed to say? Where would she get the materials? Where would she work? How would she find the time? How would Irma and Sid feel about it?

"You don't have to answer just this minute," came Opal's gentle voice. "I'm sure this is quite a surprise. It's fine if you want to think about it."

Cat sat up a little straighter. Looking over at Opal she said, "But I'd really like to have it soon. At least before St. Louis."

Ignoring Cat, Opal said to Helen, "You'd receive a handsome payment. Think about this, it would serve you well as a testament to your abilities."

"I just want to know if you're able," Cat put in. "It's a complicated undertaking."

Now Helen spoke up. She'd put together much more complicated articles and she knew exactly how she'd create this costume. "I would need your measurements."

Cat turned the paper over. "I already thought of that. I'm quite accustomed to working with tailors."

The measurements had been carefully scripted on the paper. "I can have the cloth ordered and sent by train from Cincinnati. Arriving day after tomorrow."

Beneath the measurements—which Helen recognized, having worked with similar numbers many times—was written out other numbers.

Pointing to the other numbers, Cat said, "Five dollars. That's the price I'm willing to pay for your work." Laying a dollar bill on the table and scooting it over to Helen, she said, "This is my deposit. The other four dollars will be wired you to when I receive the finished product."

Helen could scarcely breathe. She'd never earned money of her own before. Of course, she earned a salary at the shop, but that was different.

When she could finally speak, she said, "Perhaps I could ask Irma and Sid if they might allow me to use the shop after hours."

Opal gave a soft clap of her hands. "Oh, that's a wonderful idea, Helen. If you need me to put in a good word, you just let me know. I've become fast friends with the Sid and Irma." Then she added, "And we do give them plenty of extra business on our way through."

Helen didn't think she'd need Opal's input. She was pretty sure she could handle making the request on her own. It'd only be for a few evenings. And they closed early on Saturdays. A few more hours would be available then.

Cat pushed back her chair and stood. "A deal then?"

Helen wondered if they could hear her heart pounding. She nodded. "Yes." Clearing her throat, she added, "I accept your offer."

"I'll send Ralphie to the telegraph office to dispatch my fabric order."

"It's at the train station," Opal offered. "But Ralphie knows where to find it."

"I'm off then," Cat said. Handing the paper to Helen, she added, "See you at the show tonight." And with that she stood and walked away with a regal poise that must stem from many stage appearances. As Cat disappeared through the door, Helen tucked the dollar bill into her handbag.

Brett did indeed play the calliope. As she left the boat, Helen heard that musical steam machine pumping out lively strains of *Oh Susanna*. She smiled to herself, wondering how much money changed hands at the beer hall. When she walked by the place, the chairs and benches out front were empty, the previous occupants had no doubt gone home to supper.

Helen knew supper was waiting for her at the Gabler house. Her food would be in the warming oven. Ma would make sure of that. Even before they came to live with Aunt Linnie and Uncle Osborn, the Gabler household was a noisy place. Now it was even more noisy. And crowded. Seems a ruckus was brewing every hour or so. Plus, their terrier Wooly added to the chaos.

Helen never minded. In fact, she loved the entire Gabler family, but it concerned her that the four of them served up an extra burden. Aunt Linnie, who was Ma's sister, insisted they were no bother. Helen never believed her. Love can only go so far with so many mouths to feed.

Helen and Ma, along with Alice and Seth slept in the attic. Uncle Osborn had gone to great lengths to fix it up, building a sizeable partition to create two rooms. It allowed Seth to have his own space away from the females. At twelve, he needed a little privacy. Helen and Alice shared a bed, while Mama and Seth each had their own beds. The bedsteads had been brought from the farmhouse. As had the bureau and the washstand. A few things were salvaged before the landlord insisted they vacate the farm.

If Ma missed having her own house, and most especially her own kitchen, she never complained. Who knew where they would have ended up if the Gablers hadn't taken them in?

Once the sun waned, the temperature had dropped. Helen welcomed the warmth of the Gabler kitchen, and the aroma of stew met her. The little ones came running to meet her.

LeRoi, who was nine got to her first. "The tickets. The tickets. The tickets," he belted out in a crazy sing-song voice. "Can we see the tickets?"

"Please Helen," echoed Mindy Mae who was seven. "Can we?" Mindy Mae seemed to dance rather than walk. Tripping across the kitchen, she said, "Are they in your pocket? Your dress pocket? In your handbag? In your shawl?"

Shy Esta Belle whose age was between her brother and sister hung back watching. But Helen knew she was just as excited.

Through the door that led to the front room Helen could see Alice curled up on the sofa. She had a book in her hands—as usual. She and Alice shared a love of books. Especially books filled with poetry. From where Helen stood, she could see the book was one of Sandburg's. Alice looked up and gave a smile and a little wave.

From her handbag, Helen drew out the bright red tickets and spread them on the kitchen table. "One for each of us," she said. "And in the front twelve rows. Special seats."

They stared at the tickets, but no one touched them. It was as though they were awestruck. Helen knew they were dreaming of what excitement the evening would hold.

"Take off your wraps, Helen," Ma said. "I'll get your supper."

"I'm sorry to be so late."

"The boy came," LeRoi said. "He delivered a message from you right to our doorstep." His dark brown eyes flashed as he talked.

"That was Ralphie," Helen said as she hung up her hat and shawl on the hall tree hooks. "He's the cabin boy."

"I want to be a cabin boy," LeRoi said. "He didn't look like he was much older than me."

As Aunt Linnie came into the kitchen, LeRoi ran to her. "Mama I want to be a cabin boy on the showboat. Can I be a cabin boy? Can I please? Will you let me? Huh?"

Aunt Linnie put her arms around her son and ruffled his dark-brown curly mop of hair. "I don't see any reason why not. You can be anything you want to be. But let's get you through a few years of school first."

The bowl of stew held a small portion. Helen was thankful for Ma's corn-pone slathered in butter to make up for the lack of a large helping of stew.

As she was eating, Seth and Uncle Osborn came in the backdoor ushering in a whoosh of cold air. Once they had moved in town from the farm, Uncle Osborn had quickly taken Seth under his wing. The two had been working on another project out in the shop. Osborn Gabler's reputation as a builder, and as one who created most anything from wood, was known not only Chancey's Bend, but the surrounding region. The two were covered in sawdust, which Aunt Linnie scolded them for not dusting off out on the back porch.

"Hurry now. Get cleaned up. We can't be late."

Uncle Osborn looked over at Seth, who now stood almost eye-to-eye with his uncle. "Late? Say there, Seth old boy. You reckon we're supposed to be going someplace?"

Joining in the fun, Seth shrugged his shoulders. "Beats me. These women are all the time wanting us men to clean up. Maybe it's a trick."

LeRoi ran to his Papa and said, "Papa, it's the showboat. Did you forget? We're all going. And in the first twelve rows. Helen brought the tickets. Didn't you Helen? One for each of us."

Helen poured molasses over the last of her corn pone and tried not to laugh as she ate.

Now Mindy Mae was jumping around like a jack rabbit. "We're going to the showboat. We're going to see the show. All of us, Papa." Looking over at her older cousin, she added, "Even you Seth. You're coming with us." Which brought laughter from everyone in the kitchen.

This is what Helen loved about living here. The laughter. The fun. The love. While she had loved her Pa dearly, and knew he loved his family, he'd been an unsmiling man who seldom if ever enjoyed a good joke. Unlike Uncle Osborn who never tired of creating fun every chance he got.

Wagons and buggies parked randomly all around the landing as the farmers had loaded up their families and came into town for the big event. Even a few new-fangled automobiles sat here and there. Seth always said that as soon as he saved up enough money, he would have his own automobile—which Helen could never imagine happening.

As they walked together down River Road, they merged with dozens of other families. Possibly the entire population of Chancey's Bend would be seated in the grand auditorium. From two blocks away the boat, lit with its hundreds of electric light bulbs, was transformed into a floating fairyland. Children hopped and danced about, finding it impossible to simply walk along with the crowd.

Pulsating sounds of the music from brass band filled the air, adding to the gaiety and excitement.

Alice walked close to Helen with her arm tucked into her sister's. "What was the delay at the show boat?" she asked in a soft whisper as though she had detected there might be a secret involved.

Helen didn't dare look into Alice's eyes for fear she'd let it out. As yet, she'd told no one about the special offer from Cat, the Broadway star. She gave a little shrug. "Oh, it was just Opal wanting to know more about the work we'd done at the shop for them."

At that Alice squeezed Helen's arm a little tighter. "I guess it's all right if I don't believe you."

Now Helen laughed. Her sweet sister was so in tune with others around her. Perhaps it was because she was so quiet. In her quietness, she had more opportunity to observe. And to listen. Alice listened past words that were spoken. She and little Exa Belle were much alike in that way. Listening and observing.

Helen whispered. "Smarty pants. You'll know soon enough."

Coop was standing on the deck, close to the point of where show-goers embarked, holding a megaphone he shouted his greetings to one and all. Shouting out how glad he was to see them. How great the show was going to be. And on and on. Coop was created perfectly for that role. Opal sat in the ticket booth taking tickets, and Ralphie showed the people where to sit.

Now they could see the members of the band, dressed in their spiffy uniforms, standing in formation on the second deck. Their rousing music was interspersed with Coop's greetings, all in a well-rehearsed rhythm.

As Helen approached the stageplank and stepped up on the deck, she looked down to watch her step. Just as she stepped foot on deck, she looked up to see Brett Lochlann looking right at her.

As he moved toward her, Helen's throat went dry. "Hello again," he said. "You heard it didn't you."

He was speaking directly to her. To her. In the midst of the moving crowd of people. She knew he was talking about his playing to calliope. She nodded. Her family members were casting questioning looks in her direction.

Stepping closer, Brett said, "I guess they're waiting for you to hand over the tickets. Here. Let me help."

Carefully, politely, he herded the family through the space beside the ticket booth, giving Helen room to step up and hand the tickets to Opal. Taking the tickets, Opal gave her a wink and said, "Enjoy the show."

Helen nodded and smiled. "We appreciate the tickets."

Once inside the lobby area, Brett said, "I know Osborn here, and Linnie, but goodness mercy me, how these little ones have grown since I left town. I never would have recognized them."

At that, Uncle Osborn shook Brett's hand and welcomed him back to Chancey's Bend, then introduced him to Ma, Alice, and Seth. Then he said, "And looks as though you are already acquainted with Helen?"

He made it a question. Which they all were wondering.

Brett again looked right at Helen making her stomach do strange flips. "Helen gave a vote in my favor to the old men who congregate at the beer hall," he explained. Then at the shocked looks, he chuckled and added, "Outside, I mean. We were outside the beer hall."

At that moment, Helen found her voice. "He was kind enough to relieve me of the bundles I was delivering from the shop."

"It was quite a load," Brett added, as though he had to explain why he had lent a hand. "Oh here, we're all standing in the way. I'm sure you will all be sitting down front. I'll take Ralphie's job and lead the way."

And he did just that. Acting as though he were an usher, he led them to one of the front rows that had just enough empty seats. There he stopped and let them file in. Helen happened to be last.

"Thank you again," she said to him. "And you did a swell job of playing the calliope."

"It's a fascinating instrument. I appreciate the compliment." Giving a little nod, he said, "I'll see you later."

Again, she knew that was simply a polite statement. As in, he would see her if he played the piano at church.

Chapter 4

The show opened with the electric footlights lighting up in a blaze of glory, making the place as bright as a sun shiny day. Few people in Chancey's Bend ever experienced electric lights. The lights could have been the whole show and it would have been a rewarding experience. But that was barely the beginning.

A man entered from the wings of the stage in front of the curtains. In his arms he held a wooden dummy. He sat on a high stool already in position on the stage. The man proceeded to make it seem for all the world, as though that dummy were really talking. LeRoi would later remark, "I knew it was the man talking, but I sure couldn't figure out how he was doing it." To which they all agreed.

Using crazy, silly jokes, talking back and forth with the dummy, the ventriloquist succeeded in keeping the entire crowd in wild laughter.

Once the ventriloquist took his bows, Helen saw Brett get up from his front seat and make his way to the piano sitting at the far right at the base of the stage. Band members were positioned in the orchestra pit. She could barely see the tops of their heads. Now the curtains glided open and the drama, entitled "Honest Hearts," began.

Cat played the lead role of the damsel in distress, and Helen followed her every move, watching how she changed emotions, interacting with fellow actors, and yet still looking out to interact with the audience. She guessed all that talent stemmed from working on a Broadway stage in New York City. What a fascinating life Cat must lead.

Throughout the drama the band played the background music, aided by Brett on the piano.

The printed program stated that during the intermission, the *soubrette,* Cat Callahan would perform. As the curtain now closed, they could hear the noise of the set behind the curtain being changed out.

Coop, who played the damsel's farmer-father in the drama, strode out on the stage, still in costume—denim overalls, faded flannel shirt, and a wide-brim straw hat, complete with bits of straw sticking out from under.

Speaking to the crowd he explained how fortunate they were to add a Broadway star to this season's billing. Saying how thankful he and Opal were that Miss Cat Callahan had chosen their showboat, *Pleasures A-Plenty.* "She'll be out here on this very stage in just a few minutes. And boy oh boy, are you in for the treat like none other you've ever experienced here in Chancey's Bend."

He chatted on a bit thanking the town and the townspeople for such a fine welcome. "This is only our fourth stop as we launch a new season. We're right on time as the ice floe up river broke up earlier than usual this year. We're heading all the way plum down to Vicksburg."

Helen knew his chatter gave Cat time to change before her intermission solo number. Shortly, he glanced over to the wings and evidently received the nod that Cat was ready.

Her stage entrance brought audible gasps from the audience. The lights played on her golden curls and reflected the twinkling spangles on her dress. It was the flaming-red dress that Helen had mended that afternoon. The length of her dress came barely to her calves, showing ruffled pantalettes. In her hand she carried a matching ruffled parasol which she opened and spun round and round as she strolled to center stage.

The song "Don't Dilly Dally on the Way," with its rousing melody and fun lyrics had the crowd laughing and clapping. Cat's clear soprano voice floated out like sunshine, filling the entire auditorium. Her shoes clicked on the wooden stage keeping with the tempo, and Brett's fingers flew up and down the keyboard making that old piano rock.

As the music faded out and the song closed, Cat gave sweeping curtsies and ran offstage, but she was instantly applauded back for an encore. This time she sang a song entitled, "I Love A Piano," and once again, Brett brought the melody to life.

No matter how much the audience clapped and cheered, her part was over. She would be hurriedly changing costumes for the remainder of the drama. A poetry reading was followed by an acrobat number—involving the two acrobats everyone had seen in the parade that afternoon. While they were quite entertaining, they couldn't hold a candle to Cat Callahan.

During the intermission, Uncle Osborn went out to the lobby and purchased bags of candy for each of them. "Since we got in here free of charge, I think I can break for a little candy," he told them as he handed out the bags.

Prizes were tucked into selected bags, and both LeRoi and Esta Belle were the lucky ones. But Mattie Mae put up such a fuss for not getting a toy, Esta Belle gave hers to her sister. In the end, it didn't really matter. The candy was a special treat, as was the entire show.

The showboat gave Chancey's Bend something to talk about for days following. Theirs was a shallow landing, thus they never saw the bigger show boats. Smaller ones would regularly dock, but *Pleasures A-Plenty* seemed to be the favorite. That was due in part to Coop's personality, and the way he came into the town and made friends with the people, along with purchasing many of their supplies from the locals.

Sid and Irma also had had tickets for the show and sat just a few rows behind Helen and her family. The entire show—and especially Cat's performance—became the source of their conversation the following day at the shop. That conversation presented the perfect moment for Helen to tell them about Cat's offer. After explaining how it had all played out, she held her breath as she had no idea how they might respond. Would it make them angry that Cat had not asked them to create the costume?

She should have known better. Their excitement nearly exploded. Irma actually gave her a hug. "You are one blessed young lady," she said. "For someone your age, this is a chance of a lifetime."

Sid, in total agreement, said with a wave of his hand, "And you can use everything right here in the shop every evening."

Their responses brought hot tears to Helen's eyes. That was the very thing she wanted to ask, but feared to do so. Access to the shop would be necessary, since there was not an inch to spare at the Gabler house.

They wanted all the details. What did the costume look like? When would the materials arrive? Was there a deadline to finish it? And on and on they talked. As the three of them studied the drawing, Irma gave a few tidbits of advice, which Helen received gladly.

Like clockwork, the package bearing the materials arrived at the shop two days following Cat's telegraphed order.

"All the way from Cincy," the delivery boy announced as he burst through the shop door making the bell ring with a flurry. Helen was sure he wanted to stay and gawk, but from the look of the basket on his bicycle, he had other deliveries to make.

"Thank you, Davy," Sid said. Digging in his pocket he pulled out a coin, which Davy caught in midair.

With a quick nod he was off and going.

"Let's go to the back," Irma suggested. Helen took that to mean they didn't need any random customers coming in and seeing the special delivery.

Cutting the twine with her large tailor scissors, Helen lifted the lid from the box. There tucked into soft pink tissue paper were the layers of silk, satin, lace, and tulle, all in varying shades of lavender, lilac, and deep purple. Helen ran her fingers over them, sensing the texture of each. Beneath the fabric were placed a dozen or so small embroidered fleurettes. These she would stitch onto the sleeves.

Also touching the fabric, Sid said, "Quality. High quality."

"You'll going to have such fun with this," Irma chimed in.

The excitement in Irma's voice matched that which was near to bursting inside Helen. She knew in her heart she would have gladly taken on this assignment with no pay.

"Here's how I see it," Sid was saying, "we have two or three alterations waiting. Whenever you finish those, if nothing new comes in, you can start creating your patterns."

"One more thing," Irma put in. "We know you'll be here after the shop closes. Please close the front blinds, and only keep the lights on here in the back."

Irma handed Helen a key to the front door. The key hung on a length of string, which Helen slipped over her head and tucked it inside her bodice.

"And," Sid added, "do not stay past ten. We still need you to be ready to work the next morning. Understand?"

Helen nodded. "I understand." Sid was perceptive. He realized once she got started, she'd never want to stop. She'd be tempted to work all night.

Not only was lilac her favorite color, lilacs were also her favorite flower. While not many books graced the Heise home—mostly they read from the Bible—they did own several books of poetry. She and Alice from little up, had fallen in love with Walt Whitman's "When Lilacs Last in the Dooryard Bloom'd," and challenged one another to memorize complete segments.

In the dooryard fronting an old farm-house near the white-wash'd palings,
Stands the lilac-bush tall-growing with heart-shaped leaves of rich green,
With many a pointed blossom rising delicate, with the perfume

strong I love,

With every leaf a miracle—and from this bush in the dooryard,

With delicate-color'd blossoms and heart-shaped leaves of rich

green,

A sprig with its flower I break.

And indeed, in their dooryard at the Heise farm, not one, but two giant lilac bushes grew. In spring-bloom-time, the heady fragrance wafted in through open windows. Living in town, those lilac bushes was one thing she greatly missed.

By closing time, with the measurements laid out on the table in front of her, Helen had the pattern pieces, cut from old newspapers, all completed. She surprised herself that she'd made that much progress. By ten, she had the bodice and sleeves basted, ready to use the Singer treadle. If she hadn't promised Sid about stopping at ten, she was sure she would have stayed all night. The joy at working with these beautiful fabrics knew no end.

Donning her wraps, she stepped out the front door of the shop, and turned the key in the lock. The wind had picked up and the chill hit her face. From out of the darkness a figure appeared, making her jump and gasp.

"Hello Helen. Sorry. I didn't want to frighten you."

It was Brett.

"I knew you were working late and I asked your Uncle Osborn if he would permit me to carry you to the house." He waved across the street indicating the Lochlann delivery buggy, sitting there all hitched up and ready to go. On the side of the buggy written in bright blue letters were the words, "Lochlann's Hardware."

Helen had seen it often as the Lochlann's hired help, an older fellow with a long white beard, made deliveries around town. No words would come to her. He'd asked Uncle Osborn?

"It's a bit nippy out," he said, tugging at his coat collar as if to prove his point. "And I know the street lamps end at Carson Street. It'll be mighty dark up by the Gabler house."

He paused, waiting for her to speak. "Well, do you trust me and old Horace here? He's known me most all my life. He knows every street and every road in and around this town." He then removed his hat and gave a sweeping bow. "Your carriage awaits.

At that she had to laugh. "This is very thoughtful of you. You're right about the streetlamps ending at Carson Street. And I'm not too fond of the dark."

"It's settled then."

Taking her by the arm, he led her around the back of the wagon to the other side where she could easily step up. After she settled in, he came around and took his place in the driver's seat. Clicking the reins, he urged Horace to move to a quick walk. The wagon's wooden overhang worked to lessen that chilly night wind.

"Horace came into the family when I was about eight or nine," he told her, chatting like they were old friends. "Clever little me thought it uproariously funny to have *Horace the horse.* Mother and Father weren't too keen on the idea, but I pressed the matter. And as you can see, I won that battle." This came with a low chuckle.

He turned to look at her, but she could barely see his face in the dark. "So, how's the costume-creating project coming along?"

With every passing streetlamp, she could catch a glimpse of his laughing eyes. He seemed to laugh a good deal, and his open expression made it easy to receive him. She just had to ask. "And pray tell how does the hardware man know what goes on in the tailor shop?"

Another laugh. "So, I'm the hardware man, am I? And here I was convinced I was now the main calliope man in town."

Now she couldn't hold back her own laughter. "Yes, you did well on that account. But you failed to answer the question."

"Okay. I'll stop with the joking. Remember, I played accompaniment for the star of the show. And she happened to mention it."

She felt silly. Of course, they would have spent time in rehearsals. It made sense that Cat might have mentioned it, but that still didn't explain why he actually asked Uncle Osborn about giving her a ride home.

They were past the streetlamps, and indeed it was dark except for the glow of lights spilling from the windows of the houses along the way. Horace plodded along up the hill that loomed at the edge of town and down the other side. Soon they were approaching the Gabler house.

"I suppose I should have asked you first," he was saying as the wagon drew a stop at the front of the house. "I hope you don't think it cheeky of me. It was a lucky guess on my part that you'd work late. I didn't like to think of you walking alone in the dark and the cold." He paused a minute, then said, "You never answered my question. How's it coming along?She took a short breath not sure how much of her heart to share. "Very nicely. And thank you for asking. Not often do we have such fine fabrics to work with at Briggs."

"We? But you're the only one working on the costume. Am I correct?"

She was thankful he couldn't see her blushing. "You are correct."

"You must be a very skillful seamstress. To be trusted by a Broadway soubrette."

Having no answer for his kind compliment, she made a move to get out of the wagon. He touched her arm. "Wait. Let me help."

It was obvious Horace wasn't going anywhere. Brett laid the reins across the seat, jumped down, came around, and lifted her down, leaving her breathless. She'd never been touched by a man before other than Pa and Uncle Osborn. Pa, not often, because he wasn't all that keen about hugging. Uncle Osborn, on the other hand, seemed to be a born hugger.

"How many nights will you be working late?"

"I'm not sure. If I can work all day Saturday, I may be finished before next week."

"At least tomorrow night and Friday then?"

She nodded.

"May I escort you home those nights? As I said, I should have asked you first. I apologize."

"Please. No need to apologize." Her words were coming easier now. "I'm very thankful to be spared not only the dark, but that brisk March wind as well. Thank you for your kindness."

Just then the front door opened, spreading golden light into the front yard. Aunt Linnie called out, "Hey there, Brett Lochlann. Come on in here and help yourself to a bowl of ham and beans. And cornbread too. It'll warm your tummy."

Again, taking Helen's arm, he gently led her up the front walk to the porch. "Thanks for the offer, Linnie, but Horace isn't used to being up this late. He might very well want to sleep in tomorrow and Father wouldn't be too happy with me."

Turning to go, he said to Helen, "Tomorrow night then?"

"Yes, thank you. This time I won't jump out of my skin."

Doffing his hat, he walked back to the wagon. She stood there for a moment as the sound of wheels crunching and hooves clopping faded into the night.

Chapter 5

Even though she was the creator of Cat's gown, she was in awe of its beauty. She seemed to know intuitively exactly how each piece should be connected to the next. That included the sweeping train and its tiers of ruffles. If someone were to ask how she knew, she would have shrugged. Because she had no inkling. The ideas, the thoughts, the plans, were just there. All in her head. And she loved every minute of the process. She continually thanked the Lord that she'd been given this amazing opportunity. As sections came together and hung on the dress form, Helen couldn't help but stare at it.

The family enjoyed razzing Helen about Brett, especially LeRoi, the more vocal of the group. "Helen has a beau," he would taunt in his sing-song voice. Naturally, the little ones echoed his words, laughing all the while.

Helen never minded the teasing, but the problem with this teasing was that it allowed her very little space to sort things out in her own mind. Thankfully, working on Cat's costume in the evenings gave her time to ponder Brett's actions, but still brought her to no conclusion.

On Friday evening, as once again the Lochlann wagon pulled up to the
Gabler house, Brett asked what time she might stop working on Saturday. The
shop closed at noon on Saturdays, which gave her the entire afternoon to work,
so she wasn't sure.

She thought for a minute. "Probably around six or so." Then she quickly
added, "But it'll still be light. And there's been no cold wind." Which was true.
With each passing day the warmth of a Kentucky spring had spread over the
hills around Chancey's Bend. "I can manage the walk home…"

With his usual laugh, and looking straight at her, he interrupted and said,
"Well, then, may I carry you home for absolutely no earthly reason other than
that I want to? No longer the gallant warrior, complete with the courageous
charger…" He waved toward Horace, which brought out her laughter. "…com-
ing to the rescue of the fair damsel in distress."

It sounded like a line from the melodrama from the showboat. And not only
did it sound like a melodrama, Helen had great difficulty believing his sincerity.
Did Brett Lochlann truly want to spend time with her? He'd spent two years at
a music conservatory. Surely there'd been sophisticated young ladies galore for
him to choose from. Why her? A nondescript country girl who knew so little
about anything.

She guessed the only way to find out was to let out the fishing line and see
how far this fish would take it.

After a long pause, she answered, "Yes, Brett Lochlann, you and your courageous charger may carry me home tomorrow for no earthly reason."

They were still sitting in the wagon, and for once, Aunt Linnie had not flung
open the front door. At Helen's answer, in the darkness, she heard Brett release
a sigh. "Thank you, Helen. Thank you for trusting me."

Later, as she lay in her bed in the attic, trying to fall asleep, she was overcome
with wonder and bewilderment. Over and over, the question came—*Why me?*
Of all people. *Why me?*

The drive home on Saturday seemed different somehow. First of all, it was
light out. She could clearly see Brett's expressions. She was struck by the kindness in his face. The cloudless sky allowed the sun to chase away the chill that

had permeated most all of March. A soft warm breeze stirred the tiny leaves that were just now budding on the trees. Even the conversation seemed different.

He had asked her about life on the farm. Had she milked cows? She definitely had. Had she fed chickens and gathered eggs? Yes to that question as well. Had there been a garden? What's a farm without a garden? And the most interesting part to Helen, was that she began to lose the awkward feeling and was able to share her thoughts.

Even after she and her family had left the farm and moved to town, she never gave much thought to her feelings about living there. But she had to admit, she did not miss all the hard work. Or the mud or the dust—it seemed to always be one or the other. On the other hand, she greatly enjoyed Aunt Linnie's garden in the back yard, and they all shared the work of the harvest—snapping beans and shelling peas, gathered around on the front porch chatting together. Most of all, she loved her work at Briggs Tailor Shop.

Brett, as it turned out, was a good listener. His interest was sincere. He truly wanted to know. But it was the next day—Sunday—that she learned more about him.

Embarrassing her to tears, he came up to her as she stood there on the board walk outside the church. Once again, he had played the piano for the service. Helen found herself fascinated by his playing. So much so, she left off singing, didn't even look at the hymnal in her hand, and just watched Brett play. That he'd studied for two years at the conservatory showed forth in his skills.

Helen was waiting for her mother and Aunt Linnie, both of whom seemed to never stop talking with the other ladies. The littles were running around the churchyard playing with the other children. Alice and Seth had already started walking to the house. Brett caught her standing there all alone.

She watched as he approached and walked right up to her. Who all were watching them? People were still milling around before heading home for Sunday dinner. And in a small town like Chancey's Bend, people talk.

"Miss Helen." He removed his hat. "May I walk you home?"

Still somewhat bewildered by his advances, she allowed herself to give a nod. "Yes, you may." She wanted to add something like, "I'd like that very much."

But it sounded so forward. So bold and unbecoming. Instead, she just let him lead the way and set her pace by his side.

She'd ridden in the wagon with him, she'd allowed him to lift her down each time, but now they were walking in step with one another. It was an entirely new sensation. She was unable to look at his face because the board sidewalks were treacherous, especially wearing her Sunday pumps. She was forced to watch her step. But just the knowledge of his tall form beside her sent shivers up her spine and made her pulse race.

First, he thanked her for accepting his invitation to walk her home, then he complimented her, saying her suit was attractive and looked very becoming on her.

She was wearing her two-piece burgundy suit with the long overskirt, all trimmed in navy satin. It was the first garment she'd made for herself after receiving a few paychecks and building up her savings. Irma helped her choose the fabric, and then allowed what she called her *employee's discount* when she made the purchase. Helen hadn't known such a thing existed, but was pleased.

"I'm sure that's your creation," he said after she'd thanked him for the compliment.

"It is." Then, attempting to be conversational, which she was learning she wasn't very good at, she said, "I enjoy hearing you at the piano. With no disrespect, I prefer your playing over Mrs. Bechtel's."

"If two years at conservatory didn't advance me much past Mrs. Bechtel, father would need to ask for a refund." Then he added, "And me too—agreeing with you that I mean no disrespect."

Helen couldn't help but laugh at that. "How did you make the decision to attend the conservatory? Seems like a big step to leave home for two years."

"It was simple. I just wanted to hear Mother and Father yell at one another."

At that, Helen stopped in her tracks. "What? Do you mean that?"

He took her arm to get her moving again. "Of course not. Not really. But that's what happened. I don't know if you know this, but all Father has ever wanted is for me to take over the store and be in business with him. And all I ever wanted was to play the piano. And the organ."

"And the calliope." She was now swept up in this saga.

"Can't forget the calliope," he agreed. "As you probably know, Mother is British. *Very* British, I must add." His imitation of his mother's accent was perfect.

"I didn't know." She rarely had need to go to the hardware store, and Brett's mother had only been in the tailor shop a couple of times that Helen could remember. Even then she'd never had a conversation with Ruth Lochlann.

"She and Father are nothing alike. No doubt at all that they dearly love one another, but when I come into the picture, they've never come into agreement."

"Have you been playing all your life?"

"Almost. Perhaps that was the problem. Mother insisted I start piano lessons when I was barely five. Father said he would allow it, but he would still be training me in the hardware business."

Now he glanced over at her. "The wrangling began quite early. I guess the most difficult part was when Mother discovered I had a natural, innate talent on the keyboard."

"You're an only child?"

"I am. Mother had lost two other babies before I was born." He paused. "Both were boys. I'm not sure how that affected either one. But I just know it had to be heart-wrenching."

"You then, became the sole source of each of their dreams."

"That would describe the situation perfectly."

They were quiet for a time as they navigated the hill up to the Gabler house. And no board walk. Just gravel.

"Mother discovered the conservatory in Cincinnati. She did learn that the qualifications were demanding. Only a small number of applicants were accepted."

He once again took her arm as they approached a rough place in the road. Fascinated with learning his story, she opted to listen.

"My clever mother used that as her bargaining chip. 'Conway,' she said, 'since the chances of his meeting the qualifications are slight, what would it hurt to just let him try? At least we'll better know the measure of his abilities.'" Now Brett laughed. "Oh, my poor father. Put his foot right into the trap. I was accepted immediately."

Helen let her laughter join in with his. It was funny. "Your mother never doubted, did she?"

"Not for a moment."

"What does the conservatory prepare you for? Not just playing for the hymn singing in the church in Chancey's Bend."

"Interesting that you would ask. Few people in this town have ever asked that question. The leaders at the conservatory put out feelers for positions for their graduates to play with an orchestra, or travel on concert tours, or to play accompaniment for stage performances—as I did for Cat Callahan."

"Much more than I would have thought. I have no knowledge of that world."

"It definitely surprised Father, who thought it would all come to nothing."

"Has he softened then? Not angry at your choice?"

They were at the Gabler house now. She could see Seth peeking through the parlor curtains. Back down the road the rest of the family were taking their time, enjoying the spring day.

"Softened? That might be a correct statement. I don't think he'll ever lose that feeling of disappointment. From the time he opened the store, and carefully built up a strong business, his goal was to have a son step in and take over."

As LeRoi, Esta Belle, and Mindy Mae came running up, Brett greeted each of them, engaging them in conversation, a skill Helen was sure he'd learned growing up working in the hardware store—the ability to talk to most anyone. A skill Helen would love to possess. Perhaps one day.

Aunt Linnie invited Brett to stay on for Sunday dinner, but he politely turned her down. "Mother doesn't know I've gone off in the opposite direction. She's in her kitchen right now, at the stove, a stirring spoon in her hand, tapping her foot and exclaiming, 'Now where is that boy?' Because to her I expect I'll always be her boy."

Aunt Linnie and Uncle Osborn laughed, because they knew Ruth Lochlann well. As a builder, Uncle Osborn had cause to be in the hardware store quite often.

Brett walked down the front walk toward the street. Tipping his hat, he said, "Miss Helen, are you still working extra hours?"

"I am."

"See you tomorrow night then?"

"Yes. Thank you."

And with that, he was gone, stepping quickly back down the road.

And once more, Helen was in total disbelief.

Chapter 6

C at's costume was close to completion. Sid and Irma raved about Helen's skills. At Helen's request, Irma did daily inspections and gave a bit of guidance along the way. But for the most part, the project laid fully in Helen's grasp. She had truly surprised herself, because at the outset the feeling of overwhelm nearly consumed her. Irma kept telling her not to think of the whole costume, but just one piece, and one section at a time. That advice helped.

Helen had never received a telegram before, but that Monday, one arrived for her at the shop. It was from Cat. She was asking Helen if there might be a completion date. Reading it, Helen's heart pounded and her stomach lurched. Up until that moment, she'd felt no pressure. She simply worked along at her own pace.

It took both Sid and Irma to calm her down.

"Of course, she's anxious to have her new costume," Irma said, "but she wouldn't want quality to be sacrificed for speed."

"Irma's right. As usual," Sid said. "I'll send a quick reply that we are overseeing the work and that it's coming along splendidly."

"Let's give her a date of a week out," Irma suggested, "even though it looks to me like you have only a couple days of work to go."

"When it arrives sooner, she'll be elated." Sid took pencil and paper and scribbled out the short reply. He handed it off to Davy from the telegraph office who stood at the door patiently waiting. As always, Sid grabbed a coin from his pocket and tossed it to Davy who responded with a wide grin and a nod.

Helen found herself telling Brett all about it as he drove her home that evening. The more time she spent in his company, the less tongue-tied she felt. She wanted to share things with him, and he was a great listener.

"Performers are a special breed of cat," he told her. "High strung. Easily rattled. I've spent a good deal of time working with them. I learned to stay calm as they sounded off in their seeming desperation."

This bit of information helped, as well as Sid and Irma's encouragement.

As they approached the Gabler house, Brett asked her a strange question. "Do you ride horses? As a farm girl, I suspect you do."

"Are you referring to a plow horse? I'm pretty good behind the plow."

It took Brett a minute to catch her joke. But then his laugh sounded out. She'd grown to love that laugh. So free and easy.

The wagon was stopped now, and he flicked the end of the reins against his free hand. "Well now, that wasn't exactly what I had in mind. I was more thinking of a saddle and a bridle."

She gave a nod. "I'm pretty good. The three of us rode Pepper to school when we were little. We took turns riding her out through the pasture to get the cows in."

She had no idea where this was leading.

"I'd like to invite you to go riding with me next Saturday afternoon. Will you have the afternoon free?"

Now the loss for words returned with a vengeance. She hesitated, fearing her stammering might sound like a child.

Brett didn't seem to notice her discomfort. He went on, "Mr. Bechtel has a couple of fine mares at the stable that he's willing to rent out."

Her mind whirled. Did Brett Lochlann just now happen to be checking out the stable for two horses to rent? Or had he been planning this? And for how long?

She managed to say that she felt the costume would be completed before then, and that her Saturday afternoon would be free. She then added, "I accept your invitation to go riding."

With one last flick of the reins, he laid them down and jumped out of the wagon. Coming around to lift her down, he told her, "Thank you Helen. I was so hoping you'd agree. There's something I want to show you."

Saturday seemed eons away. She told no one. She felt as though she were hugging a wonderful secret.

Irma was correct that Helen was well able to complete the costume on Wednesday. Helen had removed it from the dress form and carefully folded it.

From the mercantile, they commandeered a wooden fruit crate. It was like a joyous party as the three of them lined the crate with old newspapers, then layers of cloth scraps, and last of all, layers of tissue paper. The lavender and purple dress lay safely tucked in like a baby.

"I think you should add a note," Sid said.

Irma agreed. "Helen, I think Sid has a great idea there. This was your creation from start to finish." From her own desk in the back, Irma fetched a sheet of parchment stationery and handed it to Helen. "Use your creativity, my dear."

Helen took a pen from the holder on the counter, dipped it into the ink bottle and began to sketch. She drew the bare outline of a dress with flounces. Below the sketch, she penned, "Custom Designs." Below that, with a large flourish, she created two inter-locking H's for her initials. Holding it up, she asked, "How about this?"

Sid gave a whistle. "Perfect. And before you send it, make another copy so you don't forget. This needs to be saved."

"Just a moment. I have another idea."

Irma disappeared into the back. Helen heard the door to the storage room open and close. Irma returned with a wide swatch of ivory-colored satin. Handing it to Helen she said, "Take a few minutes and embroider your crest."

"But, my work..." The day wasn't over. Work remained to be completed. And they'd already spent time packing the dress.

Patting her arm, Irma said, "Nonsense. No rushes in here today. Now do as I say. Embroider the edges as well so the satin won't fray. Go on now."

The idea kindled inside of her as she sat down at her table in the back room. First she drew out the letters and the sketch on the fabric, then embroidered it all with embroidery thread of deep purple.

She wanted to just sit there and bask in the beauty of her finished product, but time was ticking away. Irma held the dress taut as Helen carefully, and securely stitched the satin label inside the bodice.

A girlish joy exploded inside her causing her to want to dance and skip all around the shop. She just had to contain it. Her creation lay in that crate, bearing her own private label. Even if this were the only garment she ever produced, it didn't matter one whit. She felt nothing could surpass the joy of this moment.

Sid attached the lid on the crate with short pieces of wire. Then he telephoned for the train-station porter to come fetch it. It bore the Greenville, Mississippi address Cat had given Helen. Sid also sent a telegram to let her know her order was on the way.

Two days later came Cat's reply.

LOVE IT STOP FITS PERFECT STOP WEARING TONIGHT STOP BALANCE WIRED

The exhilaration Helen felt was beyond her ability to describe. Her plan had been to give the money to Aunt Linnie. After all, they were living there rent-free. But as she and Mama discussed it privately, Mama said no to that plan. "Give them one of your dollars, Helen. Keep the rest. Tuck it away. You never know when you're going to need it."

Trusting Mama's wisdom, she did exactly that.

Chapter 7

H elen prayed for clear weather for Saturday. Spring rains visited the Kentucky hills with great regularity in late March. When Helen jumped out of bed early, she ran to the window to witness that golden ball ascending from the crest of the far eastern hill. The sight of bright blue skies, decorated with soft puffs of clouds, reflecting pink from the sunrise, served only to heighten her anticipation of the day ahead.

By now the whole family knew she was going riding with Brett Lochlann. Alice was confident her sister was being courted, and had no qualms in saying so. Ma just smiled and kept her thoughts to herself, which Helen appreciated.

The younger ones? That was a different story. Helen never tried to hush them, which as she knew, would only egg them on.

Barely able to eat breakfast, she left the house and arrived at the shop early. Now that she had her own key, she kept the blinds down, and went straight to her work table, hoping the time would fly by.

When Sid and Irma arrived to find her working, they simply smiled and exchanged knowing glances. They, too, knew about her special day.

At straight up noon, Brett arrived, riding a glossy chestnut mare, and leading another that matched perfectly, except for its four white socks. Dressed in Levi's, denim jacket and a Stetson, his whole demeanor seemed altered. After tying the mounts at the rail, he entered the shop.

Helen had watched his arrival through the window near her table. She quickly folded the trousers she was hemming, cleared her table, and fetched her shawl. They had planned ahead that they would go to the house and she would change into something more suitable for riding.

As they rode out of town, the direction Brett took was one Helen had never traveled. For a time they followed clear, well-defined trails. But soon he led off into dense woods where she saw no trail at all. A comfortable silence existed between them as they rode.

The air was filled with the fragrances of spring. Primroses, crocuses, and daffodils made a show of their fresh, reborn colors. Overhanging branches of the trees, in different stages of budding, gave off a soft, pale-green effect as the sun shone through. Skittering in the brush meant the horses scared up a rabbit, or perhaps a hedgehog or a skunk. Above them the blue jays and crows scolded them in harsh tones, while the song birds simply took flight and soared into the bright blue sky.

After riding for the better part of an hour, Brett reined in, turned around to her and said, "You're probably wondering, but I do have a destination in mind."

She laughed. "That's good to know. That way I'm convinced we're not lost."

"Nope. Not lost." Pointing ahead, he said, "It's just over that hill."

"You're sure? It looks like all the other hills we've been over." She smiled as she spoke. Because truthfully, she wasn't concerned in the least. A feeling of safety and security filled her. The trust she experienced with Brett surprised her.

With his hand raised like a cavalry commander, he said, "Forward ho."

Watching him as he rode, it was clear that Brett was at home in the saddle, as though he'd ridden all his life. This puzzled Helen, knowing he grew up as a town kid. There weren't many *town kids* in Chancey's Bend, since the majority of the population lived on small farms out in the country. As she herself had.

As they topped the hill to which he had indicated, he stopped and she brought her horse up beside him. There in the small narrow valley lay the remains of what had obviously been a homestead. The buildings were in ruins, and the fences in disrepair, but the trees, shrubs, flowering bushes, and flowers still thrived.

"Come on."

Now she rode beside him rather than following behind. As they neared the place, Helen could make out that dozens of the bushes were lilacs. At some moment in the far distant past, some homesteader had cared to plant a grove of lilacs. Helen could only stare.

Slowly she dismounted and still holding the reins walked over to the nearest bush where she could see that each branch hung heavy with buds, showing the slightest hints of the purple blossoms to come. Touching a cluster, she leaned in and there was the slightest hint of the heady fragrance.

She turned to look up at Brett's face as he beamed out a smile to her. "A little birdie told me that lilacs are your favorite flower. So, I thought I'd share this with you."

Off his horse now, he stood beside her. The moment was almost too much to take in. It was beyond her comprehension that someone would do this for her.

"Enough lilacs for you?" he asked in a low voice.

"More than enough." She looked over at him and soaked in that kind, open face. "Of course, there can never be too many lilacs."

The pounding of her heart forced her to step away from him. She tied the reins to a close branch and simply strolled in and out among that amazing stand of lilacs, lightly touching the glossy, heart-shaped leaves. She'd never been in such a heavenly spot in her entire life. She'd like to camp here and wait till every tiny blossom opened. Under her breath, almost whispering, she began reciting,

"WHEN lilacs last in the dooryard bloom'd,

And the great star early droop'd in the western sky in the night,
I mourn'd, and yet shall mourn with ever-returning spring."

Brett stepped in right behind her. She wasn't aware he stood so close. But his voice came clear.

"Ever-returning spring, trinity sure to me you bring,
Lilac blooming perennial and drooping star in the west,
And thought of him I love."

Shocked, she whirled around. "You know that poem?"

"I do."

All she could do was stand there dumfounded. And he went on.

"In the dooryard fronting an old farm-house near the white-wash'd
palings,
Stands the lilac-bush tall-growing with heart-shaped leaves of rich
green,
With many a pointed blossom rising delicate, with the perfume
strong I love,"

In unison they recited the next...

"With every leaf a miracle—and from this bush in the dooryard,
With delicate-color'd blossoms and heart-shaped leaves of rich
green,
A sprig with its flower I break."

"How did you come to know it?" she asked.

"A British mother who insisted I read, appreciate, and yes, even memorize poetry."

Stepping forward, he enfolded her gently in his arms. Whispering into her hair, he said, "Perhaps she had a mother's premonition that I would one day meet someone—someone I would care about and that that someone might love lilacs."

At that, Helen felt him kiss the top of her head, and fire shot all through her.

Still and all a gentleman, he released her, took her hand and said, "Now we're going to have lunch right over there on that dilapidated porch."

"Lunch?" Helen's mind was still a cloudy muddle.

"See those bulging saddle bags? That's lunch in there."

Only at that moment did she realize she was hungry. Food had been the furthest thing from her mind.

Brett set about unfastening the bedroll behind the saddle. From inside the canvas he pulled out a well-worn quilt. "I'll spread this out, and you can fetch the grub."

Lunch consisted of fried chicken, biscuits, boiled eggs, apples and sugar cookies the size of a large saucer, heavily sprinkled with cinnamon and sugar. Helen couldn't believe it all fit in the two saddlebags.

Their voices and laughter filled the air as they ate. It wasn't until much later that Helen recalled how easily the conversation had flowed. They talked about everything, from what foods they liked, their families, to the state of Chancey's Bend—Brett felt it was past time for a paved street and concrete sidewalks—to their dreams for the future, to the war in Europe.

Helen wanted to know how he'd become so adept at riding which he then explained that at age seventeen, he'd spent a month working on an Oklahoma ranch where his aunt, uncle, and cousins lived.

"That definitely explains it," she said as she took the cookie he handed to her. "But am I to believe you spent a month away from your piano?"

With a chuckle he said, "How intuitive you are. And the answer is no I did not. An old upright, out-of-tune piano sat in their front parlor."

"And you made great use of it?"

"I did at that. Every evening. A command performance. Even though I was dog-tired."

"You love playing that much."

Pensive for a moment he replied, "That much and more."

After cleaning up and repacking, they walked around the property and into the woods. Still talking. Even when they were quiet, the silence never felt awkward, but comfortable.

Helen never wanted the perfect day to end. Before leaving, Brett took out his knife and cut two sizeable branches from one of the lilac bushes.

Handing them to her, he said, "They may just wilt," he said. "But then again you may get to see them bloom."

Arriving at the Gabler house, both dismounted and as they stood there Brett handed her the lilac branches and thanked her for the day.

But she demurred. "I'm the one who owes all the thanks. This outing was your idea. And you even furnished lunch. I enjoyed every minute. But most especially lilacs."

"We'll go back when the lilacs are in full bloom. That is, if you agree."

"I would love that. I agree fully."

She watched as he rode down River Road with the other mount in tow. When he'd gone only about a block, he turned around and waved. She hadn't moved. She returned the wave.

What had she ever done to deserve the ardent attentions of this wonderful man?

Chapter 8

The quiet in the shop on Mondays, matched the quiet in town, as though people were slowly waking up from their Sunday rest. But late in the day on this particular Monday, the atmosphere changed. From her work table, she could hear people shouting. Out the window she saw clusters of shop owners gathered in front of the stores. Their voices loud and agitated.

Presently, Sid pulled back the curtain at the door and said, "Just came over the wire, Helen. Our president done declared war." Jabbing his thumb toward the street, he added, "That's what all the ruckus is about."

Pressing her hand against her midsection, she felt she might be sick. For months people talked, fussed, argued, and debated about America entering the war, but Helen never believed it would ever happen. Europe seemed to her as another planet, totally removed from her small corner of Kentucky. Her mind couldn't catch hold of it.

"What does this mean, Sid?"

With a shake of his head, he said, "It means everything will be forever changed."

How she was supposed to work after that announcement Helen wasn't sure. On her table lay the pieces of a suit ordered for the banker's wife. It had to be just so. She ran her hand over the soft worsted wool as though to steady herself. Something here in front of her was actually the same as it had been a few minutes earlier.

The next morning as she walked down River Road toward the shop, she heard the newsboys shouting as they carried newspapers that had recently been thrown off the train.

As she came closer, she caught sight of ominous-looking, three-inch headlines:

STATE OF WAR DECLARES PRESIDENT

It lent stark reality to the situation she'd wanted to ignore. Last evening as the family talked about it, Uncle Osborn surprised her by agreeing that this was necessary. "We can't let those Huns keep sinking ships, and making moves to rule all of Europe and the British Isles." With a wave of his hand he added, "Our boys will show 'em what for. I guarantee it."

The bells on the shop door gave off their familiar friendly jingle as she entered. Sid and Irma had the open newspaper spread out on the counter.

"Helen, come look at this."

As Helen took a closer look, she saw rotogravures showing various cities where long lines of young men stood ready to volunteer to go and fight.

Irma just shook her head and in a soft voice said, "Who would have ever thought so many would be ready to go and die?"

The sadness in her voice brought hot tears to Helen's eyes.

"Now Mother," Sid chided. He always called her Mother when no customers were in the shop. "No need to give in to hopelessness. With our boys over there, it'll be over and done in no time. Probably be home by Christmas."

It was much later that Helen learned those hopeful words about Christmas were something Sid had read in the newspaper.

The following Friday they learned that Congress voted to support President Wilson's decision. No turning back now.

One Sunday after church, Brett invited Helen to come to his house for dinner. "I'd like you to hear how I play music other than church hymns."

She was both nervous and elated at this special invitation. While she'd seen the Lochlanns around town, in church, and on a very rare occasion when she entered into their hardware store, she didn't really know them. Ruth Lochlann seemed aloof which Helen found somewhat intimidating.

After informing Ma that she wouldn't be home for Sunday dinner, she walked alongside Brett to the Lochlann house. Helen had little knowledge of who lived where in Chancey's Bend. Each morning, she walked to the shop, in the afternoon she walked home again. (That is until Brett started fetching her in the delivery wagon.) That was about the extent of her days. She had no need to explore the rest of the town.

Brett was nearly always the last one out of the church. He wanted to make sure all the music was put away and things set in order. Then he visited with the townspeople as though he were the pastor. Finally, when he was free, they walked together north of town. Leaving River Road, the side road took on a slight incline.

"If I'd thought ahead, I would have harnessed up Horace."

Not thinking about the walk, which she was enjoying immensely, she asked, "Does your mother even know she's having company for Sunday dinner?"

Giving a soft chuckle, he answered, "Well of course she does."

Helen sighed. "Oh good."

"I whispered it to her near the close of the sermon. Right before I went up to play for the closing hymn."

Playfully, she smacked his arm. "Brett! You can't do that."

Ducking as though she'd thrown a punch, he said, "What? It's my mother, I guess I can if I want to. And besides, she loves company." He looked over at her and gave her that wide grin of his. "Especially *this* company."

The large, two-story house sat on a small knoll overlooking the Chancey River. Large, but unpretentious. White clapboard and sporting dark blue shutters, it was encased in a wide wraparound porch, complete with a porch swing which matched the blue of the shutters. The house spoke of neatness and order. Flower beds were coming alive with a rainbow of spring blossoms.

She could see a few outbuildings in back the house. A small barn, chicken house, corn crib, and a stable. More went on here than simply a family who owned the local hardware store. It appeared a great deal more profitable than the farm she'd been used to during her growing-up years. Perhaps something could be said for having a thriving business *and* a farm.

Conway and Ruth did all they could to help Helen feel at ease, creating easy conversation as they ate. Conway teased his wife about her cooking, noting how once she married him and moved to the South, she had to "stop boiling and start frying."

She easily accepted the teasing, and Helen could sense the comfortable bond between the two.

"Nary a body would know about fried anything where I came from," Ruth said in her own defense.

"You learned well," Helen said. And it was true. Her cooking rated right up there with Aunt Linnie, who could throw together most anything in the kitchen and it turned out like a gourmet dish.

"I would hope so," Ruth replied. "Going on twenty-five years of cooking for this man of mine."

Ruth had a way of holding her head high, chin lifted. The graying curls, even though tucked into a low, twisted braid at the nape of her neck, escaped in loose tendrils about her face, which she habitually swept back with her hand. The gray-blue eyes expressed kindness and gentleness at which Helen marveled, remembering what Brett had told her about the loss of two babies.

Helen had known women who allowed grief to harden their heart, and their countenance. But that wasn't the case with Ruth Lochlann.

Conway's gentle manners matched his wife's. His square jaw, covered with graying chin whiskers lent a kind of strength. A man of strong character. A businessman with integrity, which was a treasure in a small town where everyone knew everyone's business.

During the conversation, Helen learned that it had been her Uncle Osborn who built their house. "We worked together," Conway said with a smile. "But obviously he was the builder and I just hammered a nail here and there."

"A lot more than that," Ruth put in. "He's a wee bit modest, my Conway is."

Helen wasn't surprised as she knew her uncle was known as a reputable builder throughout the entire region.

At one point in the conversation, Ruth asked about the costume Helen had created for Cat, the singing Broadway star. Helen glanced over at Brett, quite surprised that he had shared that information.

Giving a slight shrug and a look of guilt, he said, "It wasn't a secret, was it?"

"I think you're the talk of the town," Ruth interjected. "After all, telegrams were coming and going, and the telegraph operators were never known for holding their tongues."

Helen tried to answer their questions, but still, the entire experience remained difficult to express in words.

Brett seemed to note her discomfort and kindly directed the conversation to other subjects.

The dinner had begun with oyster stew, followed by a large platter of fried river fish. Bowls of fresh peas, snap beans, fresh radishes, and new potatoes, which Conway proudly announced were from his wife's garden. Small cups of honey accompanied the yeast rolls.

When dessert arrived—light-as-a-feather golden sponge cake, smothered in strawberries--Helen was forced to request a small portion. She felt stuffed. But she noticed the two men had no such compunction.

As Ruth began clearing the table, Helen stood up and joined her, stacking the empty plates. "No need, my dear," Ruth protested with a wave of her hand.

"I'm used to this. We all pitch in at the Gabler's. Even the little ones."

"I'm quite sure of that, but I believe Brett requires your company in the parlor."

Brett, now standing beside her, held out his hand.

"Go on now," Ruth said. "Enjoy your time together."

Helen nodded and accepted Brett's hand. Leading her into the parlor, she saw the massive, grand piano. The beauty of it left her speechless. Tapestries at the window were drawn back allowing spring sunlight to stream in and reflect on the glossy black of the instrument.

Brett motioned to a tufted chair of deep forest-green, positioned close beside the piano. "This is for you," he told her. "You sit here."

Making herself comfortable, she watched as he sat down, adjusted the bench and began to play. The effect was nothing like church hymns. Likewise, his facial expression was nothing like when he played church hymns. Later, he would explain how he loved the hymns, but felt restricted. As her personal concert began, he told her each composer, naming Mozart, Beethoven, Handel, and the explosive compositions of Rachmaninov.

Losing track of time, Helen sat transfixed, much of the time with eyes closed, as though she longed to soak it in through her skin to carry with her wherever she went. Brett, too, appeared lost to anything but the music. This gave Helen yet another totally different glimpse into the inner workings of this man.

It must have been over an hour that sped by, when at last Conway and Ruth entered the room, breaking the spell. Helen wasn't sure if she resented it, or welcomed it. "It's now our turn," Conway said with a twinkle in his eye.

Brett looked over at Helen and smiled. "Get ready." Reaching over to a stack of pale-orange music books atop the piano, he handed a copy to his parents, one to Helen, and opened one in front of him.

Shifting into a totally different mode, Brett started with *Polly Wolly Doodle*. Once they wore that one out, he progressed to, *The Old Gray Mare, There is a Tavern in the Town, Oh Susanna, There'll Be a Hot Time in the Old Town Tonight*. And what would a songfest be without rounds? By the time they moved through *Row, Row, Row Your Boat,* and *Three Blind Mice,* the laughter nearly outpaced the singing.

All three Lochlanns could boast marvelous voices, so at first, Helen hesitated to chime in for fear of messing things up, but they kept waving at her to join them. Finally, she simply forgot herself and entered fully into the fun and laughter. She couldn't remember ever having such a wonderful time.

Out of breath and still laughing Ruth said, "I think it's time for coffee and second helpings of cake."

Brett pushed back the bench and stood up. "I vote in favor of that plan." Looking over at her with those clear blue smiling eyes, and giving a little bow, he said, "Requesting the pleasure of your company, ma'am."

He continued to take her off guard. She never knew what was coming next. From the deeply-serious concert pianist to this little-boy, fun-side of him.

Accepting his hand, she simply said, "Request accepted."

If she thought the surprises were over, having shared dinner with Brett and his family, being the solo audience of a concert performance, then taking part of their raucous, laughter-filled songfest, she was sadly mistaken. Nothing could even come close to what came next when he walked her home.

Although the afternoon was waning, the warmth held. For which Helen gave thanks, since she had no wrap. After all, she thought that morning that she would be attending church service, then returning home.

Conversation along the way was sporadic, with Brett talking about such things as how the city fathers needed to decide once and for all to pave River Road, and pour concrete sidewalks. "We need to keep up if the town looks to grow and bring in more businesses."

She gave her agreement. After all, she was forced to navigate the rough, uneven wooden sidewalks every day on her way to and from work. Plus, the dust and mud of the unpaved main street of the town, truly did make it seem they'd never entered into the new century.

They were almost out of the short business district, into where the sidewalk ended and tree-lined neighborhoods commenced, when Brett, after taking a deep breath, said, "Helen, I'm scheduled for a concert in Cincinnati this coming Friday."

He'd stopped walking now and turned to look at her, making her heart melt. The statement mystified her. Why did he want her to know about this upcoming concert?

"I'll be playing with the symphony, but also I've been requisitioned to play Rachmaninov."

Helen had never seen Brett so nervous. His hand was in his trousers pocket, then out again, and back in. He pushed his hat back and then said, "I know this is very forward of me, but..."

She didn't know what to do to calm him. "Yes?" she said as kindly as she could.

"I want very much for you to be there with me. To experience a real concert. Not just in the parlor."

The invitation took her totally by surprise. But she knew very well that such a trip would never meet Ma's approval. The moment that thought flitted through her mind, he quickly added that Conway and Ruth were going as well.

"The concert will be at the Opera House. We'll stay at the Statler Hotel." Now his hat was in his hands. "Mother and Father will see to it that you are looked after."

He threw his head back and let out a good belly laugh. "I'm not doing very well with this, am I? I'm not very practiced. I didn't mean you need to be looked after like a child."

"It's all right. I knew what you meant."

And while she knew his meaning, she was still puzzled as to the why of all of this. Why her? Of all people. The backwoods Kentucky farm girl. Why was he inviting her to his concert?

Still holding his hat, he reached out to take her hand. "I understand this is not only forward of me, but sudden as well. If you want to think about it, you can give your answer later."

In her whirling thoughts, she wondered what in the world would she wear. She had nothing suitable for such an occasion.

"It is a surprise, Brett, and I'm so honored that you would want me there. I will need to think about it. And talk with Ma."

"Of course." He started walking again, replaced his hat, but kept hold of her hand.

As they approached the Gabler's front door, he asked if he could once again take her home from work the next day. When she accepted, he added, "Perhaps you'll have the answer then?"

He phrased it in a question.

"I will, Brett. I promise. I'll answer you tomorrow."

Releasing her hand and doffing his hat, he walked backward a few steps smiling at her. As he turned and hurried down the road, he raised a hand and waved.

Her heart refused to slow down, even after she lay in her bed that night trying to sleep. It all seemed like a dream

Chapter 9

L ate that evening, she'd told the family of the invitation and asked Ma
what she thought. They were sitting up late, enjoying conversation
out on the front porch. The little ones had been asleep long ago. Helen
purposely waited to share her news, not wanting their noisy voices disturbing her thinking. She was already befuddled enough.

"You're a woman now, Helen," she said. "I trust your judgement. If you
want to go, and since Mr. and Mrs. Lochlann are in attendance, I see no
harm."

Ma turned to her brother-in-law. "Osborn? Your take on this? She's
living under your roof."

Aunt Linnie, not unkindly, answered for him. "We been a-knowing the
Lochlanns for many years. I'd trust them with my life."

Uncle Osborn nodded. "It's time for you to see the world outside this
little burg, Helen. So much out there to see and learn about."

"Brett's courting you," Alice leaned over and whispered in her ear making her blush.

Twisting her handkerchief in her lap, Helen said, "What in the world will I wear?"

"Now don't you worry, my dear," Ma said. "God will provide."

Surprising her, Seth spoke up. "Hey sis. He asked you. Seems to me that's what matters."

That gave everyone a good chuckle. After all, it did come down to that. She was still in disbelief. Brett had actually asked her.

"Oh, my word," Irma said, her face wreathed in a bright smile at hearing the news. "This is getting a little bit serious." Calling to Sid, who was already at work in the back, she said, "Come here, Sid. You gotta hear this."

Like with her family, Helen was reluctant to put too much emphasis on the thing. She wished everyone would stop blowing it out of proportion.

Sid's eyes sparkled. "Well now. That's exciting, Helen. It's time you have a look at the bigger world," waving his hand to take in all of Chancey's Bend. "Bigger'n this place anyway."

"That's sorta what Uncle Osborn had to say."

"He's right," Irma agreed.

"Seems to me, you'll be needing off work Friday," Sid said.

Helen was nervous about asking. She'd never asked for a day off before. She'd never even been sick and unable to work.

She nodded. "Train leaves first thing Friday morning."

"That's fine, Helen. You go and have a great time." This from Irma.

As she hung up her wraps, Helen hesitated a bit. Another favor was needed. "Sid? Irma? I was wondering. Do you have a nice fabric I could purchase? I'll need to make something that will be suitable for a concert in the big city."

"Aw pawsh," Irma said. "You got no time for that. Sid, watch the store. Helen and I got business to take care of upstairs."

In all the time of working at the shop, Helen had never been in their upstairs apartment. She was amazed at how neat, tidy, and compact it was. Perfect for the two of them. She remembered Irma saying they had left the bit city, left their big house, and were perfectly suited for this life in little Chancey's Bend.

"Now then," Irma said pointing to a chair in the kitchen. "You sit there a minute. I think I have just what you need."

After a few minutes she returned carrying several outfits on padded satin hangers. "Remember, my dear, we lived in the city for years and I attended many operas, dance reviews, symphonies, lectures, and dramas." Giving a laugh she added, "And I was a bit smaller around the middle than I am now."

"Oh, but I couldn't..." Helen started to protest.

"Of course you can. These just been a-hanging in here doing no one any good."

Hooking the hangers over kitchen cabinet door handles, she smoothed them down, then one by one, brought them to Helen showing the front and back. Each one more stunning than the other. Helen felt breathless. She let her fingertips linger over the elegant fabrics of each. By now she knew quality fabric, and these were definitely that.

"Well? What do you think? Will one of these fit for the concert?"

"Irma, you're so kind. I was at loose ends having no idea what I might wear. This is beyond my ability to believe. Mama said God would provide." Looking back over them, she said, "I believe my choice will be the gold lamé."

"Ah. I hoped you'd choose that one. Because..." Grabbing the other hangers she disappeared back into the bedroom. Returning with a wide-brim hat in hand, she finished her sentence. "..I just happen to have the matching hat."

The band around the crown echoed the gold lamé of the dress, complete with a large bow and streamers down the back. The effect was striking.

"Now shoes, and I think we'll have you all outfitted." Once again Irma disappeared through the door.

Helen would have loved to have had a glimpse of all that was stored in that room.

"Your foot is small like mine. At least one of these pairs should fit."

After trying them on, Helen chose the black patent with the decorative buckle and ankle strap.

"Good choice. Even though they're a bit big, the strap will hold them in place. Don't want to be losing a shoe like Cinderella." Irma tucked the pair back into a white shoebox.

"Cincinnati is a noisy place," Irma was saying later that afternoon as they worked together in the backroom. "It'll be a bit of a shock at first. More automobiles than you've ever seen. Trolleys moving at great speed and clanging their bells. Buildings so tall you can hardly see the tops. Almost like they're in the clouds."

"Do you miss it?" Helen asked as she created small stitches hemming a flowered skirt.

"I did at first." With a hand cupped to her mouth, and in a fake whisper, she said, "Don't tell Sid. I'd never admit it to him. He was so happy to get away from it all. He grew up out in the country on a farm, so city life never suited him." She smoothed out the trousers in front of her and placed one of the cuffs under the needle of the Singer and set the treadle moving. "But now? I'm so used to Chancey's Bend, that even when we go to the city to purchase merchandise, I can't wait to get back to the peace and quiet."

Chapter 10

The city turned out to be all that Irma described and more. Helen didn't express her thoughts aloud, but in her mind it was like a thousand showboats. Bright lights everywhere.

She'd never before ridden on a train. She'd never before ridden in an automobile. And definitely, she'd never before experienced a hotel. It required all her mental power to remain composed, and not to gaze about her like a small child at a carnival. Conway and Ruth took her under their wing as Brett parted from them upon their arrival. Rehearsals at the Opera House required his presence.

The taxi cab that carried them from the station to the hotel parked at the front entry and waited for Brett. A burgundy canopy, trimmed in glossy gold fringe stretched from the front door of the hotel to where they stood at the street. As Conway motioned for the doorman to come fetch their bags, Brett stepped closer to where Helen was standing and explained to her that he would be at rehearsals at the Opera House all afternoon.

"But I'll be with you for dinner tonight," he assured her. To his mother, he said, "Shall we eat in the dining room?" He motioned toward the hotel.

Through the spacious side windows, Helen could see a room filled with tables covered in white cloths, replete with china, silver, and crystal. How would she ever manage to eat in such elegance?

Ruth nodded. "Let's do. It'll save time."

"I agree," Conway chimed in.

"It's settled then." Giving them a quick salute, Brett climbed back into the waiting yellow taxi that rumbled as it sat there waiting. "Till tonight then." And he was gone.

"Come dear." Ruth gently took Helen's arm. "Let's get you settled."

A boy, no older than Seth, dressed in a blue-grey uniform, replete with rows of brass buttons, carried their baggage and led them to an elevator. Another first for Helen.

When the elevator operator asked for the floor number, Conway said, "Third floor."

As the gold grillwork door closed, the operator turned a crank, and the little cage began to move. Helen held her breath. For a moment she feared they would be trapped inside and be unable to escape. But no sooner had the thought flitted through her mind, the operator turned the crank again, the cage stopped moving, and the grillwork door opened.

"Third floor," came the announcement.

Down the carpeted hallway they went, with Ruth still holding Helen's arm. It gave off a measure of comfort that Helen sorely needed.

Their rooms were situated in a row down the hall with Helen's first, the next for Conway and Ruth, and the furthest one for Brett.

"I'll take our bags, and Brett's," Conway said to his wife. "You take care of our girl here." He smiled at her as he said it. Helen had no doubt he knew full well that she was nearly dumbstruck by all these new experiences.

"By all means." Ruth took Helen's bag from the uniformed boy and turned the key in the door. As it opened, Helen saw a spacious room. Never in her life had she had a room to herself.

A wide four-poster bed, sporting a flowered spread and snow-white pillows, dominated the center of the room. Against the opposite wall sat a walnut-colored vanity, set with a wide oval mirror above, and pink tufted bench placed in front.

Setting Helen's bag near the bed, Ruth stepped to the windows and drew back the heavy draperies. Motioning for Helen to join her, Ruth said, "Come look. You have a great view."

Ruth's statement was definitely true. The room was on the street side of the hotel, and she could see all the automobiles, trolleys, and horse-drawn drays, coming and going at a frantic pace. How could so many people be in such a hurry to get where they were going?

The site of many young men in military uniforms left Helen disconcerted. It was also true on the train as soldiers nearly filled the car in which they were riding. It definitely brought the reality of war into focus.

"You can hang your things in here." Ruth opened the chifforobe. "We're going to take a walk later. Would you care to join us? Or would you rather rest until this evening?"

Helen didn't have to think for a second. "Oh, I would very much like to go with you. I'm ready to see all there is to see."

Ruth chuckled. "Freshen up, then. We'll come get you in about an hour."

Not only a room to herself, but also an adjoining bathroom. Removing her hat, she laid it on the vanity bench. Dreamlike she entered bathroom and gazed around. A soap dish on the lavatory held an embossed lavender bar of soap. Picking it up, she was startled to breathe in the deep scent of lilacs. How fitting.

"Just like you, Lord, to give me this sweet message. Thank you."

Their walk later that afternoon, took them to shops where Ruth made a few small purchases. At one place where Conway waited outside, Ruth looked over boxes of silk hosiery. Turning to Helen, she asked, "Which do you like?"

Helen had only known cotton stockings. The smiling clerk spread out several pair across the glass-covered counter—black, gray, cream, white—and some with lace patterns throughout. This is what she remembered seeing Cat wear. Elegant to the extreme. She could only imagine the cost. Pointing to the cream pair with lace at the top, she said, "These are lovely."

Choosing three pair, including the cream pair, Ruth paid with folding money. To the clerk, she said, pointing to the cream pair, "Wrap these separately."

As they walked to the front entrance, Ruth handed Helen the package containing the cream hosiery. "These, my dear, are for you."

No words would come. If she opened her mouth, Helen knew she would merely stammer and sound juvenile. She simply whispered her thanks and graciously received the package that Ruth handed to her.

"Wear them tonight and enjoy your special time here."

Brett's expression when he first saw her in the gold lamé dress—complete with ribboned hat, patent shoes, *and silk stockings*—made her fairly certain he cared about her. Still, in all this time, he'd not expressed his feelings for her, which meant she was left to interpret from words and facial expressions. This particular expression was priceless.

The feeling was certainly mutual, as she'd never seen him in tails and tie. He was strikingly handsome, and as they entered the dining area of the hotel, she noticed other young ladies in the room gazing at him. She certainly couldn't blame them.

Lively conversation around the table that evening gave her no time to think about being nervous. Brett regaled them with tales of the rehearsal sessions. He'd found the piano to be slightly out of tune, resulting in an emergency call for a tuner to show up. And while members of the symphony were gracious and congenial, it was the soloist who created the most problems.

"High strung," he told them as he cut into a thick steak. "I'm convinced all entertainers are inherently high strung."

"Perhaps it's their way of hiding a case of the nerves," Ruth suggested.

"That could be," he said, "but they seem to use their nervousness to create problems—imaginary problems I might add—and in turn make everyone else around them miserable."

"Other than high-strung singers, and out-of-tune pianos," Conway put in, "how did it go?"

Brett laughed. "I did make it sound disastrous, didn't I?"

"A wee bit, perhaps," his mother agreed.

"Once the tuner left, and I went through the numbers with the symphony, it went well."

"Are *you* nervous?" Helen wanted to know. She couldn't imagine performing in front of an entire theater filled with people watching your every move. He looked at her for a moment making her wonder if she'd spoken out of turn. She quickly added, "I know I would be."

"Good question, Helen. The answer is, no matter how many times you play before an audience, there's always a measure of nervousness. It's natural."

"But you don't create problems, or make others miserable," Ruth added with a laugh.

They'd ordered ice cream for dessert. As Brett's spoon clinked on the crystal stemmed bowl, and as he spooned out the last bites, he asked, "Is that a question or a statement?"

"Oh, a statement, of course."

And that's the way it went. Easy and relaxed conversation all through the meal, until time to hail a taxi cab to take them to the opera house.

If Helen had thought the hotel resplendent, the opera house put it in the shade. In gentlemanly fashion, Brett hooked her hand in the crook of his arm as they advanced up the wide front Opera House staircase. At the entrance to the theater, he leaned down toward her and whispered, "I'm glad you're here to experience this part of my life. Thank you for accepting my invitation. Will you say a prayer over me?"

So startled, she could barely speak, she whispered a short prayer of blessing over him, and later, for the life of her, couldn't remember a single word she said. But he smiled and thanked her. Before releasing her gloved hand, he gave it a soft squeeze setting her heart pounding.

He gave the three of them over to the usher to lead them to their special seats near the front, and then he was gone.

Not sure what she expected, Helen was amazed to find that the concert elicited a wide range of emotions, taking her from being close to tears, to wild excitement. As the music rose and fell in waves, filling the room to nearly bursting, it swept her up in its magic.

Watching Brett at the grand piano on a stage in front of hundreds, far exceeded being a one-person audience for the *concert* in the parlor at his house. When she dared for a moment to take her eyes off the platform, and look around her, she sensed that every person was also caught up in the electrifying grasp of the music. Were concerts always like this?

That Brett played throughout the entire program surprised her. He played for every number, with seemingly little effort. So confident. So in control of every movement and every piece played. Then there came the piano concerto in which he truly commanded audience attention. Backed up by the symphony orchestra, the harmonies baffled her—amazed that so many different instruments could create such a glorious sound.

Sitting there spellbound she wondered how could such a talented, gifted, brilliant pianist—possibly heading for a professional career—ever think twice about her? A small-town, backwoods, farm girl. It made no sense.

Those thoughts returned to her later. Much later. After the magic had subsided; as she tried to settle down in the strange and spacious hotel room. She stood at the window and watched the traffic, which seemed never to slow down or quiet down, even at this late hour. She very nearly buckled under the weight of her thoughts. At what point would Brett Lochlann come to his senses and realize Helen Heise was no catch?

Chapter 11

Returning to her own world in small town Chancey's Bend turned out to be more difficult than Helen thought it might be. The city noise and lights had not overwhelmed her. Indeed, she would like to have tasted more of what it had to offer.

Only the sight of so many soldiers disturbed her. On several street corners she saw tables set up, behind which loomed large signs proclaiming Red Cross fund-raising. Gathered around the tables were smart-looking soldiers and sailors. Helen never remembered seeing navy uniforms. For the matter, she'd not seen many uniforms at all. Ever.

Nurses in pale-blue dresses, covered by pure white aprons with a bright red cross embroidered on the bib, stood chatting with the soldiers. Their starched white caps lent to them an aura of courage and confidence. Watching them, Helen wondered what compelled them to want to be a nurse? Especially now at a time of war.

Posters in store windows encouraged citizens to buy Liberty Bonds. Helen had no idea what Liberty Bonds were, but it must have something to do with money needed to fight a war.

Her first night back home, in her own familiar bed, in her familiar attic bedroom, she tossed and turned as sleep fled. Once she heard Alice's soft snores, she took a deep breath and said, "Ma?"

"Hm?"

Crawling out of bed, pulling her wrapper around her, she tiptoed to Ma's bed and crawled in beside her, soaking in the warmth and the love.

"I need to ask you something. My feelings are a jumbled mess. How am I supposed to know what's real? Or am I just giving in to wishful thinking?"

Giving Helen a soft pat on the arm, she said, "Am I to guess you're referring to your feelings for Brett Lochlann?"

Helen had to chuckle. "That's a correct guess."

"What you want to know is if you are truly in love with him."

"Yes. I so want it to be real. But I'm so afraid it's not."

"That's understandable. Because all these emotions are new to you. It's like trying to find your way through the woods, taking a direction you've never taken before."

Snuggling closer to Mama, she said, "That's a perfect way to describe it."

"When you're away from him, are your thoughts still filled with him?"

"Yes. It's maddening."

"And when you're away from him, are you counting the hours until you get to see him again?"

"Yes."

"When you see him, when you're near him, is you heart doing flip flops?"

"And my stomach too."

"I think we're getting somewhere."

"Oh Ma. That could just be a girlish crush."

"True. Could be. Let's go this direction. Name three qualities, or characteristics that you do not like about Brett Lochlann. That you absolutely cannot stand."

Helen thought for a few moments. "Oh Ma, I can't think of any. He's such a gentleman. He's courteous. He cares about how I feel and what I think. He goes out of his way to make sure I'm taken care of. Even making sure Ruth and Conway watched over me in Cincinnati. He's talented. He's handsome. And..." She paused.

"And?"

"Before he went back stage, just before his performance, he asked me to pray for him."

"Just you?"

"Hm hm."

"Not his parents?"

"No. And they were standing nearby."

"Helen, it appears that you are in love with a Godly man who is in love with you. My advice to you is to enjoy the journey." Giving Helen a hug, then a gentle shove, she said, "Now get back to bed and get to sleep so I can get to sleep."

Kissing her mother's cheek, she replied, "Yes, Ma. And thank you."

Thick green underbrush had flourished since they last came along this trail. It made for slow going for the horses.

"Should have grabbed my machete," Brett joked as he guided his horse in front of Helen going single file.

Helen didn't mind going slow, as she drank in the sights and sounds of springtime. Each tree now sported full leaves from the smaller persimmon and dogwood, to the towering oaks, black walnut, river birch, and others she recognized from years of wandering through the forests that surrounded their farm. As the spring breeze moved through the loblolly pines and hemlocks it gave off a familiar sighing sound.

As they approached the clearing, Brett waited for her to catch up. Her anticipation continued to build knowing the lilacs now would be in full bloom.

She wasn't disappointed. The sight took her breath away. A array of lavender lay before them.

"Come on." She clucked at her horse, taking her into a trot. "We need a closeup, so we can take in all that sweet scent."

Helen never imagined there could be a place so lovely. She found herself wishing she could thank those settlers who cared enough to nurture this flowering forest.

After dismounting and securing the horses, Brett took her hand as they strolled through the maze, stopping here and there to pluck a cluster and enjoy the distinct lilac aroma. The warmth of the May sunshine worked to enhance the aroma so that it filled the air.

Later, after enjoying lunch that Ma had packed—because Helen insisted it was her turn—they sat side-by-side on the old quilt they'd spread out on the porch of the deserted house.

They had hardly stopped talking since Brett came to fetch her at the Gabler house. Now that Helen had done as Ma instructed, to enjoy the journey, she felt much more comfortable in their conversation.

Now Brett drew in an audible breath, reached over to take her hand, and said, "Helen, I hope you know how much I care for you."

Here came that flip-flopping of her heart, as Ma called it. "I know you care, Brett. You've made that quite clear. But how much? That you haven't made clear." Her forward reply surprised her. But it was what she'd been longing to know for weeks.

Reaching his arm around her shoulders, he pulled her close. "How much? Let's just say, I'm crazy in love with you."

Turning now to look straight into her eyes, he added, "If it hadn't been for this dad-blamed war, I would at this moment be begging you to marry me."

Everything inside her wanted to say, *Forget the war. Please beg me to marry you.* But she held her peace and let him have his say.

"This war has changed everything. I've been trying to ignore it, but as more of our young men from Chancey's Bend are signing up, I see it can't be ignored."

Helen's throat constricted till she felt she couldn't breathe. Where was he going with all this?

"Our trip to Cincinnati, seeing all the soldiers, the sense came over me that I'm being disloyal to my country."

Fearing what words were coming next, she gently lay her head on his shoulder and felt his arms closing about her.

"I've enlisted, Helen. I leave on Monday."

The sobs came unbidden. No amount of will power could stop them. At the very moment when she felt her life had direction and purpose and meaning, it was being snatched away. She couldn't bear it.

He continued to hold her and graciously let her cry. "I hope these tears mean that you care as well. I've hoped that for a very long time."

Finally, when she could catch her breath, she whispered, "I do care, Brett. I love you deeply. With all my heart."

Tucking his finger under her chin he lifted it, then brushed away the tears from her cheeks. Pulling out his handkerchief he handed it to her. "You're beautiful, even when you're crying."

Dabbing at her eyes, she could scarcely believe she was hearing his kind words. All her days of wondering were over. Now she knew. Now she felt secure in his love for her.

"Tell me, Helen. If I were begging you to marry me today, what would your answer be?"

Managing a smile, she answered, "I would yell out a yes at the top of my voice so it would be heard all the way back to Chancey's Bend."

"The very words I'd hoped to hear." Leaning over, he gave her a light, sweet kiss, full on her lips. "I can't ask you now. It wouldn't be fair. But I will ask one thing of you."

"What is it?"

"All I ask is that you wait for me. You are lovely, and other men will be seeking you out. Please wait for me. I will come back to you."

She reached up to stroke his cheek. "I will wait for you Brett Lochlann. No matter how long it takes."

When they arrived back in town, Brett went inside the Gabler house with Helen to tell her family his news. He'd told his parents the evening before.

In answer to her question of how they had reacted, Brett said his father masked his emotions. "But Mother cried, and asked if there was any way I could get out of going."

"And you explained that you could not."

"The draft has already begun. I don't want to stand around waiting for that news."

Everyone in the Gabler household was gathered in the spacious kitchen. As they entered, Wooly jumped up from his place by the back door and trotted over to Brett, tail wagging in greeting. It was a surprise for the family to see Brett come in. This was a first. All eyes were on them, as Helen announced that Brett had something to tell them.

Ma had the large enamelware coffeepot on the burner, and Aunt Linnie was taking down plates and cutting large pieces of frosted chocolate cake. As she set plates around, she directed the younger ones to sit at their small table off to the side of the room. Then she motioned for Brett and Helen to sit at the table.

As they sat down, and before all the filled mugs could be passed around, Brett explained his enlistment. And that he would be leaving the following Monday. Uncle Osborn didn't seem surprised. Ma couldn't suppress a gasp. Sweet, sensitive Alice jumped up and ran upstairs to her room. Her reaction displayed exactly how Helen felt. She wanted to run away and never have to face this awful truth.

Ma then stepped over to Brett, placing a sizeable slice of cake in front of him, she patted his shoulder. "We're all very proud of you, Brett. I know this was not an easy decision."

Brett looked up at her. "I don't think it's any secret how I feel about your daughter, Freida." Reaching over, he took Helen's hand. "I've asked her to wait for me. And when I return, that's when I will formally ask you for her hand."

Smiling, he looked around the room, and added, "I guess I'll have to ask all of you. She belongs to all of you."

Seth spoke up and said, "You betcha. Uncle Osborn and I will be watching over her for you."

LeRoi got up from his place, came over to Brett's side. Standing straight and tall, he said, "I'm going to be a soldier and fight right alongside of you, Brett."

"Thanks for your offer LeRoi. But the whole thing will be over by Christmas. I'll be back before you're old enough to enlist."

Helen remembered that Sid had said almost the very same words. She wondered how they could be so sure. She didn't feel sure about anything. Before all this whoopla, she'd never been interested in the newspapers that arrived at the shop. But now she read the front pages just as soon as Sid and Irma were finished.

Stories of German U-boats sinking unarmed American freighters. Numbers of British soldiers dying and wounded on the front lines. The Germans using mustard gas to disable soldiers. And how everything was bogged down within trenches dug for miles along the front lines. It was all so ugly. And so terrifying. And her beloved Brett was headed right into the thick of it. The very thought made her feel sick.

Chapter 12

They made quite a showing at Chancey's Bend train station, all coming to see Brett off. He'd been notified that his first destination was a newly-built training camp named Camp Sherman in Chillicothe, Ohio.

"At least it's not halfway across the country," his mother said as she dabbed at the tears on her cheeks with her flowered handkerchief.

The chuffing of the train came on like a monstrous, evil threat, bearing down on them to carry away the precious love of her life. Helen could hardly believe the sight of the train filled to overflowing with dozens of young uniformed men hanging out the windows waving at them—all of whom were leaving their homes, their families, and for many, their lovers. A heartbreaking realization.

Each member of the family in their turn, gave Brett hugs and handshakes, but when he came to Helen, he pulled her tightly to him till she could feel the scratchy wool of his uniform, the scent of which she would never forget. Unlike their first kiss, this one was full of ardor and passion. Any other time, she would have been embarrassed beyond words. But not now. Not this special moment. Everything in her wanted to hold him close and never ever let go.

"I love you, Helen," he whispered. "You are my sweet Lilac Love."

That brought a smile to her lips. "I know now. And I love you too, my darling."

In a matter of minutes, he was aboard, waving to them from the train window along with all the other soldiers. Slowly and steadily, the train began to move, picking up speed. They all stood there watching it grow smaller and smaller until it became a mere speck in the distance.

Helen thought surely, she'd wake up from this bad dream and her life would go back to normal. But now, nothing was normal.

In the weeks that followed, everything turned bleak and empty. Had Brett really taken up that much of her life? Possessed that much of her heart? Of her soul? Oh, how she hated this war. Everything about it was wicked, evil, and most of all, unfair.

Thankfully, Brett's letters came with great regularity. And she wrote to him nearly every day.

He described the acres of newly-built barracks that filled the camp. "It's like nothing you've ever seen," he wrote. "And they all look alike. You don't want to get lost or you'll be sleeping with a whole regiment of strangers." He seemed to be able to make light of his situation.

As the weeks progressed, he told of more and more new war exercises in which they were involved.

We dig trenches, we shoot guns—big guns, we build pontoon bridges, and we eat lots of bad food. I sure do miss home cooking. And of course, we march. And we march. And then we march some more. Everywhere we go, we march. Oh, and did I mention sit ups, and pushups, and all kinds of fitness programs?

In a later letter he wrote,

It's difficult to explain, Helen, but when we are all decked out in our uniforms, marching in formation, with every man in perfect unison, and with the drill commands being shouted out, one can't help but experience a burst of pride in our hearts. Even more so if the band is there to play rousing march tunes. It's exhilarating. I admit I'm quite surprised at that emotion.

But what did she have to write to him? Nothing. Every day was the same as the day before. She didn't even want to get up in the morning. She dreaded going to the shop. Nothing was the same as before. She caught Mama and Aunt Linnie exchanging worried, concerned looks. Let them be worried. Helen just didn't care.

After six weeks of training, Brett was scheduled to come home on a week's furlough. From there, he explained in a letter, he was being shipped to Camp Gordon, Georgia. Farther away from her. She counted the days which dragged by maddingly.

One evening as she was coming up to the house, she met Alice who was on her way out the door with her large tapestry bag hooked on her arm. When had her younger sister become so grown up? With her hair pinned up, her chic little hat tilted just so, she'd turned into a woman almost overnight.

"You're going out?" Helen asked, puzzled.

"I'm knitting with the Red Cross women at the high school gymnasium."

"Knitting?"

"I mentioned it to you last week. Don't you remember? We're knitting socks for the soldiers."

Completely embarrassed, Helen didn't remember, but faking, she said, "Oh yes. Now that you mention it." Then she asked, "What about your supper?" It sounded silly after she said it,

With a shake of her bag Alice said, "I have apples and a sandwich in here."

They were standing together on the front porch now, and Alice said, "Please come with me, Helen. I'm finally getting acquainted with other women in this town. They're all so nice. It's such a good time. When I asked you before, you never even answered me."

Helen felt herself flinch. She didn't want to have a *good time.* All her good times had left on the train weeks ago.

Alice reached out and gently laid her hand on Helen's arm. "You know, you still do have a beau. One who adores you. He just happens to be in another place at the moment. Excuse me for being forward but you're acting as though you've completely lost him."

Where had this wisdom come from—out of the mouth of her younger sister? Alice had only just turned thirteen. Was she right? Had Helen been acting as though she'd lost Brett forever?

Alice gave her no chance to reply. "I can only hope that someday I'll have someone who loves me like Brett loves you. You are greatly blessed." Removing her hand from Helen's arm, she added. "I'd like to think you'd act like it. Do you want Brett to come home on leave and find a despondent, dispirited girl waiting for him? Why you barely eat. And you never talk to your family who loves you."

The words hurt something awful. Was Alice right? Was she being self-centered—all wrapped up in her own feelings of loss? It wasn't helping anyone. And certainly not herself.

Taking a different tack for self-preservation, Helen said, "You were always better at knitting that I was."

Alice laughed. "And you were much better at making all our clothes. But there are ladies, oh and young girls too, who know nothing about knitting and everyone is learning together. Won't you come? We'll be there until eight." Tripping down the front porch stairs, she said, "I'll be watching for you. I'll be your teacher. Ha. Won't that be a good joke."

A few more steps and Alice turned about and said, "Think of it this way. Our soldiers need warm socks. Someone this very moment may be knitting a pair of socks that Brett will wear."

And she was gone.

Helen didn't go that night. But the feelings of guilt finally overwhelmed her, especially after Alice's remark about someone knitting socks for Brett. Her sister had hit home.

Alice's description was correct. It was a warm, friendly group, some accomplished in the art of knitting and could turn out socks and warm mufflers at a high rate of speed, and others who'd never held a pair of knitting needles. Everyone joined in and helped one another. Helen allowed Alice to teach her. The straight knitting she caught onto quickly. It was turning the heel of the socks that provided the biggest challenge.

It was here, in this group of women in the community, that she realized she was not alone in her grief and loneliness. One young wife was the mother of two toddlers and now she had no husband to help out or support. Another lady told that two of her sons, only eighteen and nineteen years of age, had enlisted on the same day. Her home was now bereft of two of her children.

As this mother said, "I never expected they would be under my roof forever. I could be resigned to their leaving to go out in the world." Fighting back tears, she added, "But not to war."

And so it happened, that through this female companionship, Helen found the time of Brett's absence more tolerable.

When he did come home on a week of leave, she wasn't despondent. The week was magical as they spent nearly every waking moment together. To her great surprise, Sid and Irma invited Brett to come inside the shop and sit with Helen as she worked. A kindness she never expected, and a kindness she could never repay.

Many hours were spent at the Lochlann home. Helen had no desire to steal Brett from his parents. They needed time with him as well. And he was at the keyboard much of those hours. He described it as being like cool water to a man dying of thirst. He'd never in his life spent that much time away from a piano.

This time when Brett left, Helen took special effort to constrain her emotions. She felt a new level of maturity, in full realization she was not alone. Families all across the country were in this same predicament. The war had changed everything and changed every person.

"Wait for me, my Lilac Love. I will come home to you," he whispered as once again they stood beside the monstrous train that waited to carry him away from her.

"There'll never be anyone else for me," she replied. "I'm yours forever."

A parting kiss and he was gone from her arms and waving to her from the train window. She held her tears until she was alone that night in her own bed. Only then did she allow herself to give way to the flood of emotions.

The very next day, Helen sat hemming a pair of trousers, wondering how she would ever get through these days of routine sameness. Yes, there was her loving family who doted over her. Yes, she had her work. Yes, she enjoyed the friendship of the ladies in the knitting group, but still, life felt so empty.

At mid-morning, Irma came to her table carrying a letter that changed everything.

"Look here, Miss Helen. You got a letter from the *Pleasures A-Plenty.*"

"I did? A letter for me?"

Irma laughed. "I guess so. You just happen to be the only Helen Heise I know." Waving the letter, she added, "And that's the name I see written right here on the envelope."

Taking the envelope emblazoned with the picture of the showboat in the corner, Helen simply stared at it for a minute. Maybe Cat needed another costume. That would add some sparkle to her dreary days.

"Well, you gonna just sit there and look at it?"

Sid stuck his head through the curtain at the doorway. Making a silly face, he said, "Hey kiddo, we're dying to know. I didn't get no letter from Coop and them. I'm green with envy."

Helen couldn't help but laugh at Sid's silliness. After opening the envelope and pulling out the letter, she followed the swirling, precise penmanship signed by Opal. Scanning it quickly—it was quite lengthy—she looked up at Sid and Irma.

"Did the boat sink?" Sid asked. "You look a might peaked."

"What is it?" Opal chimed in.

Helen just shook her head. "This is unbelievable. They want me to come and join the crew."

"Join the crew? On the showboat?" Sid was coming closer now, obviously full of curiosity. "But you don't have any acting experience. What'll you do?"

Helen continued to stare at the letter in disbelief. "Just listen," she said.

My dear Miss Helen,

All of us here on the showboat pray this letter finds you well. I guess by this time, all this war nonsense has visited Chancey's Bend. It has definitely visited Pleasures A-Plenty. Can you hear us all the way down the river yelling OUCH?

We are losing young men right and left. Which means we are in search of extra hands. In a meeting of our remaining crew, your name came up. I don't know if you realize that you became an object of appreciation after the skilled work you did on Cat's costume. (We all still rave about it.)

Now you're no doubt wondering what you would be doing on a showboat. Here's the answer.

Work on the boat is never done. Even if we still had all our young men, we would still need your skills as a seamstress. So there's that. But there's cooking, cleaning, stage set up and take down.

And believe it or not, you will be needed on stage. Don't worry, you won't have to learn lines. (That is, unless you want to.) But you can wear an old shirt and overalls, pin your hair up under a straw hat, and walk on as the farmer's son. Several roles in the dramas need similar walk-ons.

Oh, and Cat said she would very much like to have you help in the role of her secretary, assisting with her correspondence.

That's about it. How does it sound? If you are willing, we can talk about salary later. We are fair in that regard. And just think, you can eat all you want pretty much for free. Plus, you'll see sights you've probably never seen before.

Send us a telegram and just say yes or no. (And we're all hoping it will be yes.) If yes, we'll quickly send money for a train ticket. And let you know our exact location.

Respectfully,

Opal Cooper

Now it was Sid and Irma's turn to stare.

"Don't that beat all," Sid said. "Now don't that just beat all. You on a showboat."

"Don't get in a hurry, Sid," Irma said. "Leave her have time to wool this over in her head. This isn't a small decision."

Putting his arm over his wife's shoulder, Sid said, "Irma's right. As usual." Guiding Irma toward the door, he added, "Let's let her alone with her letter."

For the present moment, Helen had no idea what her decision might be.

Chapter 13

"Alice, let's eat supper with the family tonight. I have something to share. And I want you to be there."

Helen had intercepted her sister as she was in the kitchen preparing her bag to attend the knitting group. Aunt Linnie and Ma stopped their tasks of preparing supper and gave questioning looks.

"I hate to disappoint the knitting group," Alice said. "We all need to carry our own weight."

"Is everything all right, Helen?" Ma set the crockery bowl of mashed potatoes on the table.

"Yes. Fine. It's all fine. Everything's fine." Helen had no idea what to say. She just wanted the family to sit down and listen, and then help her make this decision. "Where is everyone?"

Aunt Linnie laughed. "Everyone is where everyone usually is this time of day. You just haven't been here."

It was true. She hadn't been home in the evening since she started attending the knitting group. But in a few minutes, Aunt Linnie had rounded up the little ones from down the street where they were playing with neighbor children. And Seth and Uncle Osborn came tromping in from working out in the shop.

"Wash up quick," Ma instructed. "Helen had something on her mind to say."

LeRoi came over to Helen. "What is it? Are you going to run away and get married?" Making gaga eyes, he crooned, "Helen's so in love, so in love, so blindly in love."

Aunt Linnie came at him from behind and grabbed him by the ear, making him squeal. "LeRoi Gabler, where are your manners?" she demanded. "You owe your cousin an apology for your rude behavior."

Rubbing his reddening ear, he mumbled an apology.

Giving him a little shove, Aunt Linnie said, "The sooner you wash those filthy hands of yours, the sooner we'll learn just what's going on. You're holding everything up."

"Aw, I'm not that dirty," he grumbled. But stepped a bit quicker to the lavatory.

At last, prayers were said, food was being passed, and Helen drew the letter from her skirt pocket. She took great effort to keep the envelope tucked away. She didn't want anyone to know where the letter came from. Clearing her throat, she said, "I received this letter today. It came to me at the shop."

The family knew that Brett's letters came to the mailbox at the house. Helen looked around at the serious expressions. Not wanting to keep them in suspense, she started by announcing that the letter came from Opal Cooper. A heavy silence filled the room as she read through the entire letter—even LeRoi held his peace. When she came to, *Respectfully, Opal Cooper,* she folded the letter and tucked it back into her pocket. Still no one said a word.

"Well," she said, "isn't anybody going to say something? What are you thinking? Should I go? Should I stay?"

Alice's voice quavered in a whisper, she said, "How will Brett know where to send your letters? He won't be able to find you."

"I know the showboat has a tight schedule." This from Uncle Osborn. "Their itinerary is laid out months in advance." Looking over at Helen, he added, "All Helen has to do is send him a copy. He'll send the letters to each destination."

Ma agreed. "Well of course. You can't tell me all those crew members go without mail while traveling."

LeRoi, fidgeting in his chair piped up. "I want to go, Helen. Let me go. They need men. I know I can be of help. I can do those things they need."

Aunt Linnie gave him a stern look. "Son, you're not going anywhere until you have at least two more years at the school. Then you can go wherever your heart leads you."

"I'll probably go out west and be a ranch hand. Ride horses and herd cattle."

His comment bought laughter, and the seriousness of the moment was lessened some.

Helen truly thought everyone would have strong opinions and help her make her decision.

"Ma?"

Helen tried to read her mother's expression. Tears glistened in her eyes. "Oh Helen. You know I'll miss you fiercely. You are such a light in my life." Motioning around the table, she added, "In all our lives."

As they voiced their agreement, it brought Helen to tears. Was she ready to leave this warmth? This love? But even if there had been no war, if Brett still been here and they married, they surely would not live in Chancey's Bend. One way or the other, her destiny would lie outside this tiny backwater town.

Then Ma added, "If you say no to this opportunity, I think you will always regret it."

Aunt Linnie said, "I agree with Freida. With Brett away, what's to hold you here?"

"It's like Opal said in her letter," said Uncle Osborn, "when would you ever have such a chance to travel and see places you've never seen before?"

It was Aunt Linnie who said, "I think we should pray about this."

"Agreed," Uncle Osborn as he motioned for everyone to take hold of hands.

As each one prayed over her, and then offered their encouragement, Helen's excitement began to build. It was at that moment she realized that she really wanted to go. She wanted to travel. She wanted to see new places and meet new people. So, it was settled.

As she entered the tailor shop on her last day, she saw a large box sitting on the front counter. In it lay the gold lamé dress, matching hat, and black patent pumps she'd worn in Cincinnati.

"I want you to have these," Irma told her.

The loving words, the caring gift, brought tears to Helen's eyes. "I'm not sure I'll have a place to wear these," she said. "I think I'm going to be peeling potatoes in the galley and swabbing the decks." Her attempt at humor was an effort to hold back a flood of tears, waiting to fall.

Irma wrapped Helen up in a strong hug. "Believe me, Helen. A woman never knows when she might need a fancy dress," she said.

Then Sid was there, hugging her as well. "You're like our very own daughter, Helen. I hope you know that. We're sure enough gonna miss you."

He took the box and handed it to her. "Irma's right, as usual. You never know when a fancy dress will come in handy. Take this with our blessings. You'll think of us when you wear it."

They prayed blessings over her before she went out the door.

Now it was her turn to board the train and wave out the window, after being hugged by about a dozen townspeople. After joining the knitting group, the number of her acquaintances had grown.

Saying her good-byes to Brett's parents, and to Irma and Sid, turned out to be almost as difficult as with her own family. Seth and Uncle Osborn had painted a large sign sporting a picture of the likeness of *Pleasures A-Plenty*. The sign read:

Pleasures on board the Pleasures A-Plenty
Will multiply exponentially,

With the arrival of Helen Heise

A few tears were shed, but for the most part it was a joyous occasion. Everyone appeared to be happy for her and wished her well.

It wasn't until the rocking train was far down the tracks that the fear crept in. What in the world was she doing? What had she been thinking? This was a wild and crazy idea. The other time she rode the train, Brett had been by her side. And Ruth and Conway were sitting across from her doing all within their power to make her feel at ease.

Now she clasped her gloved hands in her lap to keep them from shaking, and swallowed hard around the lump forming in her throat. This train was taking her away from everything she'd ever known.

At that moment, her thoughts turned to Brett. He probably had these same feelings when the train had carried him away. At least she knew where she was going and knew what was ahead for her. Brett had had no idea. As she began to pray for him, the fear subsided somewhat.

Groups of soldiers were scattered throughout the train cars. Mesmerized by the landscape flying by her window, she hadn't realized that a group toward the far end of the car were watching her. As she took notice, one of the men smiled at her. Quickly she returned her gaze to the scenery out the window.

After a moment, she felt movement and looked up into the eyes of a handsome soldier. Hat in hand he said, "Traveling alone, young lady? Would you like company?"

Feeling the heat rising to her cheeks, she replied, "Yes. Well, I mean no. I'll be meeting someone."

"Your sweetheart?"

This was the opportunity to squelch this. "My sweetheart, my *fiancé*, is stationed in Georgia. Today I'm on my way to visit friends."

Thankfully, the word fiancé cancelled the advance. "I understand," he said. "Sorry to have bothered you, miss. You have a good journey."

"No apology needed." After a pause, she added, "Thank you for wearing the uniform."

Giving a little salute, he returned to his seat. After that, she made sure to keep her eyes averted. Just a lonely soldier boy, she thought. And he meant no harm.

The closer they came to her stopping off point of New Madrid, Missouri, the nervousness returned. What if the showboat had been detained? What if no one was there to meet her? What would she do?

Presently, the porter came through the car announcing the next stop of New Madrid. Helen felt the train slowing, and saw the station outside the window. A much bigger station than in Chancey's Bend. As the train lurched to a stop, she picked up her two suitcases, which seemed a pitiful small amount of belongings. But Opal insisted she would need very little. "Most everything will be provided," she'd said in her most recent letter.

The letter had arrived quickly following Helen's telegram letting them know of her decision to accept the offer. In her letter, Opal expressed the joy and excitement of the *Pleasures A-Plenty* crew at her decision.

As she now walked through the train car with a suitcase in each hand, she kept peering out the windows, hoping to see a familiar face. Then she was at the door, stepping down to the platform, when a shout went up.

"There she is! Helen! Over here."

Coop was there striding toward her with Ralphie close by his side.

Was everyone getting off at New Madrid? She wasn't used to so many people in one place. She maneuvered through the crowd, sensing great relief that Coop was indeed right there to meet her.

Ralphie took her bags while Coop faced her and gave a deep bow, sweeping his captain's hat off as he did so. "Miss Helena. We are honored that you would grace us with your presence."

His loud greeting caused people to stop and gaze their direction, which in turn caused Helen's cheeks to flame. No one could ignore his get-up. The entire community no doubt knew Coop as the showboat captain, just as they did in Chancey's Bend.

Hooking his arm in hers, he suddenly shouted out, "Ho there, folks. Just look-a here, would you now? This is our newest crew member, Miss Helena."

Leaning down, he said softly, "Helena is more of a proper stage name, don't you agree?"

Never in her life had she given thought to her name. Certainly not in regard to being a *stage name*. And she liked how he pronounced it Hel-eena. He gave it an elegant flair.

"Come tonight," Coop called out as they made their way to a waiting wagon, with a slouched-shouldered, bearded, gray-haired man in the driver's seat. "We'll make formal introduction then."

Ralphie placed Helen's bags in the wagon bed then hopped up beside them, dangling his long legs off the back. Coop gave her a hand up where she seated herself by the old man who smelled like horses. Coop climbed up beside her, as he gave one last yell to the crowd. "The name says it all, folks. *Pleasures A-Plenty*. Come see for yourself. Enjoy the pleasures. You won't want to miss it. At Weatherly's Landing. Band strikes up at six. Show starts at seven."

Helen had heard Coop's booming voice before, but never this close. If it hadn't appeared rude, she would have clapped her hands over her ears.

The wagon moved slowly down the street toward the river. New Madrid, larger in size and population than Chancey's Bend, could boast many more stores and houses, and automobiles. So many automobiles. The sight and sounds of the chugging machines seemed to be everywhere. Some were even enclosed, like the one she experienced in Cincinnati. She remembered Brett's father making the comment that in a few years there would be no more horses on the streets, only automobiles. Helen couldn't fathom such a thing. But it looked to be true in this place.

As the wagon jolted around a corner, the vast, wide Mississippi River came into view, gentle waves sparkling in the midday sunshine. And there, sitting proudly at the landing, were docked the showboat and the steamboat *Odyssey*. Helen's new home.

Chapter 14

This landing was nothing like the muddy one at Chancey's Bend. Here the town had laid out smooth concrete right down to the water's edge. As Helen made her way across the wide stageplank, there stood Opal on the deck smiling, waving, and shouting her greeting. Her lively manner instantly put Helen at ease.

"Howdy Miss Helen. Welcome aboard. Now as a resident, not just a visitor."

On her heels came Coop, who announced to everyone within hearing distance, "No longer Helen. I want to introduce to you our newest troupe member, Heleeena."

"Oh my." Opal gave Helen a gentle hug. "Isn't that just like Coop? Already christened you with a new name."

"I guess so."

"And how do you like it?"

Helen thought for a brief moment. "I like it. Yes. I do. I like it a lot."

Suddenly the deck was swarming with actors, band members, Odyssey crew, and even the cook from the galley. Each one coming up to give handshakes, to welcome her, and calling her Helena. It was a bit overwhelming.

"You're a mighty fine sight, Helena," said a band member whom she remembered as one of the cornet players. "Every dad-burned human being of the male species seems to think fighting a war is more important than putting on a show."

"Now Richard," Opal said, "we mustn't be reproachful of our fighting men."

Surveying the crowd gathered around her, it was obvious most were gals and older men. Too old, Helena supposed, to be marching away to war.

As the excitement of her arrival wound down, Opal and Coop led her into the auditorium and up the side stairs. She remembered when she went up those same stairs the day Cat placed her order for the costume. But now she was led off the opposite direction where the stairs forked. They came out on the far side of the deck and there Coop opened the door to her room.

After setting her luggage down inside, he patted her on the shoulder. "Helena, I surely hope you're gonna be happy with us."

"Aw Coop," Opal said, pushing him out of the way, "of course she's going to be happy. Who on this boat ain't happy? Now get on outta here so's I can get her settled in."

Coop gave Helena a wink and a grin, and was gone.

The room, while small, was neat and tidy. Never before had she enjoyed space of her very own. Except for the hotel in Cincinnati, but that was only two nights. This would be hers and hers alone. For who knew how many days.

A small bed, covered with a patchwork quilt took up one corner. A braided rag-rug lay beside the bed. In the opposite corner sat a desk and chair where Helen knew she'd be writing letters to Brett. Opal pointed out the two drawers in the desk. "You can keep your personal things in here," she explained.

A wooden washstand butted up against the desk, complete with pink-flowered pitcher and wash bowl.

"And this..." Opal picked up a bucket and long rope that sat beneath the washstand. "...this is for drawing your own water."

Helena couldn't help but laugh. "From the river. I'll be drawing water from the river."

Waving toward the window, Opal said, "There's plenty out there, wouldn't you say?"

Helena turned around, gazed at the view out her window, and was instantly mesmerized. The wide river made the Chancey River seem like a little creek. The Mighty Mississippi stretched out ahead as far as the eye could see. Realizing that this would be her view for the days and weeks to come caused a thrill of excitement to course through her.

"Now you put your things away, then come down to the Odyssey and Cook will make sure you have a good lunch. We've already eaten. Then come to the stage and we'll talk about your tasks for tonight. Since you're a new arrival, we'll start you with something simple. Tomorrow, you can study a walk-on role."

Helena nodded. Not only was she now living on the showboat, but she would actually be a part of the show. It was almost too much to take in.

Cook, Helena soon learned ruled her kitchen with an iron hand, but she was an excellent cook. The lunch set before her consisted of a bowl of venison stew, sourdough bread with rich butter, a flowered china plate overflowing with a pile of ripe strawberries and blackberries, and apple pandowdy for dessert with a pitcher of cream to pour over it.

Food at the Gabler's, while always sufficient, rarely offered enough for anyone to have seconds. After finishing off her first lunch on the showboat, Helena felt stuffed to the gills. This experience was already like a dream come true.

Before she had left the Gabler home, LeRoi was set on teasing her that she would be sick from the rocking of the boat. "It's never still," he said. "Remember how it felt when we were at the show?"

Helena had to say, she never remembered anything except the excitement of the show. But once he brought it up, she wondered if indeed the rocking might make her sick. Thankfully, it was quite the opposite. The rocking along with the sounds of lapping water, lulled her to sleep. Her first night, she slept soundly and didn't awaken until the first bell rang at nine.

That alone seemed humorous to her. Back in Chancey's Bend, she was accustomed to getting up and getting ready for work much earlier. How could she have slept so late? Possibly due to the excitement of her first day on board. The stress from travel, and the nervousness at handling the tasks assigned her.

Opal had walked her through detailed instructions. She showed Helena how the stage consisted of several rolled curtains, some toward the back of the stage, some closer to the front. In between the curtains were what Opal called *flats*. Flats were made of heavy canvas stretched on wooden frames. One side showed painted images of bushes and greenery for outdoor scenes. The other side showed painted images of wooden paneling to portray an interior scene.

During the dramas, at Opal's signal, Helena was to pull out the flats, turn them about and push them back on stage. It was, Opal explained, the task of a stage hand, but her assistance would free up one of the stage hands to then serve as a walk-on for the play. During the intermission, Helena helped Ralphie sell bags of candy to the happy crowd of show-goers.

Every part of the showboat functioned like a well-oiled machine. Each member of the troupe knew their place, knew their lines for the drama, and knew exactly where they were supposed to be at any given time. That's no doubt why Opal had Helena positioned in a stationary spot for the entire show for her first night.

Even backstage, the show pulsated excitement from Coop's opening monologue to the closing songs. For Helena the highlight of the show was when Cat Callahan sang, "Peg 'O My Heart," dressed in the lilac and purple costume Helena had created. For the finale, the Broadway star brought down the house with "Johnny Get Your Gun," which even though it was an old minstrel song, it seemed in this wartime to be the perfect number.

The letter Helena had received from Brett the day before she left Chancey's Bend, assured her he was agreeable with her decision. She'd given him the news as soon as the telegram went over the wire to Coop and Opal. In his letter he wrote:

In a much different way, you're aiding in the war efforts. In times like these, people need a lighthearted break. The showboat provides that break. I know the crew must be overflowing with thanks for your presence.

I will keep the itinerary you enclosed in a place where I can refer to it often. It will be like my rifle practice—attempting to hit the target by sending letters to the right place at the right time.

Reading his response brought much relief. Helena couldn't help worrying over how he might take her news. His humor about comparing mailing letters with his rifle practice reassured her of his agreement with her decision.

Ralphie, and Taimah, the tall, muscular Creek Indian, were the first ones off the boat at each landing. After securing the vessels at the landing, they headed to the post office to pick up the mail. Helena soon learned that every crew member looked forward to mail. And she definitely included herself in that group.

Miraculously, at the very next town after New Madrid, two letters from Brett awaited her. He must have sent them the very moment he learned about her new adventure.

The letter described the rigorous training in the horrendous summer heat there in Georgia. He noted, "I've never sweated so much in my entire life. I suppose I've lost ten pounds."

He also said his orders to be shipped over to France would be coming soon.

Of course, she'd known all along that that would be his destination. But reading the letters in the privacy of her small room, those words hit hard. She was forced to lie down across her bed for a few moments just to catch her breath and pray.

Being on board *Pleasures A-Plenty* had helped to quell the fears that tried to invade her thoughts. All the *what ifs*. Every newspaper was emblazoned with long lists of the dead and wounded. Now, on the showboat, she was too busy to consider all the *what ifs*. Rarely did she even see a newspaper, let alone have a spare minute to read one. Then, with the arrival of Brett's letters, once again the reality came crashing down.

Surprisingly, Helena quickly stepped into the rhythms of the days, and the nights, of the showboat. Most of her walk-on roles were that of a young boy. As Opal had described in her original letter, the costume might consist of overalls, flannel shirt, with her hair pinned up beneath a straw hat. In other roles she was a beggar with ragged clothes. Or a bad boy, in shirt and trousers, who was always getting into trouble. Eventually she was given a few lines in order to "made the scene more realistic," as Opal explained.

Even starring in a male part, Helena still had to wear stage makeup. "Without it," Opal explained, "in the glare of footlights, your face takes on a pale, pasty look—rather like a ghost."

And so it was, Opal meticulously taught, and Helena learned, how to apply stage makeup. She couldn't help wonder what Brett would think if he saw her in face paint.

Due to their lack of leading men, Coop dyed his graying hair and mustache and played the young hero, and sometimes even the evil villain. Dual roles kept him running backstage to the green room throughout show time to make quick costume changes. Ever the consummate showman, he could pull it off with great finesse.

In addition to her stage appearances, Helena was assigned several odd jobs such as cleaning chores and lending a helping hand to Cook who seemed to always be in a bad mood.

None of this did she mind. She'd been accustomed to hard work all her growing up years on the farm. She was ready to help wherever needed. Opal often said that Helena had come aboard to "light up the place."

While cast members habitually slept in due to their late hours the night before, the crew of the Odyssey rose early, firing up the steam engine, casting off and heading downriver to the next stop on their tight schedule. She had grown to enjoy the peaceful ride, watching the passing scenery which ranged from farms and small settlements, to dark-green thick forests, to wide-open pastureland. She'd never imagined how restful a boat ride could be. Nothing like a noisy, rattling, rocking train.

Every Sunday morning, without fail, Coop gathered all his underlings in the galley for a church service. Only a very few declined his invitation. They sat around the long tables with their Bibles in front of them.

No long sermons. No hymn books. Coop in his strong baritone voice led in the hymns that most all of them were familiar with. After a few songs and prayers, he took his Bible and read a passage. Often it was an account such as Gideon, or Jonah, or David and Goliath. To the story, he would add his own words of encouragement and exhortation. As he closed in prayer, he always prayed that the horrendous war would end quickly and all the fighting doughboys would return safely.

During the times when Helena had been assigned no tasks, and if her letters to Brett were caught up, she would rummage through the racks of costumes which seemed to be in constant need of repair. The crew, especially the actors, voiced their appreciation.

When patching, altering, and repairing the costumes, Helena liked to sit on the deck outside her room. She'd created a red-and-white striped canvas canopy that she stretched from the deck roof down to the railing. This cast a welcome shade in the midday heat.

One afternoon, as she was working, Isobel, their young ingenue came down the deck toward her carrying the chair from her room.

"Mind if I join you?"

Not waiting for answer, she plunked down her chair and settled herself with a deep sigh. Helena welcomed the company. Little by little, she was making friends with the cast and crew. Isobel played mainly the child parts because of her small stature. But, Helena reasoned, also probably because Cat Callahan had top billing and received the roles of the main characters. But it was clear that Isobel was happy to take whatever roles came her way.

Motioning to Helena's canopy, Isobel said, "This is such a great idea. Can you make me one?" Tucking one leg under the other as she leaned back, she said, "Oh never mind. I'd rather come over here and share yours."

Helena had to laugh. "You're welcome under my canopy any time. Even if I'm off doing other things."

Motioning to the pile of costumes spread at Helena's feet, Isobel said, "No one in our crowd cares a whit about patching and darning. We're thankful you do."

Smiling, Helena replied, "Sewing's my God-given gift. I've been sewing for my family since I was a little girl. Making almost all our clothes. Then we moved from the farm, and I became employed in a tailor shop in Chancey's Bend."

"I know about that," Isobel replied with a nod. "Every gal on *Pleasures A-Plenty* turned green with envy when we saw the creation you made for Cat. We'd heard about you before Opal ever invited you to join."

At that moment, two other troupe members, hearing the voices, came out from their rooms and, each bringing their own chair, joined the circle. Their voices helped draw attention away from Helena's blushing from Isobel's compliment. As they arranged their chairs so they could chat, she let the flow of the friendly voices, and thrumming of the Odyssey, ease her into a state of contentment. Threading her needle, she moved from patching rips and torn hems to reattaching missing buttons.

Two of the female crew members, Isobel, being one of them, had husbands who'd gone off to war. They shared what news they knew, which wasn't much. All the newspaper reports implied the war wasn't going well. But truth was hard to come by. "It's all propaganda," Coop often said.

The other girl who'd been left behind was Myra, the acrobat and high wire artist. Helena remembered them from the parade on River Road in Chancey's Bend. She'd also seen photographs of the amazing aerial stunts Myra and her husband, Lendon, had performed together. Demonstrating deep courage, she'd continued on alone. Helena had often heard Myra say, "I'm only half here. My other half's in France."

Myra's wiry body was as flexible as a piece of string. Headstands, handstands, back flips, balancing on a chair, riding a unicycle around the stage—then standing on the seat. She amazed the crowd with her seemingly impossible body contortions. Her performances filled time between acts of the drama as cast members changed costumes and stage hands rearranged the scenery.

Myra's finale consisted of walking the high wire strung above the audience from one end of the auditorium to the other, a feat that drew audible gasps from all those who gazed upward.

It was up to Ralphie to *spot* her, which was what Lendon had always done before he left for the war. As Ralphie said, watching and being ready to catch should Myra fall, made him as nervous "as a cat in a roomful of rocking chairs."

Coop made certain the high wire was checked then rechecked, by at least four crewmembers. He was adamant in his insistence to keep Myra safe.

"I don't want no rifle-toting doughboy coming after me 'cuz I let his sweet darling be injured while he was away saving the country."

Crew and cast knew he was only half kidding. Everyone adored their Captain.

Chapter 15

If Helena had thought she might become friends with Cat, she was mistaken. Cat didn't appear to be overly friendly to anyone on board. Wherever small clusters of cast and crew gathered to chat, Cat was never among them. Of course, she had to be present for meals, but she scarcely if ever joined in the conversations. She did, however, reach out to Helena a few times, asking her to come to her stateroom and draft letters.

Most of the correspondence had to do with her acting career, letters written to agents, stage directors, and producers. Helena got the drift that Cat was on the showboat only as a brief respite from her hectic acting life, a life which demanded a great deal of travel, deadlines, rehearsals, and late-night engagements. Rehearsals on the showboat happened at the first of the season and that was it. The only exception was if a cast member had to step into another role. Even then it was a brief practice because nearly every member knew each other's lines. They'd heard them at every presentation.

Cat let it be known that come fall she was destined to leave the quiet showboat life and return to New York. When she thought about it, Helena was bothered that even though Cat enjoyed top billing on all the advertising, was blessed with room and board and a nice salary, the Broadway star seemed ungrateful for any of it. However, Helena never dwelled on it. Cat went her way, Helena went hers. Even when Helena worked with Cat, the conversation was centered only on the tasks at hand.

Cat's costumes remained in her stateroom—a room that was larger than most of the others—rather than being mingled with other costumes that were stored backstage. Every Saturday, Cat handed over a dollar to Helena for not only writing letters, but also for the extra work of seeing to it all dresses, hats, props, and hosiery were in tip top condition.

Even with the extra chores, Helena still took time to write long letters to Brett nearly every afternoon. Unlike when she lived in Chancey's Bend, where each day overflowed with sameness, now she had countless things to write about. New sights and new experiences awaited her at every stop.

One day, Opal asked Helena to locate a band uniform that might fit her, and to join in the march up main street along with the band.

"But I play no instrument. I can barely peck out *Chopsticks* on the piano."

The two of them were sitting and chatting in the orchestra pit in front of the stage. Opal reached over and picked up a cornet case, flipped up the silver latches, opened the red-silk-lined case, and brought out the instrument.

"Can you do this?" Opal proceeded to fiddle with the valves.

"Sure."

Reaching back into the case, she pulled out the mouthpiece. Placing it against her lips she sputtered into it. "Can you do that?"

Again Helena said, "Well, sure. But that's not..."

Opal laughed. "Remember Helena, on the showboat, it's all about *show*."

Placing the mouthpiece firmly onto the cornet, she put it up to her mouth, then fiddled with the valves. "Like this. Here you try it. Put it up tight against your lips, blow, and see what happens."

Doing as Opal instructed, Helena sputtered a few sounds, and imitating Opal, made the keys go up and down.

"Perfect. Good job. Believe me, Helena, no one in these backwater villages knows anything about playing a cornet, and they won't know that it's all a show. And we desperately need more bodies in that band. Our drummer and xylophone player are now playing louder than ever to make up for the lack."

And so it happened at the very next landing, Helena smartly decked out in a band uniform, complete with the hat, marched up and down main street, making a great show of playing her cornet. At first she was nervous, but then it began to be such great fun, she could hardly wait until next parade. Plus, the exhilarating feeling of knowing she was an important part of bringing a bit of joy to a grieving nation.

Little did she know, but she was about to be assigned yet another role in the show. Opal surprised her one day by asking if she might have a recitation she could give. One that all ages might enjoy. "The more double roles we assign, the more time needed between scenes," she explained.

Without even a thought, Helena blurted out, "I can recite, 'When Lilacs Last in the Door-yard Bloom'd.'" As soon as she spoke it, she wished she hadn't. That was *their poem*. Hers and Brett's. What was she thinking?

At Helena's answer, Opal's eyes lit up. Clapping her hands, she exclaimed, "I love it. It's perfect. Walt Whitman. How much of it can you recite?"

Helena hesitated. She could recite it in its entirety, but since it was a requiem, some parts would be too solemn for the show. Then she said, "Parts of it are sad. Perhaps I should choose something different."

"Oh no. Please. I love Whitman. Let's look at using the Lilac poem. We'll sit down together and choose which verses to include and which ones to avoid. Meet me on my porch in an hour."

They'd been the last ones at the lunch table in the galley when Opal had asked her to hang back so they could talk. Now as they got up to leave, Opal added,

"Feel free to choose any dress from the wardrobe for your recitation. Something fancy."

It was then than Helena explained that she already had a fancy dress. After describing her gold lamé, Opal agreed it would be perfect.

By this time, Helena had no fear of the stage. She performed in front of the footlights in nearly every show. But standing on the stage, alone, with hers as the only voice, brought on a new level of stage fright. That plus wearing the dress she'd worn the night she'd been with Brett made her miss him intensely. She remembered how he gazed at her with loving eyes that night.

The backstage dressing room was always a flurry of activity before and during every performance. Sitting there in front of one of the mirrors, preparing for her recitation, she cradled her face in her hands fighting tears. Myra came and sat down beside her and patted her arm.

"It's all right, Helena. We all get a case of the nerves. I still do to this day."

Shaking her head, Helena said. "It not just that." Looking over at her new friend she said, "It's this dress. And the Lilac poem. All overflowing with memories of Brett."

"I understand. You know I do. For years it was always Lendon and me. Just the two of us performing. Now every single time I perform, I miss him desperately. As though part of me is missing."

Covering Myra's hand with hers, Helena was overcome with shame. "I'm so sorry Myra. How selfish of me. I was totally wrapped up in my own problems." Taking a deep breath, she added, "We can do this. As God gives us the strength. We can do this."

"That's a girl." Standing up and tugging on Helena's arm, she said, "Come on. Almost time for you to go on. By taking this role, you're helping every member of the troupe."

Boldly Helena stepped out in front of the foremost curtain, footlights glaring in her eyes. And she began, softly at first...

O powerful western fallen star!
O shades of night—O moody, tearful night!
O great star disappear'd—O the black murk that hides the star!

O cruel hands that hold me powerless—O helpless soul of me!
O harsh surrounding cloud that will not free my soul.

From the wings, she heard Opal's loud whisper, "Louder. Stronger."

After a deep breath, and a lift to her chin, she projected her voice to the back of the auditorium.

In the dooryard fronting an old farm-house near the white-wash'd
palings,
Stands the lilac-bush tall-growing with heart-shaped leaves of rich
green,
With many a pointed blossom rising delicate, with the perfume
strong I love,
With every leaf a miracle—and from this bush in the dooryard,
With delicate-color'd blossoms and heart-shaped leaves of rich
green,
A sprig with its flower I break.

After the show, Helena was showered with praise. Most importantly, from Coop himself, exclaiming how well she did. "You had the audience in the palm of your hand. Your voice inflections are phenomenal. I would have thought you came up through some New York acting school."

She did recall how good it felt to hear the sound of the applause. And after Myra's encouragement, she'd had no fear at all.

Brett's letters were sometimes waiting in batches at the post office in the next town. She sorted them according to dates on the postmark—France postmarks now—to keep them in order. He described the sight of thousands of uniformed American troops disembarking and landing on the shore, then all marching away to the training camps that General "Black Jack" Pershing had set up for them. Brett wrote that he had had a glimpse of the famous general, but only from a distance.

"Now it's back to tedious and boring training and marching," one letter read. "Oh. And then more marching and training. Highly frustrating. Wearisome."

Further on in the letter, he wrote:

No signs of moving us to the front, but we have seen troops coming back from battle. I won't describe. Just to say "ghastly." We've met a few American boys who came over before us to serve in the ambulance corp. I'm proud of them, but cannot even begin to imagine how difficult that job would be. And dangerous since they go as close to the fighting lines as possible to quickly rescue the wounded and deliver them to the hospital posts.

The first hospitals to be reached are tents. Yes, tents. And with winter coming on.

I know you are praying for me my sweet Helen, but include prayers for the many others as well. Great suffering here.

She'd told him of her name change, but she realized that being thousands of miles away, and not hearing it repeated many times a day, he would be reluctant to use Helena. After all, he'd only known her as Helen. He'd fallen in love with Helen.

Early in her showboat journey, Helena had been much too busy to think about what might lie ahead for her, but as the summer began to wane, it suddenly occurred to her that she'd made no plans for when the season was over.

Coop explained that *Pleasures A-Plenty* never traveled all the way to New Orleans as did the other showboats.

"Those big boys can have it," he said one day as they were eating lunch. "We prefer to travel the smaller tributaries that the big boats can't handle. And don't want to handle." Breaking open a steaming yeast roll and slathering it with butter and honey, he added, "They take the high road and we take the low road. But we still make a lot of money. Plus, the backwater towns are our most loyal customers."

Vic, the donkey trainer who was sitting across from her, spoke up. "We like how they sometimes pay us in meat and potatoes."

"Don't forget the elderberry jam," added a voice from the other end of the table.

From there they began calling out their favorite items the farm people brought in payment—pickled okra, string beans, beets, bunches of onions, pork rinds, plucked chickens, and on and on they went.

Helena had stopped listening. It had been at that moment, when Coop mentioned not going to New Orleans, that the thought came to her that this would not last forever. The more she thought about it, the more she knew she had no desire to go back to Chancey's Bend. Not after all this fun and excitement.

That realization surprised her.

But then what? She had no idea.

Their turnaround point, occurring in early August, was Vicksburg. Going north, against the current required more firepower from the Odyssey. At the bigger city docks, they took on coal to fuel the *Odyssey*. Helena enjoy watching from the vantage point of the back deck, as all deckhands joined in shoveling coal from the shiny black mounds piled up on the dock, into deep wheelbarrows, across a gangplank, then dumped into the bin on the steamboat. Dripping with sweat from the sweltering heat, they hardly paused as they worked till the bin was sufficiently filled. Helena marveled at their strength, and at the balance required to maneuver that barrow down the narrow gangplank.

The galley may have been hot, but she never minded helping Cook with meal preparation. A hand-written schedule posted on the galley door listed who worked when.

"It wasn't until we started losing our cast members to the war effort," Opal had told her, "that we began to ask for volunteers in the galley to assist Cook. Before that, we would never have thought of such a thing. Still, even now, we never require it of anyone. Totally voluntary."

Cook obviously had her pick of the help. After Vic assisted one time, Cook demanded that he go back to tending his trained donkey, Mr. Crinkle. "The bloke smells like his jackass," she was heard saying, "and he can't peel a spud worth a plug nickel."

Vic only laughed and winked. Many cast members suspected he planned that out like a stage play. It was a minor incident. No one really cared. Who didn't love the playful Mr. Crinkle and his caretaker, Vic?

A few weeks after the turnaround, Helena was in her usual place, under her awning, stitching together a new clown outfit for Vic. While he seemed to be content with the existing costume, Helena thought it could be much more colorful. She'd also designed a new bright-red neck ruff consisting of many more layers of netting than the one he'd worn for a couple of seasons. Vic definitely soaked up the special attention.

Opal, who usually remained on her own special porch, graced with the potted palms and her canaries singing from their white cages, came and sat with the few cast member who had gathered with Helena.

The Queen of the showboat was never without her record books in which she logged most every detail of the showboat operations. Helena wagered that no president of any large business was as meticulous as Opal Cooper.

Opal sat quietly posting into the log books from a batch of sales receipts and listening to the chatter, which usually consisted of nothing much except how the dramas could be improved, what they liked and disliked about the food, and which landings were their favorites. Sometimes talk turned to families and home.

It was during one of those conversations—about family and home—that Opal turned to Helena and asked, "How do you feel about your return to Chancey's Bend?"

It was a subject Helena preferred to avoid. While she wanted to see her family, the return would make missing Brett that much more painful. It was already almost more painful than she could bear. Everything little thing in Chancey's Bend would remind her of her days of being courted and falling in love.

She continued stitching the ruffles on the clown suit for a moment, letting her mind wander. Then she gave a little shrug. "I'm not sure."

"I'm asking because in my years in this business, it's rare for a cast member to perform in front of friends and family. But this will be happening for you. I wanted to bring it up ahead of time. If you want to take that night off, I would understand."

The comment wasn't at all what Helena was expecting. It was Brett who consumed most all her thoughts—not her family.

Shaking out the clown suit and holding it up for all to see, the cast members piled on the compliments, claiming that Vic would be the best-dressed clown-donkey-trainer on the showboat circuit.

"Wish you'd created it at the beginning of the season," one stated.

"But I only just thought of it a few days ago," Helena replied.

"No matter," Opal said. "If he returns to us, and I hope to God he does, he'll have it all next season. And we still have a month of shows before we winter."

"To answer your question," Helena said to Opal, "I don't believe I'll mind at all performing at Chancey's Bend. Really. I'll be fine."

And she was fine with the performance. She had warned her family ahead of time that she would be marching in the parade pretending to play the cornet. She didn't want that to be a surprise to them. And her recitation of the Walt Whitman poem went smooth as silk. After the show her family flocked around her heaping praises on her.

In the hours between the parade and show time, she had stopped by the tailor shop to say hello to Irma and Sid. They'd hired a new seamstress, but as Irma said, "Helen, she can't hold a candle to you. Your sewing skills just can't be beat."

Helena told them to take special notice of Vic's costume which she'd designed and created. And as Coop had always done, now it was her job to hand out free tickets. Only this time no costumes were delivered for repair. The repairs were being taken care of by her on a daily basis. But Coop told her to give tickets to the Briggses anyway.

Then she headed to the Gabler's only to find that the little ones weren't so little any more. They'd each one grown, and all were talking at once. Seth, quieter than the others, came to give her a hug and now towered over her. How could have grown so tall in such a short time? In his soft voice, now lowered an octave, he told her how much he'd missed her.

They all fussed over her, hugs were given all round. Alice tugged at her to come sit close. Helena had missed them too. While it was a good feeling to be with them again, she knew this was no longer her home. She was a different person than the one who'd left a few months ago.

Because her time was so limited, Aunt Linnie had invited the Lochlanns for supper. Only for a few minutes did the conversation turn to Brett. Helena could tell the pain of missing him was as deep for his parents as it was for her. He was, after all, their only child.

Over dinner she delighted them with tales from the showboat. She hadn't realized how many funny and interesting stories she had to share. But it was a lively cast and crew, and a different town every day.

After the Lochlanns left, it was time for Uncle Osborn to show off his new Model-T parked in a separate garage behind the house. A garage? Helena could hardly believe it. Now his woodworking shop sat flanked by a special building that housed his automobile.

Mama came up to her and said, "We have another surprise to show you."

After Uncle Osborn cranked the Model-T to life and backed it out, they all piled in.

"Where're we going?" she asked. "I've got to get back to the boat."

"This'll only take a minute," Uncle Osborn told her. "Then I'll personally drive you to the boat. You needn't walk."

He drove just a short way out of town. There in a wooded lot, a house was going up.

Alice grabbed Helena's hand. "It's ours, Helen. Uncle Osborn and Seth are building it for us. For Ma, and Seth, and me." Then she added in a wistful voice, "I wish you had time to walk over and have a closer look. I could show you where my room's going to be. I'll have a bedroom of my own."

Helena didn't want to say that she'd had a room of her own for many days now. That would be unkind. She could sense how this new house pleased her sister.

"And I'm helping," LeRoi said. "I'm learning to build. Papa says I'm doing a darn good job too."

"I did say that." Uncle Osborn turned the Model T around and drove back toward town. "And it's true. I'm building a team of builders."

His clever choice of words brought laughter all around.

Then Mindy Mae chimed in. "Someday our builder team will build a house for you and Brett, Helen. When he comes home from being a soldier."

The statement took Helena by surprise. Of course, they didn't know. She'd told no one. No one in her family knew that she never ever wanted to live in Chancey's Bend.

Even her lame attempts at explaining about her new name went unheeded. She would always be Helen to them. She let it rest. It didn't matter.

After the others had gotten out of the car at the house, Uncle Osborn drove her down River Road, back to her other home, her new home. On the way she couldn't help but notice gold stars mounted in the front windows of several houses. Each star represented a soldier who had died in a far distant land, and it made her heart hurt. For the millionth time, she prayed for Brett's safe return.

Chapter 16

C at's stack of correspondence appeared to be growing. Helena supposed it was because with each passing day, Cat was closer to returning to her life as a star on the Broadway stage.

Helena had heard Broadway called the *Great White Way* due to the dazzling electric lighting of theater marquees, street lamps, and large advertising signs. If the lights on *Pleasures A-Plenty* were mesmerizing, how exciting would it be to see Broadway and Times Square?

Pleasures A-Plenty had left the Mighty Mississippi and now navigated back on the smaller Ohio River. The days were cooling down and when Helena sat out on the deck, she kept her red wool sweater wrapped snugly around her shoulders. Breezes off the water were stronger and cooler than on the land.

Helena had learned that the Coopers planned to winter in Henderson. She would have liked to have known what they did all winter, but was too embarrassed to ask. She knew Opal assumed she would be returning home and had even mentioned something about getting her train tickets. Helena had no answer for her.

Then in a moment of time, the solution appeared.

Helena was in the process of folding up her wooden lap desk, preparing to leave Cat's stateroom after a few hours of work, when Cat said, "Do you have a few minutes? I have a question."

Helena wasn't sure how well she'd disguised her surprise. Cat Callahan speaking to her in a conversational tone was something new. Even after all these months of being together.

"Of course."

"Do you have plans for the end of the season? For this winter?"

Helena held her peace for a moment. The question took her by surprise and she didn't know what to say. How much was she willing to reveal? She'd been private about her decision not to return home.

Evidently, noting the pause, Cat went on. "The reason I'm asking is because if you have no other plans, would you consider continuing to work as my assistant?"

At that, Helena was even more shocked. Her words tumbled out. "To New York?"

"Chicago first. Then New York." Cat was placing stationary, envelopes, and postage stamps into the side drawer of her desk. "I understand you may need to think about it. I know it's rather sudden."

But she didn't need to think about it. To Helena, this was the answer to all her wondering and questioning. This was the perfect solution. Attempting to still her excitement, and calm her voice, she said, "I've been thinking about how to spend the off-season. I have no plans to return to Chancey's Bend. I would be pleased to accept your offer."

Cat stood, which signaled Helena's dismissal. "Good. We'll discuss further details when we arrive at Henderson."

Helena hefted up her desk in her arms and stepped to the door. As she left, she said a quick thank you. She wasn't sure if Cat had answered or not.

Chicago. New York. This was beyond her wildest dreams. She wanted to shout it out to the whole world, but she couldn't. Not yet. She wouldn't inform her family until she was on the train to Chicago. And Brett...? Well. That was confusing. Of course, she'd tell him, but wasn't sure the best time to do so. She didn't want to worry him.

Cook had prepared a heavier meal than usual. Roast leg of lamb, scalloped potatoes, snap beans, her famous dark rye bread, finished off with pineapple upside down cake. Cast member were literally groaning as they left the galley, all heading to their staterooms for a long nap. Helena was no exception.

Usually when taking a nap, she lay across her bed and read Brett's latest letters until she fell asleep. However, today she drew back the quilted coverlet and snuggled down beneath it. She'd barely finished reading one letter when she fell into a deep sleep.

At the first sound of the wailing, she thought she was dreaming, but it didn't stop. The anguished cries reminded her when back on the farm, an animal would be caught in a trap that her father had set. It took a few moments to come to her senses. This wasn't a dream. Sitting straight up, she could tell it was coming from the lower deck. The wails were growing stronger. Louder. More intense.

She jumped up, slipped into her shoes, ran out the door and down to the far end of the deck. There she saw Myra cradled in Opal's arms and many of the troupe crowded around. Opal was guiding Myra to a deck chair that someone had brought.

Craning over the rail, Helena could see that Myra was clutching a telegram. Oh, the dreaded telegrams. Everyone knew about them, but few people actually talked about them.

The wails of anguish were now interspersed with discernable words. Myra was crying out Lendon's name as she nearly doubled over in grief. "No. Please. No. Not my Lendon. My life. My soul. Please no." Words gasped out between deep uncontrollable sobbing. Helena felt she would be physical ill just listening.

At first, she wanted to hurry down to be part of the support, but by that time, they were lifting Myra to her feet. Helena heard a snippet of someone saying, "...get her to her room."

At that moment, almost like magic, there was Taimah. He stepped up and lifted Myra in his strong arms as though she weighed no more than a feather. He whispered something to Opal. She opened the auditorium doors and waved him inside.

Myra's stateroom was down a few doors from Helena's. Quickly she retreated to her own room, sat down at her desk, laid her head on her arms and wept. She had no control over the vicious thoughts—what if that telegram had been for her? What if it had been Brett? Oh how she hated this infernal war.

Getting through the show that night demanded the strength, courage, and steeled determination of every troupe member. It was their job to bring joy and happiness to an entire town.

The high wire was not strung up that night. And there was no acrobat number. But the show must go on. And it did. Helena later wondered how they did it. She witnessed an even deeper level the mettle of the people that made up the showboat team.

Myra's sister was coming on the train to take Myra home to New Jersey. No one felt she should travel alone. The mourning widow stayed mostly in her room. Opal sat with her much of the time and made sure Myra's meals were brought to her.

It was decided that the sister should meet them in Henderson. She was given a warm welcome, made sure she ate with the troupe, slept on a cot in Myra's room before the two of them left the next day. All the crew and cast were there on the showboat deck to say their good-byes, giving Myra hugs and comforting words. But as Helena knew, no amount of words would ever dull the pain of Myra's loss.

Helena remembered back when it was just the two of them chatting, and Myra told how she and Lendon had grown up together, both in show-business families. They had been building their act together since they were children.

In comparison, Helena had known Brett for only a short time. Even at that, she grieved his absence and longed to see his face, hear his voice, and feel his arms wrapped tightly around her.

Her heart hurt for Myra.

As Helena and Cat disembarked the train in Chicago's Union Station, and once their luggage was assembled around them—which included Cat's large trunks—Cat hailed a taxi cab.

The first impression Helena had of Chicago was the aromas that seemed to hang in the air. It was nothing like being aboard the showboat with river breezes cleansing the air. Chicago just smelled nasty. It wasn't until later that she learned when the wind was right, she was smelling the stockyards, and the meat packing plants. Apart from the nasty smells, even the very city itself lacked the sparkle that she remembered from Cincinnati. Instead it was rather dull and colorless. What it lacked in sparkle, it made up in noise.

Cat had requested that the taxi driver to take them along Michigan Avenue to view the harbor before being let off at their hotel. Helena had only thought the Mississippi was wide and grand, but out past the harbor, the white-capped expanse of Lake Michigan seemed to go on forever. More water than she'd ever seen. The driver made it a point to explain that Chicago dispatched many freighters and war ships from this harbor over to England to help win the war.

No matter where they went, it seemed to Helena there was little or no conversation that didn't include the war. She understood, but still felt it wearisome.

The *Auditorium Theatre* resided in the massive Auditorium Building which, to Helena, resembled nothing more than a European fortress. The tall square building sat on the busy Ida B. Wells Street in the South Loop. In addition to the theatre, offices and a 400-room hotel were housed in that building. On the train, Helena had read the details of the place in a brochure Cat had given her, and she ogled over the opulence of the theatre. Naturally she thought they would be staying in one of the fancy rooms in that hotel, but she thought wrong.

Their hotel, located three blocks away, turned out to be much less glamorous in style and décor. Cat's trunks were delivered to the theatre, her smaller suitcases she kept with her. The man at the desk verified their reservations and called for a young boy to take their bags.

Their rooms were small, the furnishings sparse, and the rugs worn bare and faded. Helena's room was a few doors down the hall from Cat's. The boy opened Helena's door first and then handed her the key. After placing her two suitcases near the small bed, he stood there for a few minutes before it dawned on Helena that he was waiting for a tip. Nervously, she opened her bag and reached in for a coin. She had no idea what was expected. After all, it was a rather rundown place.

He took the coin, looked at it with a masked expression, so she still had no idea if it had been enough. Even if he'd scowled at her, she would have had a better idea.

As he left, she heard Cat call her name. She stepped out into the dimly-lit hallway to hear Cat say, "Rest a bit, then we'll go eat. Come to my room in an hour."

Helena nodded and went back into her room. Pulling back the drapes, she saw that the view was a dull-red brick building, so close she could almost reach out and touch it. That is, if it had been warm enough to even open the window. But it wasn't. In fact, it had turned quite chilly.

She thought longingly of the bolts of heavy woolen fabrics in the back room of Briggs Tailor Shop. She and Irma had fashioned many a silk-lined, double-breasted overcoat from that beautifully textured wool.

At some point, she would have to purchase a coat, because she knew if it was cold in Chicago, it would be even colder in New York. She wasn't sure how and when that could be managed. Or how much she could spend. All her savings were wrapped in a small drawstring bag which she'd sewn into her chemise.

Cat had never clearly outlined how much Helena would be earning, or how much of the expenses she would be expected to take on. She had hoped that once it was just the two of them traveling together, there would be more conversation between them. That had not happened. Other than necessary directives or bits of information, Cat acted as though Helena were invisible.

Every once in a while, Helena would hear the echo of Brett's words saying that most all performers were high strung. And even as she and Opal were saying their good-byes at the train station in Henderson, Opal said, "I hope you're making a wise decision, Helena. I know for a fact that Cat's not the easiest person to work with."

Helena thanked Opal, but she was certain this was exactly what she should be doing. And as for Cat? Well, she might be self-centered and aloof, but she wasn't a monster. Helena was convinced she could handle anything Cat might dish out.

Their noon meal was at a delicatessen—a new word to Helena. Standing at a counter along one side of the busy eatery, the two of them ate hot pastrami sandwiches and washed it down with mugs of root beer. Two more new items in Helena's life. In all her travels with *Pleasures A-Plenty,* she'd never heard of pastrami.

She was more than ready for all the new experiences that lay ahead.

Chapter 17

H elena's first view of the interior of the Auditorium Theatre was from the wings of the stage. Nothing could have prepared her for the breathtaking gold and scarlet splendor, nor the breadth and depth of the main auditorium. While the box seats were low and to the sides, the balconies were high and open and offered optimum viewing. In fact, Helena had read in the brochure that the goal of the design was that the best seats would not be reserved for the wealthiest patrons. That every seat was a prime seat. It appeared that goal had been attained.

With the help of a stagehand, Cat's trunks were taken to her dressing room. Cat's role in the drama, *A Little Journey,* was as a co-star, but she was in nearly every scene, which meant she had one of the nicer dressing rooms. A room all to herself. A sign with Cat's name in fancy script had been fastened to the door.

The large mirror on the far wall was surrounded with electric lights. On the long counter beneath was a wide array of bottles, tubes, cases, and compacts, containing who-knew-what-all. A small lavatory had been installed at the side for handy use, Helena supposed, for removing all that stage makeup.

The furniture consisted of a comfy-looking sofa decorated with scarlet and gold pillows. Of course, a brass vanity stool with scarlet upholstery. Artwork in gilded frames graced the walls. Beneath her feet a soft oriental rug made Helena want to remove her shoes and walk on it barefoot. This room was so much nicer than their hotel room, she would have preferred to stay right here and sleep on this sofa.

From the wings later that day, she witnessed what Cat referred to as a *run-through* rehearsal. No real acting. The characters simply read their parts. When they emerged from the theatre into the cold wind in the late afternoon, Cat remarked that Helena's cloth coat would never do in this place.

"Come. Let's grab a trolley."

Pulling her felt hat down further over her ears, and pulling the collar of her coat up around her neck, Helena had to agree.

Riding the trolley—yet another new experience for Helena. All the noisy trolleys coming and going seemed a strange, complex, and confusing system. Hopefully, she wouldn't be staying in Chicago long enough to have to learn it.

The area of the city where they disembarked was rundown and shabby. Keeping up with Cat's quick steps proved difficult. Trash in the streets and poorly dressed people gave Helena more of a shiver than the icy wind. Just ahead of them was a shop with a sign in the window that read: *Buy Sell Trade Rent.* The paint-chipped sign above the door read *The Second Hand Store. Chicago's Best.*

Second hand store? If Helena had not been so cold, she would have laughed. What a crazy notion. But this was exactly the store into which Cat led her. Stepping right up to the counter, Cat said to the squat little lady with glasses dangling on a chain around her neck, "We need a warm coat." Waving toward Helena, she added, "For this gal here."

Helena was certain she turned several shades of red. If there'd been a hole in the floor, she would have gladly dropped right through it. The lady whose disheveled hair apparently hadn't seen a hairbrush in several days, put on her glasses and looked Helena up and down. Putting one finger in the air, she said, "You came at the right time. I have exactly what you need." At that she disappeared through a curtained door behind her and came out carrying a coat over her arm.

Although it smelled musty with hints of moth balls, it was indeed a warm coat. It was navy wool with gold buttons and a silvery-gray satin lining. Helena pushed through her embarrassment and looked it over thoroughly, looking for moth holes, or any rips or tears, and found none.

"Three dollars," the lady said.

Cat responded, "Too much. We're in a hurry. A dollar fifty and we'll take it."

Helena was sure it was at least a twenty-dollar coat. Or more. Cat was quite the negotiator.

Pushing her straggling hair from her face, the lady waved her hand. "Hold on a sec." Reaching into a drawer below the counter, she pulled out a navy-and-pale-blue patterned muffler along with matching gloves. "Two dollars with these thrown in?"

Cat nodded. "Deal." Pulling the money from her pocketbook, Cat said to Helena, "You can pay me back later."

Taking the money before Cat could change her mind, the lady pulled a nub of a pencil from behind her ear and scribbled out a ticket and handed it to Cat. "Want 'em wrapped?"

Helena wasn't too keen on wearing this used coat. Her plan was to let it air out tonight and wear it tomorrow. However, she had no chance to protest.

Cat stepped up and lifted Helena's cloth coat from her shoulders said, "Here, let me help you with that." As Helena slipped out of her lightweight coat, Cat handed it to the lady. "Wrap this one instead."

The lady nodded and pulled a length of brown paper from the large roll on the counter. In the time it took for Helena to tuck the knitted muffler around her neck and pull on the coat and gloves, her other coat had been wrapped and the package tied up with string.

Helena had to admit, she was much warmer as they left the secondhand store and rode the trolley back to their hotel.

The next few days were filled with frenzied rehearsals, complete with the director yelling at whomever he sensed was not performing to his level of expectations. He was on the stage, moving people, waving his arms, repeating lines to show the drama effect he was looking for.

A kindly stage hand made sure Helena had a chair in which to sit as she watched the action from the wings. It had been made clear she was not allowed out in the seating area. At one point, the director surprised her by handing her a script. It was thick and heavy.

"Watch along and perhaps we could use you as a prompter."

Helena just nodded and opened the script, easily finding the exact spot. Yet another first. She never even seen a play script before, let alone hold one in her hands.

Cat turned snippy and curt on the day of the opening night. Helena wasn't put off. She'd be nervous as well if she were performing on that stage. Helena was expected to have Cat's costumes and accessories out and ready. She'd learned exactly what to do at dress rehearsal.

Opening night was a frenzy of palpable excitement and nervousness. The director did indeed use Helena as a prompter. But only as a backup. The real prompter was in a small cubbyhole between the orchestra pit and the stage. The cast could see and hear him, but he was hidden from the audience.

At the final curtain call, amidst the powerful echoes of applause and cheers, the play appeared to be a success. Only the newspaper reviews the next day would tell the tale, but for now the cast appeared to be exuberant.

Back in Cat's dressing room, Helena carefully tended to all the details of the costumes. As she was hanging up the last item, Cat said, "I'm going with the cast to a club to celebrate. You go on to your room. I'll see you in the morning."

Helena struggled to mask her astonishment. Did Cat really mean she would be expected to walk to their hotel, alone, late at night? Surely Cat was kidding. But then, Helena had learned, Cat never kidded about anything.

Cat never even walked her to the back stage door. Of course, Helena knew the way. They'd walked it every day since their arrival. But never alone.

The cold wind hit her in the face as she exited the building. *I can do this. I will do this.* She straightened her shoulders, lifted her chin, made sure her pocketbook was hooked on her arm beneath her warm coat and began walking. By the time she reached the hotel, she felt her heart would pound right out of her chest. The man behind the counter was leaned back in his chair reading a newspaper. He moved the newspaper away from his face and said, "You the one traveling with that actress lady?"

Helena, already keyed up, jumped as he spoke to her. She managed to nod as she kept walking toward the stairs.

"Your name Heise?"

Now she stopped. Again, she nodded. How could he know her name?

Reaching below the counter, he pulled out an envelope. "Letter here for you. They addressed it in care of the hotel, and Miss Callahan."

As she stepped over to take it from him, she could see it was from her family. She almost forgotten she'd given them Cat's itinerary.

"Pretty smart folks you got there, girlie. Thinking to add Miss Callahan's name along with the hotel."

Clutching her letter, she gave him another nod, thanked him and hurried up the stairs. It may have been a shabby room, but she sighed with deep relief as she unlocked her door, went inside and locked it behind her. After taking off her wraps, she collapsed in the chair by the bed and opened her letter.

Once she'd made the decision to travel with Cat, Helena faced the challenge of writing home to give her family the news. She had no idea how they would take it. The letter was from all of them, each one writing a few lines. She could feel the love as waves of homesickness washed over her.

All wished her well. Her mother added that she would rather Helena (of course, she still wrote *Helen*) had talked it over with the family before making such a serious decision. However, she added that she trusted Helena to the uttermost.

"I know you'll use your God-given wisdom no matter what comes your way," she wrote.

Inside the letter was a smaller envelope with Alice's name penned in the upper right-hand corner. How like Alice to give her a private note. As she opened it her heart hurt for wanting to see her sister and hear her voice. The note read:

I don't care what anyone else says, I am extremely proud of you for having the courage to take this step. Of course, I had so hoped you would be with us all winter, but no matter. You will be seeing places, doing things, and meeting people that I could only dream about. I guess it's permissible if I am just a little bit jealous. Follow your dream my dear sister. And write to us soon. Love, Alice

Folding the pages and placing them back into the envelope, she opened one of her suitcases and tucked the letter into one of the pouches for safekeeping.

Thinking about home, and the roomy, cozy, Gabler kitchen, she suddenly realized she was hungry. She'd not eaten since their late lunch. Now at nearly midnight, her stomach loudly complained.

Had she been a native Chicagoan, she would have popped right out the door and headed to the all-night deli. But she definitely not a native. And she would just have to be hungry. A hard lesson learned. For the rest of the run, she made sure to have a sandwich in her pocketbook. A sandwich she paid for out of her dwindling savings.

Sleep was a long time coming as she thought about the fear she'd experienced on her return to the hotel. It came to her that she'd not prayed to ask God to help her through it. She couldn't remember the last time she'd prayed. When she had unpacked, she hadn't even bothered to take out her Bible. It was still in one of her two suitcases. She wasn't even sure which one.

A few reviews for the play were negative, but most were positive. The cast members and stage hands were delighted. On closing night, the director surprised Helena by handing her a few coins and thanked her for her assistance. She had actually stepped into her role on the third night. The prompter from his small enclosure at the front of the stage caught her attention, mouthed, *Take over*, and disappeared. By that time, she was so accustomed to following the script, she felt fairly comfortable. In the few minutes of the prompter's disappearance, she'd not had to prompt anyone. After all, these were seasoned performers. But she was confident that she could have prompted if necessary.

If Helena thought they were now headed for New York, she was sadly mistaken. Cat seemed bent on informing her of things only at last minute. As they parted at the theatre on closing night—she was now walking back to the hotel alone every night—Cat instructed her to be packed and ready to leave the next morning by seven. And she was. She was seated in the lobby, with her suitcases placed at her feet, before seven.

When Cat came down the stairs and into the lobby, Helena was once again struck by the actress's beauty. She noticed how the hotel clerk couldn't stop staring. Helen witnessed it happening wherever they went. Even this early in the morning Cat was dressed to the nines. A long, cream-colored coat, complete with ermine collar, a small hat cocked to the side, and her perfectly coifed platinum hair glowing. A large ermine muff hung from a satin cord around her neck.

She stepped up to the desk as the befuddled clerk turned the register book around and handed her a pen so she could sign them out. "Have my baggage brought down," she ordered.

Helena noted the lack of the word *please*, which seemed the most basic rule of courtesy. She stood as Cat approached.

"We'll be in Cleveland for a four-day run." Then turning away, she added, "Step lively, we've a train to catch."

At that point, Helena felt she just as well be one of Cat's pieces of baggage—just something to lug along and put up with.

Rather than the trolley, Cat hailed a taxi cab in order to handle all the luggage. At Union Station, as she hurried to keep up with Cat, Helena realized with alarm that while she'd given Brett and her family the names and addresses of the theaters in Chicago and New York, she hadn't known to include Cleveland. Cat's behavior was beginning to rankle Helena's nerves.

The Palace Theater in Cleveland, while not as elaborate as the Auditorium in Chicago was nonetheless dazzling. And as with the Auditorium, the theme of gold and scarlet ran throughout.

Cat's dressing room was smaller, so wrangling her wardrobe trunks proved a bit more challenging for the stage hand. And now rather than a hotel, their abode for this run was a boarding house—a boarding house specifically for single women of the theater called the East Main House. Cat had a room to herself, but Helena shared a room with one of the understudies of another show crew.

Thankfully the girl, Ardeen, was a happy soul, kind and considerate. Another plus was that breakfast and dinner were served around a large dining room table with plenty to eat. Much better than the meager fare at the deli in Chicago.

Ardeen, an Irish lass crowned with a mop of wild red curls, encouraged Helena to stow away food and take to their room.

"We'll not always be here for the dinner meal," she said with a wink as she shoved an orange and a yeast roll into her skirt pockets. "It's crucial to pack away for later."

Helena understood. Late nights were as much a part of theater life as it had been on the showboat.

The East Main House was conveniently located in the midst of the theater district of Cleveland; hence the women were from varying shows taking a run in the city. While some degree of pride and jealousy reared its ugly head, for the most part the girls were congenial.

Helena was convinced that Cleveland could compete with Chicago's boast of being the windy city. It was the cold winds off the lake that Helena disliked and made her long for the showboat navigating the warm rivers down South.

Chapter 18

In their few days of sharing a room, Helena and Ardeen enjoyed long conversations about their backgrounds, the theater, and their hopes and dreams.

Ardeen, came from a large Irish family, and grew up right in the heart of New York city. Her Irish brogue fascinated Helena, but also surprised her that Ardeen could turn it off and on.

When asked, Ardeen explained that she'd been to acting school. "*Neighborhood Playhouse School of the Theatre* it's called. Papa wasn't too keen on the idea, but after he died, Mama and rest of the family pooled their money so I could attend. That's where I learned how to talk in different accents. It's a must for stage stars."

But Ardeen seemed more interested in learning about Helena's accounts of her childhood days on the farm, her life in a rural river town, and she was fascinated to learn about living on the showboat.

"Of course, I'd heard about showboats, but hadn't any idea what they were really like. I envy you."

"You should try it next summer," Helena suggested. "I can put you in contact with Coop and Opal."

Pushing curls away from her face, Ardeen said, "I may just do that. Sounds like fun."

Conversation about the showboat brought Cat Callahan into the conversation, followed by the details of how Helena had created a costume for the star.

"I hope you charged her a pretty penny." Ardeen's voice had an edge to it.

Helena hesitated. "Well, I didn't exactly *charge* her. I accepted what she offered." Then she quickly added that Opal was witness. "I'm sure if the price hadn't been fair, Opal would have said something."

"I know it's none of my business, but may I ask how much she's paying you now?"

Standing in front the mirror that hung on the wall, Helena had unpinned her chignon and was brushing out her long hair. Not for the first time, she wished she had a short mop of curls like her friend.

At Ardeen's question she stopped brushing and turned to look at Ardeen who was sitting on the side of the bed pulling off her hosiery. Truthfully, it had become quite worrisome to Helena that Cat never mentioned money. Ever. She hesitated with her answer. "Well, I don't really do that much for her."

"But you are in charge of her wardrobe. That's what she hired you for. And she did hire you. Is that correct?"

"And I take care of her correspondence. She has me write letters and see to it they are mailed."

"I can tell from your expression that you don't know your salary. Not the amount, nor the time it's due."

Helena heaved a deep sigh. "Oh Ardeen. You're so right. And I have no one to talk to about it." She lay her hairbrush on the dresser, walked over to her side of the bed and turned back the covers. "It's a muddled mess."

Slipping her flannel gown over her head, Ardeen said, "What you need is a touch of New York spizzerinctum."

"Spizzer... what?"

"Spizzerinctum. You know, like Hutzpah. Nerve. Guts."

Fluffing her pillow and placing it behind her, Helena leaned back. "I think I have a shortage of those characteristics."

Ardeen waved away the idea with a sweep of her hand. "That's not true. It's just that you've never been in a predicament where you had to use it. In New York, we learn it from the cradle. Just like anything else in life, it requires practice."

Helena nodded, but she couldn't imagine herself talking to Cat as an equal.

"Tell me this. Two or three years ago, did you ever dream you'd be stepping onto the stage of a showboat?"

"Absolutely not. Never entered my head."

"And did you envision yourself actually on that stage? Behind those footlights?"

Helena could see where her new friend was going. "Never."

"New circumstances. New situations. New experiences. But you did it. Now you're going to do this."

Turning around, sitting Indian-style at the foot of the bed, Ardeen faced Helena. "Let's do play pretend. I am you and you are Cat."

Helena had to laugh. "Not sure I can manage that role."

"I know. I know. Tough one. Just give it your best."

"Where do I start?"

"Cat doesn't start. Helena starts."

"Oh."

"You're on the train headed to New York. I turn and say, 'Cat, just to make sure our working relationship runs well, a few details need to be addressed.'"

"I can't do this, Ardeen. I have no idea how Cat would respond. She barely speaks to me."

"We're the scriptwriters here. We'll just pretend."

Helena gave a nod and pressed in. "Cat might answer with, 'What details?'"

Ardeen, answering in her role as Helena, replied, "'From the beginning I expected to be told my salary and how often I would be paid. Because that's how a business relationship should work.' Then you can add something like, 'We can clear this up right now. Before we get to New York.'"

"You make it seem so easy. But my stomach will be in knots."

"Was your stomach in knots when you walked on stage the first time?"

"And every time after the first time."

"But you did it."

"I did."

"You can do this. You'll be sitting together on the train. She can't get away. She needs you to press in. She needs to know you're not a pushover. If you don't do this, she'll run over you from now on." Then Ardeen added, "Were you aware she doesn't have a very good reputation?"

"How do you mean?"

"First of all, the world of the theater is small. It may seem quite vast to an outsider, but everything interrelates, and for that very reason, rumors fly freely. Some true. Some a little less than true."

"And about Cat?"

"Seem to be true."

"Any details you can give me? Other than what I've experienced myself?"

"Since you've lived it, I'll just say, your suspicions are correct. She's interested mainly in herself. As a stage actress she's highly talented. But all the accolades have gone to her head."

"Pride goes before a fall."

"Yeah. Hey. Isn't that in the Bible somewhere?"

Helena nodded. "Proverbs sixteen-eighteen. It actually reads, *Pride goes before destruction, And a haughty spirit before a fall.*"

Lying back Ardeen lifted her arms and waved them as she announced in a fake British accent, "Well, I can tell you this. When my name is up there in lights, I shall never have a haughty spirit. I shall never forget my humble beginnings from whence I came."

Helena laughed as she clapped to show her approval. "I believe you, Ardeen Miller. And I believe that one day your name will be up there in lights."

"And one day, if she's not careful, Cat may fall."

As Helena fell asleep, she rehearsed the phrases Ardeen taught her. She'd pretend she was speaking lines in a play. This would be her performance. And in the days following, Ardeen helped her practice until she had it down pat.

As usual, Cat took the window seat on the train, and always facing forward. Helena had hoped against hope they would have seats to themselves so she could get this salary matter settled. And it happened.

She wasn't going to take a chance someone might come join them and botch the moment. As they were settling in, Cat pulled out the latest edition of *Variety* magazine, which Helena had learned, the actress read religiously.

Taking a deep breath, she stepped out on her make-believe stage. "Cat, just to make sure our business relationship runs well, a few details need to be addressed."

As the words hung in the air, she realized how stiff and wooden they sounded. But she didn't care. She'd said them and that was that.

From behind her magazine, Cat gave the answer just as Helena had predicted. "What details would that be?"

"When I took on this position, I expected to be told my salary and how often I'd be paid. Because that's how a business relationship should function." Her confidence was building—her voice sounded more natural.

Still holding the magazine in front of her face, Cat replied, "I told you before. A dollar a week paid every Saturday. Food and lodging extra." Lowering the magazine, she added curtly, "You might want to work on your memory. I'm relying on you to oversee details."

An interesting reply that was. Of course, it was a bald-faced lie. Helena realized it did no good to point that out. But she did muster the courage to say, "Then this Saturday, I will be owed two dollars."

Cat gave a little sniff and returned to her reading. After a few minutes she said, in her usual cold voice, "Not to worry. You'll have it."

Smiling to herself, Helena reached into her bag and brought out pen and stationery to write a long letter to Brett. Later, she'd write to Ardeen—because she'd asked for her new friend's home address—and thank her for the scriptwriting and acting lessons. It had worked like a charm.

While the city of New York was somewhat of a disappointment to Helena, the Belasco Theater was not. She had now experienced Cincinnati, Chicago, and Cleveland. Each seemed to have its own personality and mood. But New York? No description fit. The city seemed dank, dismal, and extremely noisy. On their arrival, the gray clouds floated down to hover at the tops of the massive skyscrapers, and snow whipped around in a furious white flurry.

Rather than a boarding house, their lodging turned out to be in a ladies'-only hotel rightly named Urania House. Helena would learn later that Urania was the Greek Muse of astronomy. Astronomy. Stars. Perfect moniker for such a wide array of star-struck girls.

Many of the residents hailed from the theater. Not only the Broadway stage, but vaudeville and the follies. It was quite an eclectic group that gathered in what was known as the *parlor* located at the rear of the first floor. That spacious room was set about with floral sofas, overstuffed chairs, and tables where card games flourished. Helena enjoyed spending time getting to know the girls, but she missed Ardeen. In their short time together, they'd become pals.

Her first impression of the Belasco theater, where Cat held the starring role of the daughter in *Broken Threads,* was a heady atmosphere of rushing about, shouting voices, seeming chaos, and excited anticipation. Everything about the Belasco came off as bigger, greater, busier, louder, with an added measure of aplomb. The appearance of chaos proved to be deceiving because every person knew their tasks and rushed about to fulfill them. Opening night was a mere two days out.

The interior made the previous theaters she'd experienced pale in comparison. Here murals graced the walls, Tiffany chandeliers offered soft lighting, and all woodwork was of deep, rich chestnut hue. Overhanging balconies guaranteed fabulous seating, with large boxes set out from the second balcony. She found it difficult not to just stand and stare. But there was work to be done.

For this production, Cat's costumes were provided by the company, not her own outfits. A stagehand guided Helena down a flight of stairs to the Wardrobe Department. There she was introduced to Deborah, a lively, talkative Jewish lady who held oversight for the entire department. Defying the newest fad of a bobbed do, her dark hair lay in ringlets on her shoulders. She appeared to have a fondness for bangle bracelets and colorful rope beads that hung almost to her waist. Somehow, she pulled off the gaudy jewelry perfectly. Helena found her to be a delight.

In the central area of the Wardrobe Department sat a solid wooden desk cluttered with papers, catalogs, fabric swatches, overflowing ashtrays, and empty coffee cups. A few feet away, a wide cutting table dominated the area, wider than any she'd worked with at Briggs Tailor Shop. Across the room, an open door gave her a glimpse of the major area of the department, where rack after rack after rack of costumes awaited her. It would be Helena's tasks to have each of Cat's costumes in her dressing room at the ready for each scene.

Deborah led her to where all costumes for *Broken Threads* had been assembled. A young stagehand was there with a rolling rack to help her gather up Cat's costumes, complete with hats, undergarments, and shoes.

Helena longed to rummage through all the racks and see how each one costume had been created, but now was not the time.

The highlight of her first day at Belasco was when one of the workers from the front office brought her a batch of letters from Brett.

"Postmarked France," the lady said with a smile. "My guess is you've been waiting awhile for these."

Pressing the letters to her heart, she nodded. "It's My fiancé, Brett."

"Many of the cast member here receive similar mail, my dear. The war is a grievous time for all of us."

Her words brought back the image of Myra's screams of anguish when she received the news that her Lendon would never be coming home.

Blinking back hot tears, she thanked the lady and quickly turned away.

Chapter 19

It was pure agony not being able read Brett's letters until she was alone in her room that evening. The room was small but clean and not nearly as threadbare as Cleveland. *Small* was stretching it—tiny cubicle was more fitting. The furniture consisted of a bed, and a chifforobe. The bathroom was located down the hall.

Being alone was taking some getting used to, especially after being with Ardeen. Helena would gladly have returned to the threadbare room for Ardeen's chatty company. But also for the hearty meals where all the boarders sat around the long dining room table with several lively conversations going on at once. The Urania House offered no meals which was worrisome for Helena. How she was to keep herself fed, she had no idea.

Pulling off her wraps and her snow-wet shoes, she fluffed the bed pillows behind her back, laid on the bed and sorted the letters according to dates. The earliest dated from October and here it was nearing Thanksgiving. Such a long time.

It was clear from the tone of his letters that there was much he couldn't say. Probably not allowed to say. Phrases such as "...not much to write...," "...everything the same...," "no news to speak of...." Mostly he spoke of his love for her and recalling memories of their times together. Telling her how he was counting the days until all this nonsense was over and he was back with her once again.

Life in the trenches, he explained, was definitely not a "walk in the park." Then he added, "Or, definitely not a picnic lunch in a lilac grove." Next to these words he drew stick figures of two people walking among flowering trees. "I'm no artist, and I have no purple paint or ink, but you get my drift." She was sobbing before she finished the first letter and she still had several more to read.

At least he had been receiving her letters and seemed happy for her new life in New York. Again, she agonized not knowing his true feelings since she couldn't see his expression. Unable to gauge his reaction.

Between the street noises, and her thinking of Brett being thousands of miles away in the midst of horrific danger, sleep was slow coming. She forced her thoughts to move forward in time. She envisioned Brett performing in vast concert halls in front of eager audiences and to the sounds of rousing applause. She'd be right there on the front row as one of his most devoted, adoring fans. Perhaps the two of them would live in a nice apartment here in New York City.

Continuing her fantasies, it occurred to her that she might well be able to make connections for Brett while she was here. After all, New York boasted of being the heart of the entertainment world. She knew that pianists were even featured on popular radio programs. So many opportunities were out there. She'd ask around and gather ideas.

Life for cast members of a headliner Broadway play proved to be much more hectic that the other venues Helena had so far experienced. New York City did everything bigger and better than anyone else, or any place else. The cast spent nearly every day, all day, in endless rehearsals. The director, and his assistants, pushed and prodded the players through each scene, calling for continual repeats, demanding perfection. While seemingly relentless, still and yet, Helena found herself drinking in the pulsing energy and the excitement. She had to admit, she'd fallen in love with every aspect of the theater.

When not tending to tasks in Cat's dressing room, Helena headed downstairs to wardrobe to talk with Deborah and watch her work. She enjoyed listening to Deborah's vast knowledge of the entire department. Precise organization was crucial as she was required to retrieve any certain costume, for any given scene, at any given moment. As she spoke, she waved toward the thick script that lay on the wide cutting table. "I have to know every detail of every production and when each costume is needed."

Helena picked up the script and fanned through it. "I studied a script when we were in Cleveland," Helena said. "The director used me as a backup prompter."

"Really? You must be a quick study. That doesn't happen very often."

Helena was actually searching through the script for Cat's speaking parts. So many. On almost every page. And some were several paragraphs. How could a person memorize so many lines?

"Want me to put a bug in Mr. Cranston's ear?"

"What?"

"About your ability to prompt. Want me to tell Mr. Cranston?"

Helena was taken aback. "The director?" She'd heard and seen the director yelling at the cast during rehearsals. He could be a bear. So intimidating.

She gave a little shrug. Such a ridiculous idea—that she would have any part in a Broadway play.

Deborah pulled another dress from rack and spread it out on the table, scanning it for rips, tears, or missing hooks or buttons. "I know he seems gruff, but his bark is worse than his bite. He only yells to keep order, and to command the attention of the cast. They can be a disorderly lot if not kept in tight rein."

Helena laid the script back down on the table and watched as Deborah gave the dress the onceover. She picked up the costume and flipped it over. Her many bracelets jangled as she worked. "Well? What say? I won't speak a word unless you feel you want to take it on."

"'Even if you mention it to him, he probably has others waiting to take it on."

"Oh honey." Deborah pushed her long, dark curls away from her face. "That's not a job everyone is hankering for."

Helena took in a deep breath. "All right. I'm game."

"Consider it done. He'll be down here after rehearsals. I'll tell him then."

Helena moved around the table and took a closer look at the costume. "Hm. I was wondering how that overskirt was attached and tucked. Now I see."

"Aha. You know how to sew as well? Aren't you just full of talents."

Helena felt her face warming. She hadn't meant to boast. But Deborah instantly wanted to know more and drew Helena right in. Before she knew it, she was sharing about her contract to create Cat's costume and how she worked with the wardrobe on *Pleasures A-Plenty*.

At this point, Deborah stopped working and gave Helena her full attention. It was clear she was quite taken by this news. "I know you're employed by Miss Callahan, but I sure could use your help around here. Maybe when you have a few minutes free. Like now."

Helena was hoping Deborah couldn't hear how hard her heart was pounding. This was exactly what she'd been longing for, but she was cautious. "I guess it might be permissible."

"Well, she doesn't own you. Does she?"

Helena nearly laughed out loud. Sometimes that's exactly how she felt—that she was the property of Cat Callahan.

Days flew by as opening night drew near. Helena seldom saw Cat, and she assumed she'd see her even less once the play opened. To her everlasting surprise, Mr. Cranston agreed to allow her to at least start studying the script in preparation to stand in as an extra prompter. She never spoke to him. Messages were relayed through Deborah, letting her know that one of the assistant directors would test Helena a day or so before opening night. To her everlasting surprise, she was accepted. Once that hurdle was cleared, she spent a couple hours in her room each night giving the script a careful reading.

Deborah, ever the kindhearted one, had informed Helena where the stage hands ate lunch. The first words out of Helena's mouth were: "How much does it cost?" which made Deborah laugh.

"*Bupkis*," she replied with a wave of her hand. "Nothing. Show up and act like you belong. Just schmooze, girlie. Act like you know everyone there."

Helena had never in her life remembered being hungry. Even on the farm when they were strapped with hardly a penny to their name, Mother could always create something from the garden. Or from the canned fruits and vegetables resting on the wooden shelves in the cellar. Or she could butcher another chicken and make chicken and dumplings.

These days, she was hungry most of the time. She had no idea how to budget the little bit of money she had. A list of rules was posted in the main entrance of their hotel, one of which stated: *No food allowed in the rooms.*

She guessed it was to deter mice and bugs, but it was a rule she quickly learned she would have to break. She wasn't about to go to a café all by herself. She had no idea how to order, or how much to spend. Finally, she located a small corner grocery and bought a loaf of bread and a length of salami. Concealing the package under her coat, she hurried to her room with her illicit contraband.

Thinking ahead, she *borrowed* a butter knife from the table at lunch time. She could at least cut the bread and salami and make sandwiches. After eating, she wrapped the remainder in a towel and tucked it into one of her suitcases. The suitcase may reek of salami, but at least the food was secured.

Weather in the city remained cold, windy, and snowy, but the warmth of the theater more than made up for it, so she endured the walk of about ten blocks from her hotel to the theater. The sidewalks were nearly always shoveled so it wasn't too messy

The sad fact was that by spring she was sure her only pair of shoes would be ruined.

Now her days were divided between being stationed in the wings with the script open in her lap—they required her to sit through at least two full rehearsals—and then lending a hand to Deborah. She wasn't sure which was her favorite. It was all too wonderful to take in.

It delighted her to write long letters to Brett detailing what was going on in her new "life in the big city." She could only hope he was happy for her. Letters were so lacking in relaying true thoughts, feelings, and emotions. How she longed to sit down and talk face-to-face, to hear his voice, and to feel his loving arms around her.

One day when she entered the Wardrobe Department, Deborah was sporting a wide grin. With bracelets jangling, she waved over to the far wall next to the door that led into the wardrobe area. "Found something for you, honey. Take a look."

Helena walked over and was astonished to find a pair of buckle-up galoshes sitting there. Something she'd been secretly been longing for, but knew she could never afford.

Deborah went to her cluttered desk and rolled out her office chair, and said, "Here. Sit down. See if they fit."

In a daze, Helena did so and when she slid her foot, with her lace-up shoes intact, it felt they were made for her. They look new. Clasping the buckles, she then ran her fingers over the rubberized soles and rejoiced that no water could ever seep in. She stood and walked a few steps. It was then she realized tears were coursing down her cheeks.

"Thank you, Deborah," she said, her voice breaking up.

"Ah it's nothing. They were sitting way back in a corner. I bet they haven't been used for ages. You walking all that way in the slush, it looked like they had your name written all over them."

"I'll return them after all the snow is gone."

"Forget that. After the snow then comes spring rains. Just keep them. They'll never be missed." Touching her lips, she added, "Mum's the word."

As Helena sat back down and took off her new galoshes, Deborah said, "How about you keep them in my coat closet?" She pointed to the wardrobe door. "Just inside to your left."

Helena realized that Deborah meant to keep them out of Cat's sight.

Chapter 20

Broken Threads proved to be a long-running hit. The run continued past Thanksgiving into the Christmas season. Each night, Helena was counted on to not only have Cat's costumes at the ready, but also to be on hand as a prompter. By now she'd memorized lines for most all the characters. Not because she set out to do so, but listening to the production night after night, it just happened.

By this time, she was growing accustomed to returning to her hotel room alone each night after the last curtain went down. As she sloshed through the melting snow, bone weariness chased away any fear. The walk had become a matter of course.

In addition to the wonderful watertight galoshes, the gift-giving Deborah had presented Helena with a flowing smock. At first, Helena was puzzled, then her friend pointed out the two patch pockets. "I'd say a couple oranges, maybe even a banana will easily fit in these," she said with a grin. The wardrobe mistress overwhelmed Helena with her kindness.

Now at lunch, Helena managed to walk away from the lunch table with more food than before. One day, as she walked down one side of the table filling her plate, she glanced over and saw one of the stagehands doing the exact same thing—stuffing rolls in his jacket pockets. He caught her eye and gave a wink. After that, she felt no guilt. The food was there for all of them, and it was no crime to take what they needed. They were all hungry.

Following each night's performance, the cast members habitually gathered at Delmonico's where they ate, drank, gossiped, and talked shop until the wee hours. Similar to the showboat actors, they stayed up late, and slept late.

Arriving at the theater one morning the week before Christmas, she was met in wardrobe by an agitated Deborah. "Get off your things and get upstairs. Mr. Cranston needs you."

Pulling off her galoshes, she said, "Me? There must be some mistake? Why me?"

Helping her off with her coat and tossing it over her office chair, she replied, "How am I supposed to know? He sent a stagehand in here not half an hour ago and said to send you to his office as soon as you arrived."

"Did I do something wrong? Am I in trouble?"

Deborah held her by the arm and nearly dragged her to the door. "Go."

"Deborah, I have no idea where his office is. All I know is your place here, back stage, and the actor's dressing rooms."

"Grab any stagehand and ask for directions. It's in the other part of the complex adjacent to the theater—the office building and hotel."

Suddenly she was fear struck. Smoothing her hair back, she said, "Do I look all right? I wish I'd worn something different."

With another gentle shove, Deborah said, "You look fine. Go. Just go."

By now most of the stagehands knew her and as she went backstage one approached her saying that Mr. Cranston was asking for her. "Come on, I'll take you."

Taking the elevator to the fourth floor, they stepped into a vast carpeted anteroom where a neatly-dressed secretary sat behind a desk clicking away on her typewriter. The stagehand said, "This is Miss Heise. Mr. Cranston wants to see her."

Nodding, she flicked a button on a box on her desk and announced to her boss that Miss Heise had arrived. Helena could hear the voice coming from the box that said, "Send her in."

She never knew such a contraption existed. It was almost like a telephone, but different.

Pointing to a set of ornate double doors, the secretary said, "Go on in."

Helena turned to thank the stagehand. He smiled and said, "Think you can find your way back?"

Still speechless she simply nodded.

Mr. Cranston's massive office appeared more like a museum than a place of work. Plaques, photographs, and framed newspaper articles covered the walls. Ornate statues, and urns were set about; gold embossed planters filled with leafy ferns lent a garden effect. She wanted to stop and look at everything, but the moment she entered Mr. Cranston stood, stepped around the massive walnut desk, and strode toward her with an outstretched hand.

"Miss Heist, thank you for coming." Motioning to where two wing-back chairs faced an ornate but empty fireplace, he said, "Let's sit over here. This won't take but a few minutes."

The man was much calmer in demeanor than what she'd perceived from the wings as she witnessed many rehearsals and listened to his harsh verbal onslaughts.

"We're in a pinch, Miss Heise," he said as he pulled a cigarette from a gold case. He waved the case toward her offering her one, to which she shook her head. "Were you aware that Gwynne has taken ill?"

Gwynne, Helena knew, played the role of the housekeeper. More than a simple walk-on, she had several speaking parts. "I had no idea. But Mildred, the understudy..."

"Mildred's husband just returned from the front. She'll be out for several days. As you can see, that leaves us in a bind. Deborah in wardrobe seemed to think, due to your hours as prompter, you might know the part."

Suddenly her stunned mind whipped into a whirlwind. Was she hearing correctly?

Mr. Cranston continued, "She also said you'd been on the stage in showboat performances. Is that right?"

She nodded.

"Do you think you could handle this role until either Gwynne recovers, or Mildred returns?"

Her dry mouth caused her to have to swallow, then clear her throat. "I believe I can do that, sir."

Slapping the arms of his chair, he said, "Well isn't that just grand. This is my lucky day. Things like this seldom fall into place so easily."

"But sir, the role of the housekeeper is a much older lady."

He chuckled. It was the first time she'd ever heard him laugh. He was such a bear when working with his cast. "My dear, surely you've seen the miracles stage makeup can create. We'll have you aged in no time at all. Gray hair and all the wrinkles to boot."

As he walked her to the door, he added, "You'll be paid at the end of the month."

Paid. She hadn't even considered that. She would gladly have done it for free. With a nod and a thank you, she left the office and returned to more familiar territory.

"You're a natural. Took to it like a fish to water."

"I can't believe you've not be on stage before. You didn't appear a bit nervous."

"Where'd you come from? Just popped in out of the blue? You did great."

After her first performance, these compliments and more flew around her, and most came from the cast members. Helena fairly glowed, and tried her best to field these remarks with humility, but it wasn't easy. She was honest enough to realize it was a small part, with few lines, but still, they didn't have to bestow the compliments. And the truth was, she hadn't been nervous and felt she did well. The door of opportunity had swung open and she stepped through.

While taking off her makeup and getting the gray powder out of her hair—in her tiny, spare dressing room down the hallway from the rooms of the bigger stars—a cast member stuck her head in the door and invited Helena to come along to Delmonico's with them. She declined. Cat would be there, and somehow it didn't seem right. One night of taking on a bit part didn't seem enough to allow her into the inner circle.

After a few days, Mildred the understudy, let Mr. Cranston know that her husband, who'd been injured at the front, needed her. She had no plans to return. Gwynne was still out sick. Pneumonia, someone said. She was on the mend, but her voice was too weak for her to perform. Mr. Cranston let Helena know he was counting on her. She was more than happy to comply.

Thankfully, she was never on stage in the same scene with Cat. While Helena played her role in the production, she continued to race about fulfilling her obligations to her employer. When she had time to think about it, which was seldom, it did seem odd that she rarely saw Cat. Even if they passed one another, Cat seemed to purposely ignore her. But no matter, she was too captivated in becoming a fledgling actress to care. Meanwhile, letters to Brett, and her family, overflowed with vivid details of her newfound excitement.

In the midst of the heady excitement, a letter from Brett arrived with a hospital in France as the return address. Helena literally ran to a dark corner backstage and tore open the envelope in a panic.

"I know this letter is going to scare you silly, my love..." the letter began.

Don't be alarmed. My handsome face is still intact. (Smile, Darling. Smile.) As are both hands. It's a leg wound from shrapnel, which the doctors say might leave me with a limp. A limp I can live with, just as long as I can continue to run my fingers over the ivories.

I'm cutting this letter short so as to get it to you quickly.

No one seems to know when I'll be shipped out. Everything is slow in the Army. Signing with all my love, Brett.

It took a while to compose herself and breathe. The initial shock of seeing the hospital address brought horrific fears to surface. But she had no time to even think. Too much to do. She could reflect later that night in her room. For now, she was eternally grateful he would soon be home. She couldn't wait to tell him the connections she'd discovered of people who could assist him in furthering his career right here in the entertainment capital. The opportunities were limitless.

Two days later another letter arrived in which Brett opened his heart to explain what he was feeling. What he was planning. Stating that he was on his way home, Helena was ecstatic until she came to the part where he tells her how his relationship with the Lord has grown immeasurably while in the trenches, and now, "I want only to serve Him and preach the Gospel all the days of my life. With you by my side." The letter went on to explain that his plan was to return to Chancey's Bend and serve as a pastor there. He'd already corresponded with the present pastor who was getting on in age, and ready to relinquish his pulpit to someone younger.

It felt as though all the breath had been knocked out of her. Return to Chancey's Bend? No. Not ever. She couldn't. What about his dreams of becoming a concert pianist? Was he willing to let it all go? Perhaps he was, but she was not.

Surely, when they met together, looking into one another's eyes, she could convince him otherwise. At this point, he just wasn't thinking clearly. Shock effects from the war.

She began counting the days until he arrived in New York.

It was Christmas eve day when everything came crashing down around her. Arriving early that morning, she was greeted by a teary-eyed Deborah.

Helena rushed to her friend's side. "You've been crying. What's the matter?"

She'd never seen Deborah without her glowing smile. Perhaps a family member had died.

Deborah started to speak, but heavy sobs prevented words. She gently placed her hands on Helena's shoulders and said, "You have to go, my dear. You can't stay here."

"What? Can't stay? What're you saying? I don't understand."

"Cat. It's Cat."

Helena was shaking her head. "Cat? What does she have to do with this?" But after a minute, everything began to make sense.

"Cat Callahan is one mean woman," Deborah went on. "She went to Mr. Cranston telling him if you remained in the cast, she would quit and go with another company." Pulling out a hanky from her pocket she wiped the tears from her face, but never stopped crying. "She told him you're only an ordinary seamstress. Not an actress." After blowing her nose loudly, she added, "Cat Callahan's power in the theater is about as strong as Ethel Barrymore's. The difference is, Miss Barrymore is kind."

"But the role. The part. Who will...?"

"Cat demanded the part be edited out of the script."

Helena felt faint. Stepping over to Deborah's desk, she slowly seated herself in the creaking office chair. "I can see how that would work." Her head pounded so that she could barely hear her own words. "That role isn't necessary to the story line."

Deborah stood beside her and reached down and took hold of Helena's gloved hand, "My heart is breaking for you, my little one. I cannot express how I have delighted in your presence here."

Letting this awful news sink in, Helena's mind searched about for a minute. "Other theaters have wardrobe departments. Perhaps I can find work..."

Deborah didn't let her finish. "You cannot."

Helena look up full in her friend's face. "No? Why?"

Now the sobs began again. "You've been blacklisted."

"Black what?"

"Blacklisted. Cat has sent out word for no other theater to take you on. For any position."

"But why? Why would she do that? I'm no threat to her."

"I've heard how people are raving about you. How you stepped into that role as though you'd been on the stage all your life. I overheard one person saying you're a natural. The weak person inside of Cat is unable to handle that."

"What'll I do? I don't know what to do." Now tears were coursing down her face as well.

"Go back to your hotel, ask to use their telephone. Reverse charges and call home. You have a loving family. You've told me all about them. Ask them to wire money for a train ticket. Catch the afternoon train my dear. You'll be home for Christmas."

Helena rose to go. Deborah held her in warm hug. "Go home Helena. This is a wicked world here. For all it's glamor, it's a wicked world."

Back outside, the wind had picked up and more snow coming down. Deborah had insisted she keep the galoshes, for which she was deeply grateful. At any other time in her life, this would be the perfect Christmas eve day. How could her life have changed so suddenly? So completely?

At the hotel, she received yet another shock. Fitting her key in the lock and turning it, as she'd done every day for weeks, the door failed to open. Slowly she turned away from the door, walked back down the hallway, took the stairs to the lobby, and approached the desk.

Thankfully, since it was still early morning, none of the residents were around. The place was empty. The clerk's expression told her he was expecting her.

Holding up the key, she said, "I'm unable to unlock the door to my room."

The old geezer cleared his raspy throat. "Hadda change locks until rent's paid."

So that's how Cat dealt with her employee who was no longer needed. Just stop paying the rent.

"But my things…"

"All you young girlies are alike," he said, his voice laced with judgement. "You think you're gonna come to the big city and be a star. And most all of you wind up in a train wreck."

"But Miss Callahan, my employer, brought me here. I'm not looking to be a star. Part of our agreement included having a room. A room that's paid for."

He shook his head. "Don't know nothing about that. Just know the rent's due and owing."

"How much?"

Taking his glasses down from where they were perched on top his head, he hooked them on his nose. Opening a ledger, he ran his finger down the page. "Exactly four dollars and twenty-five cents." He then closed the ledger with a smack, peered over his glasses at her and said, "We hold a room for three days, then let it out to someone who will pay on time."

Her money was in her suitcase in her room. She'd long ago stopped carrying it around in her chemise. She was wasn't sure she had that much. It was at that moment, she also realized Cat had failed to pay her last week. Also, Mr. Cranston said she would be paid at the end of the month, but that was several days away. By then the room would be let out and who knew what they might to with her belongings.

For a moment she looked at the telephone sitting on the counter behind the clerk. "Call home," Deborah had said. But the shame was too great. She couldn't bring herself to beg to be rescued.

Turning to go, she said, "I'll be back."

"Three days," he replied.

Chapter 21

Helena's first thoughts were places where she could go to get in out of the cold. The harsh wind and blowing snow left her shivering. Not even her warm coat was enough to shut out the icy air. The library? The museum? But everything was closed. It was, after all, the day before Christmas. After an hour, she realized she was walking aimlessly, her head bent down against the wind. Powdery snow swirled around her, kicked up by the wind.

She knew about St. Malachy's on 49th. She'd seen it many times. But it was Catholic. No one in Chancey's Bend was Catholic. Do they kick people out who aren't Catholic? By now she was too cold to care.

She'd made a concerted effort to keep her back to the wind, but that was the wrong way. She needed to turn around, buck the wind, and get back to Broadway. Snow clung, melted and then froze to her face. By the time she reached the imposing mammoth front entrance of St. Malachy's she wasn't sure she had the strength to even get up the front steps. Pausing for a moment to catch her breath, she mounted the steps and pulled open one of the heavy wooden doors.

The warmth enveloped her and drew her into the dimly lit interior. Hesitantly, she moved to one of the pews and sat down. For a few moments, she gazed at the ornate wooden arches and artwork, the gold of the flickering candles. It was all incredibly beautiful. Eventually her heavy breathing evened out and drowsiness took over. Balancing on the arm of the pew, resting her head in her hand, she succumbed.

Awaking with a start, it took a minute to remember where she was. Then what had happened that morning came rushing back. She sensed a presence near her and looked up to see a priest—she guessed he was a priest—standing in the aisle beside her. He was looking down at her with a smile and a kindly expression which nearly brought her to tears.

"You were sleeping so peacefully, I didn't want to bother you," he said in a barely audible whisper. "Are you with the theater? You know, we call this the *actors' chapel.*"

She managed to sit up, straightened her hat and smoothed down her coat which was now dry. Being caught sleeping embarrassed her to no end. "I didn't know that."

"Are you new in the city?"

Helena nodded. "Fairly new. A few weeks."

"I'm Father Micah." He stretched out his hand.

Hesitantly, she took it and simply said, "Helena."

While she appreciated his kindness, she wasn't ready to talk about the mistreatment from Cat. Especially the fact that she was locked out of her room. Getting in out of the cold, and the brief nap had cleared her head. Now it came to her mind that she still had Ardeen's address folded up and tucked into her coin purse inside her pocketbook.

"Are you from the theater?" he asked again. "We often have actors come to us who are a little down on their luck." He seated himself in the pew in front of her, turning around to face her. "Are you alone?"

"I have a friend," she said as she dug into her things and pulled out the folded piece of paper. There it was. Ardeen's address. Thank goodness she still had it. And that it wasn't in her suitcases locked in her room. Ardeen would understand about Cat. She was the one who had warned her that Cat held a potential threat.

She held out the paper for the priest to see. "This is the address of my friend, but I don't know how to get there."

"Hm," he said. "Lower East Side. Easy to get to. Have you ever taken the subway?"

She shook her head. The subway was a terrifying thing to her.

"I can show you. It won't take long." He stood and added, "I'll get my wraps and let my assistant know I'm leaving. Will you wait here?"

She nodded. "What time is it? How long did I sleep?"

"It's still afternoon. And I don't have to return until evening Mass. Remember, it is Christmas Eve day."

How could I forget? she thought, but said nothing.

When he returned, he handed her an apple and a slice of buttered rye bread. "I thought you might be hungry."

Her stomach had been reminding her that it was about this time each day when she filled up her plate at the heavily-ladened table backstage at the Belasco Theater. Another wave of grief washed over her as the truth settled in that those days that she loved so much, were now over.

When the two of them stepped back outside, the skies had cleared somewhat, the wind had died down, and the snow reduced to a light flurry.

As she quickly ate her bread, she followed as he guided her down the stairs into the deep belly of New York City. She supposed people could get used to it, but the whole subway thing was very scary to her. The apple was slipped into her coat pocket for later.

As they approached the turnstile, she said, "I have a little money. How much is it?"

But he was already putting coins in the slot and showing her how to push through the turnstile. She never saw how much it was. "It's my Christmas gift," he said with a smile. And because it was almost Christmas, the subway was practically empty.

As the car rattled along, Father Micah explained how to know when and where to disembark, but Helena barely listened. Fear had consumed her. Not only the subway, but fear that she was grabbing at straws. What if Ardeen no longer lived at this address? Then what would she do? She remembered Ardeen explaining how they had been able to move to a cleaner, more well-maintained flat—her and her big Irish family. That had happened just before the two of them met in Cleveland. Perhaps they'd moved yet again.

The kindness of this man was beyond what Helena could have ever hoped for. Perhaps God hadn't given up on her after all.

He walked her all the way to the tenement building. In the small foyer, he searched the names on the mail boxes. "Miller you said?"

"Yes. Miller."

"Right here." He placed his finger on the front of the brass box where the names were posted.

Helena felt a deep sigh go out of her. *Now just let Ardeen be there.*

Third floor. Up three flights of dimly lit, but fairly-clean stairs. She didn't think he would come all this way with her, but yet again, if this was a dead-end search, she desperately needed the good priest to lead her back again.

As Father Micah knocked, the door was opened slightly by a little girl who peeked through. Good food smells wafted out the opening. "What do you want?" she said as though that's what she'd been taught to say.

Father Micah had stepped behind Helena which set her face-to-face with the girl. "Is this the Miller's residence?"

The little girl nodded. "And a couple others with different last names."

"I'm looking for Ardeen Miller."

At that the girl closed the door. They could hear her yelling, "Ardeen! Come here. Somebody and a priest looking for you."

Helena could hear the voice of her friend and she nearly collapsed right there in the hallway. Once again, the door opened and there was Ardeen, big as life, looking just as beautiful as Helena remembered. Lovely mass of red curls, bright blue eyes, full of life. In a flash she was wrapped up in Ardeen's arms, with squeals reverberating in her ear.

"Thank the Good Lord, Helena. Helena, my dear friend." Stepping back she said, "Let me look at you. Oh dear. Something's terribly wrong." Pausing she said, "Cat?"

Helena nodded. No words came. And another hug nearly squeezed the life out of her.

Clearing his throat, Father Micah said, "Well, well. This is the happy ending, just as we had prayed for."

"I'm sorry," Helena said, her voice cracking. "Ardeen, this is Father Micah. He helped me with the subway, and to find my way."

Ardeen released Helena in order to shake hands. "Please come in. We have dinner ready to set out on the table."

"That's very kind, my dear. But I'm needed back at St. Malachy's tonight."

"St. Malachy's? On East 49th?"

"That's the one."

"I've been in there many times. What a refuge in the midst of chaos."

"You must be in the theater."

"Just an understudy. But yes."

"We're pleased to serve as that refuge." He placed his hand on Helena's shoulder. "May your future days be blessed, Helena."

"Thank you." It was a whisper. "Thank for going out of your way to help me."

"My pleasure."

And at that he was gone, and Ardeen was pulling Helena into the living room and made quick work of introducing her to the family, most of the names she wouldn't remember. Some lived there. Others were Christmas visitors. But then, Ardeen said, "If you'll excuse us, my friend and I need to talk."

Leading the way to a back bedroom, Ardeen began helping Helena off with her coat, hat, gloves, muffler. "Sit down here." She motioned to the bed. After Helena was seated, Ardeen bent down, unbuckled the galoshes, and pulled them off. "Nice," she said as she held one up to inspect it.

"Now," she said as she drew a chair over near the bed so they were almost nose-to-nose. "Out with it. What happened?"

"I'm not sure I can tell it without crying."

"Then cry."

Trying to begin at the first, she told about the Urania House hotel, the play at Belasco's, and her friendship with Deborah and helping in wardrobe.

"I saw that Cat starred in *Broken Threads*," Ardeen said, "and I wondered about you. But honestly, I figured that you'd already gone back home to Kentucky."

Shaking her head, and taking another deep breath she told about being a prompter and then getting the bit part.

"Oh my. You on the same stage with Cat. I know she didn't like that."

"If it'd been one or two nights, she might have simply ignored me. But the understudy left, and the one who had the role was ill. When her recovery was prolonged, that's when Cat's anger exploded."

"Never mind all that," Ardeen interrupted. "I know plenty of places where you can get work. What with the war and all, every theater in the city needs help."

Now Helena couldn't stop the sobs. "She's blacklisted me, Ardeen. No theater will hire me."

Ardeen moved from her chair to sit beside Helena on the bed and hold her in a smothering hug. "Why that wicked woman." After a moment, she asked, "But your stuff. Where's your stuff? Did you leave it all at the church?"

"The blacklisting isn't the end. She didn't pay my rent as promised." Helena then explained about being locked out of her room. "I have money, but it's in my suitcase. I tried to explain to the clerk, but he refused to listen."

Ardeen jumped up. "Here's what we're going to do. You have a place at our table, and you have a place to live here as long as you need it. Now we're going to eat our Christmas Eve dinner, then we're going to go to the Urania House and get your belongings."

Helena started to protest. She could see there were many mouths to feed in this family. But Ardeen shushed her. "In an Irish family, there's no such thing as too many bodies."

Chapter 22

A week after Christmas, Helena found herself sitting at an industrial-sized sewing machine in a garment factory. The three-story brick building housed row upon row of the noisy machines on nearly every floor. It had been Ardeen's cousin, Deirdre, who helped her land the job. Deirdre worked at the factory and put in a good word, explaining to the manager that Helena was an experienced seamstress.

Helena soon discovered that one need not have any sewing experience. This was piecework. She sewed two pieces of a shirt together and handed it off to the girl beside her. That was it. All day. Hour after hour. The only bright spot was her ability to bring home a bit of money to help pay for her room and board at the Miller's.

With several individuals at Belasco's still sympathetic to Helena's plight, a system was set up to retrieve her mail. The office worker brought the letters to Deborah, and once or twice a week, Ardeen slipped in and picked them up. Helena had not told her family of her fall from grace. And definitely she had not told Brett. Nearing Valentine's Day, the letter came announcing his arrival date, along with the ship, and the dock where she could meet him. Just knowing it was a troop ship, and not a hospital ship, made her know he was not an invalid.

By this time, she'd conquered her fears and had learned the subway system. She still hated the noise and the hustle and bustle, but in New York, it was a necessary evil. She learned to deal with it.

Dressed her gold lame dress, she stood in the midst of the crowd watching as soldier after soldier came down the gangway. How would she know? It was a moving sea of uniforms. But then, one came down a bit slower, using a cane. Forcefully, she pushed her way through the crowd. Closer. Closer. Yes. It was him. It was Brett. As she shouted his name, he turned and caught site of her.

"Helen!"

In a moment they were together again. Reunited. Kissing. Hugging. Trying to talk, but unable to do so. A moment made in heaven. He looked splendid in his uniform. She'd nearly forgotten how handsome he was, although she could detect the underlying weariness.

His kit bag was at the depot, he explained. "But I can pick it up later."

Purposely, she revealed nothing about her recent misfortunes—that she was boarding with the Miller's, and that she was working in a garment factory. It didn't seem important at the moment. She could explain later. After they were back together for a time, then everything could be out in the open. But not now.

Ardeen had helped her make reservations at one of the nicer restaurants. Taking the subway to midtown she led the way to Guffanti's. She could tell he was impressed.

"You sure know your way around."

"It's not that difficult once you learn. Sort of like learning the Mississippi River."

Looking around at the lush setting, he said, "Can I afford this?"

She could tell by the twinkle in his eyes he was joking. "If you can't, I can. Or we can share. But it'll be worth every penny."

The food was as magnificent as the setting, and their conversation went on non-stop. She wanted to know every detail of his shrapnel wound. He answered those questions briefly, but quickly changed the subject. His comment was that he'd seen so many men much worse off.

He wanted to tell her about all the places he'd seen and buddies he'd met. "They were from all over the country—guys from the city, country, out west, up in Minnesota, and down in the deep south. We had close pals, then grieved and agonized when they were killed." Softly he added, "So many died."

He went on to briefly tell about the nightmare of trench warfare, which as he explained, "...is totally absurd. Makes no sense. No one wins. It's been an ongoing stalemate for years. It transforms good men into raving lunatics."

She listened without reply, hating that he'd had to suffer through so much. And that so many people, families, and communities were suffering as well.

As they were finishing dessert, he came to the point she'd been dreading. His future plans. As he began talking about taking on the pastorate in Chancey's Bend, she gently reached out and placed her hand over his.

"Brett, when I read your letter that told about this plan, there was no time for me to write and mail my reply. I also haven't had a chance to tell you about the contacts I've made here in the city. Important people who can help your career."

She struggled a bit to keep her voice steady and with a positive tone. "In a backwater town like Chancey's Bend will your gifts, your talents, have a chance to bloom? Or will they die?"

"I hear that, Helen, but when you come face-to-face with your own mortality, somehow things change perspective." He laid his hand over hers. "Having a career as a concert pianist seemed to lose all its appeal. I just want to serve the Lord."

"But God gave you your amazing talent to play the piano, and you love it. That's serving the Lord as well. Isn't it?"

He shook his head. She could tell he was hearing her, but he said, "I want you there by my side. Are you saying you won't come with me?"

She drew in a deep breath. "Not now, Brett. You go on back and be with your family for a time. I know they've missed you terribly. I believe once you're there, once you experience the limitations of such a small place, you'll change your mind. Chancey's Bend is simply too small for someone as talented as you are."

The spell had been broken. The softness had gone out of him. "I was so sure you'd follow me wherever I went. I guess I was wrong." He waved at the waiter to bring the check. Pulling out his wallet, he said, "War truly does change everything."

After she saw him off the next day at Grand Central Station, looking more handsome than ever in his civilian clothes, she was confident she was doing the right thing. By remaining behind in New York, she was doing him a great service. If she were to return to Chancey's Bend, they would marry, settle into a mundane routine, grow old together, and Brett would forever grieve his loss—his missed opportunity. Serving as a pastor in a nondescript, dusty old church, in a nondescript town no one had ever heard of. Who knew but in the long run, he might actually blame her for consenting and helping to kill his dreams?

He held her tight to him, kissed her forehead, and reminded her of his love for her. He whispered his goodbyes as the train chuffed impatiently, as though anxious to carry him away. And then he was gone.

She never told Ardeen the full truth. She simply said that Brett felt the need to see his parents and spend time with them, but that he would return to her soon. And she was confident that was true.

Spring was in the air. Never had Helena ever been so thankful for a winter to end. Work at the garment factory remained the same, grueling and boring. However, the fresh spring breezes seemed to breathe new hope into her heart. She and Ardeen spent their Sunday afternoons in Central Park enjoying the budding trees, the wide swatches of soft lush grass, and a kaleidoscope of flowers blooming everywhere. They carried their lunch and picnicked in the sunshine.

Letters received from Brett were short and brief telling about his sermons, and how the congregation had easily accepted him into their lives as their new pastor. The town had received him home as a conquering hero. He always closed by professing his abiding love. Helena counted the days until he would realize that his place was in the concert halls all around the country. Perhaps even in Europe. She prayed it would come soon.

It was nearing the end of March as she walked back to the Miller's apartment from an exhausting day in the noisy, stuffy, airless factory. Each payday, she was grateful she could pay the Miller's, but still never felt she was carrying her full load. Speed was the factory's byword as their supervisor relentlessly hounded them to work faster. She walked out at the end of the day with a headache and a tight knot between her shoulder blades. This particular day, she was asking herself how much longer she could endure the torture.

As she came down their street, she could see Ardeen sitting on the front stoop, obviously waiting for her. As she spied Helena, she jumped up and came running.

"Helena!" Ardeen caught her and spun her around. "Great news my friend. The flickers are hiring. They are desperate for players. I know the director. His name is Lance Sedgley. I can put in a good word..."

"Whoa." Helena broke free from Ardeen's grasp. "Flickers? Ugh. Ardeen, whatever are you thinking? No self-respecting actress in her right mind would stoop so low."

She'd heard it a million times—ever since she began keeping company with theater people. Once an actor or actress went over to the much-despised flickers, their reputation was tarnished beyond repair. Their stage career was over.

Ardeen hooked her arm in Helena's as they walked toward their tenement. "Tell me my dear friend. At this point in time, are you one of those *self-respecting actresses* you refer to?"

Helena didn't answer. Of course she wasn't. She was nothing but a factory worker. A weary factory worker.

"Hm. Just as I thought." As they reached the stoop, Ardeen sat down on the step and pulled Helena down to sit beside her. "Look at it this way. Come talk to the director. Just talk to Lance. Look around at the setup. Ask questions." Bumping Helena with her elbow, she added, "Questions such as salary."

"Pennies, I bet."

"I think you'll be surprised. Lance is convinced that moving pictures are the future in entertainment. Broadway can't go to MidAmerica, but a moving picture can." Ardeen then added, "You'll really like Lance. He's absolutely the berries."

"You know I can't leave work. I can't afford to lose this job."

"I can set up a time after you're off work. In the evening. Like maybe six or so."

Helena pulled the hat pin out, removed her hat, and laid it in her lap. She was listening. She was thinking. Ever since her short stint on the stage, she'd dreamed of the possibility of a real role. Surely the blacklisting couldn't last forever. If she landed in the flickers, that could kill her chances. She wasn't sure this was a risk she was willing to take.

Ardeen reached up and took Helena's chin in hand, turning her to talk eye-to-eye. "I'm your friend. Agreed?"

"Agreed. Absolutely."

"Then how's about you just do this as a favor for a friend."

Now Helena rolled her eyes and sighed. "Okay. As a favor for a friend. I'll take a look. But no promises past that."

Ardeen jumped up and pulled Helena to her feet. "That's good enough."

Helena paused a moment. "Ardeen. Are you doing this? This flickers-thing?"

Her friend just laughed. "You'll see. Come on. Time for dinner. I'm starved."

Chapter 23

F ort Lee? Helena had never heard of Fort Lee. "It's over in Jersey," Ardeen
explained. "The studio location."

"Not right here in the city?"

Ardeen shook her head. "They need more space than is available in Manhattan."

In the few months that Helena had lived in New York, she'd explored much
of the city, but never over in Brooklyn, or Queens, or the Bronx. But definitely
never across the river into Jersey.

As they boarded the Fort Lee ferry, memories of the showboat came flooding
back to Helena. She would never be sorry she'd said yes to that wonderful
adventure. Just being on a boat again sent her heart pumping. They stood at
the rail and watched the Manhattan skyline recede and peered across to the New
Jersey shore.

"What happens when we get to Jersey?" Helena asked as she firmed her hat
with her hand against the wind.

"They're sending a car."

"Sending a car? To get us? We're just there to talk. How can they afford to do that?"

"My dear friend, you ask too many questions. Be patient. Wait and see."

The car seemed to be destined to impress them. The friendly, chatty driver offered his hand to help them up into the open-top, canary-yellow Packard.

"Here to see Mr. Sedgley, I betcha," he said as he returned to the driver's seat.

"You bet correctly," Ardeen answered.

"We're getting more and more pretty girls like you two. All wanting to be in the moving pictures."

"I don't," Helena whispered under her breath. Ardeen elbowed her.

The car sped up a winding dirt motor road into wooded hills, which were reminiscent of the hills around Chancey's Bend. How could such wild countryside be so close to the noisy, bustling city? Soon the car stopped in front of a massive building with *L&S Artistes Film Company* lettered above a set of double doors. In fact, there was a series of buildings of all shapes and sizes. One appeared to be a towering greenhouse—all glass.

The driver hopped out and once again politely gave them a hand as they stepped down. "Need me to take you to Mr. Sedgley?"

Ardeen shook her head. "I know the way. I've been here before. But thanks."

The comment stopped Helena short. Her friend had been here before? What was going on?

The driver tipped his hat, hopped back into the shiny Packard, and drove off.

"Come on. You're not going to believe this."

As they walked through the doors, they entered another world. The vast interior was filled with dozens of sets. One replicated a living room, complete with all the furnishing, down to the damask draperies. Another depicted a city alleyway with fire escapes, laundry hanging on the lines, and trash bins. Still another mimicked a Western town with a boardwalk, a dusty street, and storefronts of that era. In among all the sets were large moving-picture cameras set on tripods.

Helena couldn't take it all in. All she knew about moving pictures was what she saw of the nickelodeons in the storefront arcades where people—mostly men—dropped a nickel in a slot and viewed a few fleeting seconds of an exhibition. This place was a far cry from a nickelodeon.

In one area she saw dozens of flats, painted with multiple variations of scenery. They reminded her of the flats behind the stage of the *Pleasures A-Plenty*.

"Didn't I tell you?" Ardeen said, squeezing her arm. "I knew you'd be surprised."

"Ah, Miss Miller." A booming voice echoed off all the sets in the place. "And you brought your friend."

Lance Sedgley's presence proved to be as large as his voice, and he seemed to bounce rather than walk. Tall, trim, and muscular, he came toward them with outstretched hand and a friendly smile. Round, black-rimmed glasses accentuated his laughing eyes, and his navy-blue, custom-tailored, suit spoke of wealth. And Helena knew all about customed-tailored suits.

Ardeen introduced the two of them, and Lance—he insisted on first names—explained that his main office was in the city, so a set would have to do for now. "Come sit over here." He led them to a *kitchen* where they seated themselves around a table, replete with china place settings.

"Ardeen has told me about you, Helena. That you have stage experience on a showboat, and you had a part on the Broadway stage."

"And everyone said she's a natural," Ardeen added.

"Just a small part," Helena said.

"Do you know anything about motion pictures?"

Helena shook her head. She didn't want to say that she called them *flickers* and that they were an abomination to all stage performers.

"We're up to two-reelers now. The public is clamoring for longer pictures. We're in a position to give them what they want." Pulling a cigarette case from his pocket, he waved it toward them. They both declined. After lighting up and emitting a blue cloud, he continued. "I love the stage. I love Broadway. But moving pictures will be the future. We here at *L&S Artistes* are pioneers. We are breaking new ground."

Helena had her doubts about becoming one of his so-called pioneers.

Then Lance surprised her by asking, "Can you ride a horse?"

"I can."

"Can you saddle a horse?"

"I can."

"Wonderful!" Leaning forward, he tapped the table lightly with his fist. "Do you know how few gals in this area know how to ride?"

"I've never had to consider it."

Waving his hand to take in the vast studio, he said, "This is barely half of where we film, Helena. Up in the hills—up above the Palisades—is where we film our Westerns."

"Westerns?"

Ardeen laughed. "Yeah. Like cowboys and Indians."

Helena remembered Brett telling her that he worked on a cattle ranch one summer. He would love this. He'd have authentic, first-hand input. Try as she might, she couldn't get him out of her head.

"Helena, I want to hire you on a two-week trial basis."

She started to protest.

"Five dollars a day to start."

Five dollars a day? To act? To ride a horse? Bent over a sewing machine for endless hours, she barely made five dollars a week.

"We're doing two films a week. If I like what I see, and if the films are well received, I'll raise it to ten."

This was incredulous.

"What about Ardeen?"

Her friend smiled. "I've already hired on. I wasn't quite ready to tell you."

Lance said, "Ardeen can't ride a horse. And doesn't care to learn. That means I can't use her in a Western. The two of you'll be starring in different types of films."

The money aside, Helena wasn't sure she could meet his expectations. When she started to protest, he said, "Don't worry. I'll work with you." His voice was kind. Nothing like Mr. Cranston's gruffness. "I'll teach you the ropes. Every step of the way. I think you'll be a quick study."

How could she turn this down? If it ruined her chances for Broadway, then so be it.

"What do you say?" Ardeen asked.

"When would I start?"

"Tomorrow?" That was Lance.

She laughed. It would be pure joy to leave the garment factory. "I'll have to tell my present employer that I'm quitting. And pick up a paycheck."

"I'll go with you," Ardeen said. "Then we'll come straight over here."

Lance stood, indicating the meeting was concluded. Again, he shook their hands and then guided them toward the door. "Welcome aboard, Helena. I don't think you'll regret this decision.

Throughout the spring, Lance's words rang in her ears. It turned out to be a vast understatement. She never for a moment regretted her decision to become a motion picture actress.

By now, she'd stopped counting on Brett's arrival. In fact, she'd stopped reading his letters. She tucked them into a lavender, satin-covered stationery box. Letters from her family lay side-by-side with Brett's. Their initial response to her failure to come home and be by Brett's side, were simply too harsh and judgmental to handle. After all, she reasoned, wasn't this her life to do with as she pleased? She'd stopped reading them as well.

On a daily basis, Lance raved about her acting abilities. He echoed what was said at Belasco's. "You're a natural."

She was having the time of her life. Even life on the showboat wasn't this much fun. She was acting, but with no lines to memorize. They barely even had a script.

To feed their creativity, Lance handed out dime Westerns for them to read and study. Early each morning, the cast sat down together and someone would come up with a title. From there they proceeded to create a story plot. This took about thirty minutes. Next, they retired to their dressing rooms and applied their makeup. Each did their own. The Indians had the most difficult task by applying brown greasepaint from head to toe.

Helena learned to create thin arched eyebrows, apply dark eye shadow, heavy mascaraed lashes, and then paint red cupid-bow lips. She and Ardeen practiced at home for hours on end and became quite adept at the art.

Once in costume, they loaded into automobiles and drove out into the countryside. The crew that handled the outdoor props, and the horses, were waiting for them. Out in the fresh air, riding well-trained, well-behaved, regal mounts, and enjoying the beauty of the hills, was a far cry from the stuffy garment factory.

The wranglers taught Helena how to make fast mounts and dismounts, even if the horse was moving. She impressed them with her courage to try whatever they asked her to do.

The men who operated the cameras were creating new ideas almost constantly. Experimenting with close-ups, crosscutting, and canvas frames to reflect or deflect light. Each day was a new adventure.

She had made it clear to Lance at the outset, that she would never submit to an onscreen kiss. Her leading man, Philip, was quite handsome. As with most men his age, he was a returning wounded veteran. He'd lost part of his hand in an explosion and was embarrassed about it. Ever the gentle director, Lance insisted it wasn't a problem, and taught him how to keep it hidden during filming.

Regarding Helena's request, Lance acquiesced saying, "We'll either have Philip turn you away from the camera and leave it to the viewer's imagination, or we'll have him kiss you on the forehead or cheek."

That was agreeable and she was thankful he was willing to work with her. Because by now she and Ardeen had attended several motion pictures, mostly those produced by other companies, and she'd seen some of those onscreen kisses. Such audacity embarrassed her to no end.

The first time she ever disappointed Lance was the day she was scripted to race down a hill where her beau was to be waiting for her. Her response was to be surprised by his appearance, and also exuberant with joy. The cameraman was perched in back of a roadster following her jaunt, getting great closeups as she ran. But rather than the required joy, Helena burst into sobs and nearly collapsed. The spot where Philip awaited her, turned out to be a grove of lilac bushes in full bloom, giving out their gentle fragrance.

She never suspected that that throwback memory would send her into such a whirlwind of emotions. She had succeeded in ruining the entire scene. It took a while to compose herself. Some of the team members were angry, others simply confused. She was at a loss to explain.

It was Ardeen who, later that day, helped explain to Lance that it was a random event that would never happen again.

"I certainly hope not," he said. "I can't begin to calculate what this cost us today."

It was the first time they'd either one seen him so upset. The scene was repeated the next day, only now far away from the lilacs.

That night she awakened from a dead sleep. She was in the lilac bower again with Brett, their voices blended together. She could hear every word as clearly as if he were standing right there beside her bed.

In the dooryard fronting an old farm-house near the white-wash'd
palings,
Stands the lilac-bush tall-growing with heart-shaped leaves of rich
green,
With many a pointed blossom rising delicate, with the perfume
strong I love,
With every leaf a miracle—and from this bush in the dooryard,
With delicate-color'd blossoms and heart-shaped leaves of rich
green,
A sprig with its flower I break.

Chapter 24

Helena and Ardeen moved into their own flat, closer to uptown. The time spent riding the subway from the Lower East Side was a waste. In their new place, they were closer to the ferry terminal. And by now they could well afford the rent.

She continued to have Ardeen pick up her mail at Belasco's once a week. Once they were settled in their new place, it became much closer to stop by the theater. However, it really didn't matter as letters to her became fewer as the months flew by. She blamed no one but herself. She was much too distracted to care. At least that's what she told herself.

Both were becoming noted stars of the silver screen. Ardeen as the more glamorous, ingénue; Helena as the reckless, adventurous, independent gal who helped corral the villain and win the day. Their credits were quickly mounting.

It was nearing the end of summer when Helena was walking down a Manhattan street and saw her likeness in a movie poster out front of a motion picture theater. Not only her face, but her name—in big bold letters. She was stunned. Of course, she knew they were out there. They worked closely with the art department where the posters were created. But to simply walk down the street and see it, now that was another thing altogether. Occasionally, if she and Ardeen were at a restaurant, they were recognized. That, too, was a new adventure.

"Mama wants us to go with her tomorrow night to the Coliseum." Ardeen was pulling out bread and bologna from the cabinet.

"What's happening?" Helena would do anything for Mrs. Miller. She'd been beyond kind and generous to board Helena after the fiasco at the Urania House. While Ardeen made sandwiches, Helena set the plates on the table in their small kitchen and proceeded to cut apple slices.

"It's some preacher. Mama called him an evangelist."

Helena knew all about evangelists. Many times, evangelists visited her church in Chancey's Bend, and there would be revival meetings several nights in a row. The whole town turned out. She remembered many people going forward to give their lives to Christ.

"Isn't your mama Catholic? Do Catholics listen to evangelists?"

Ardeen grabbed two bottles of Nehi pop from the icebox, grabbed the opener, flipped off the lids, and set them by their plates. As she pulled out a chair and sat down at the table, she said, "I thought you knew. Mama is protestant."

Taking a bite of her sandwich, Helena shook her head.

"They were a mismatch if ever there was one. After Papa was hurt in the accident at the factory, he knew he was dying, and he made Mama promise to raise all of us Catholic. She promised."

Helena had lived in that household all those months and never knew. Or knew and had forgotten. "So, who's this evangelist?"

"His name is Ian Buchanan. I've never heard of him, but she wants us to go with her. She doesn't like to go very far from home. It's in the Bronx. I think she just wants our company."

"We'll do it. For her I'd do most anything."

A large crowd had already gathered when they arrived at the Coliseum. They jostled through masses of people in the lobby, struggling to stay together and not get separated. From the vast lobby area they could hear the strains of *How Great Thou Art*. However, the hymn was being played with flourishes that sounded more like a Chopin composition than a hymn.

They mounted steep steps and came out in the top tier of seats giving them a full view of the large stage which was situated in the center of the arena, set about with chairs, the pulpit, and one large Grand piano. Ardeen and her mother were searching for three empty seats, but Helena stared at the stage. At first, she was unsure. It was far away. But as he started once again to play, she knew it was Brett. No mistaking. It was him. Right there on that stage. It was as though all the air had been sucked out of her. This was impossible. She took hold of the railing to steady herself.

"Come on, Helena." Ardeen was starting down the steps. "There're three empty seats. Right down here." When Helena failed to answer, Ardeen looked up at her friend. "Helena, what's the matter? You've gone all pale."

Touching her midsection, she said, "I think I'm going to be sick." Waving at them, she added, "You two go on. I'll just sit in the lobby for a little bit. I'll be all right."

She didn't wait for their answer. Now she was going against the crowd and was forced to push her way through. Once back in the lobby, she didn't stop there, but stepped outside. She needed to breathe. Needed air.

What in the world was Brett Lochlann doing in New York? At this Coliseum? With this evangelist? But then, how would she know anything about his life? She long ago stopped reading his letters. She was sure by this time, he was married to some sweet, local girl, and was building a home and family. He was too handsome, too good and kind, to remain single. And if not, surely he would have tried to contact her knowing she lived in the city.

Going back inside, she sat down in the lobby area. They were using microphones and loudspeakers inside the vast arena, and she could hear every word. She heard when the evangelist stepped up to the microphone and first of all thanked his pianist, Brett Lochlann, before he began his message.

Helena realized she'd not heard a sermon for many months. Later, she wasn't sure which was more disturbing, seeing Brett, or the Word of God that seemed to pierce her very soul. Following his message, the evangelist called people forth to receive Jesus as their Savior. Then he called those who had fallen away from their faith. That, of course, included her, but she had no intention of going into that arena.

As they rode the trolley back to Manhattan, Mrs. Miller fussed over her. Both of them were concerned, as the flu was becoming more prevalent in the city. Helena so appreciated their caring attention, but nothing they could say or do would ease the pain in her heart.

As she struggled to fall asleep that night, once again the haunting refrain came flooding back in a rush...

In the dooryard fronting an old farm-house near the white-wash'd palings,
Stands the lilac-bush tall-growing with heart-shaped leaves of rich green,
With many a pointed blossom rising delicate, with the perfume strong I love,
With every leaf a miracle—and from this bush in the dooryard,
With delicate-color'd blossoms and heart-shaped leaves of rich green,
A sprig with its flower I break.
With the perfume strong I love. With the perfume strong I love.
With the perfume strong I love. Would it never leave her confused thoughts?

Chapter 25

"California? Is this a joke?"

The entire group—performers, crew, wranglers, cameramen, even the cooks who prepared their meals every day—were gathered together in the glass studio. It was the building that Helena first thought was a greenhouse, but in fact, housed yet another studio where light was taken full advantage of.

Bedsheets sewn-together, strung up on rods, were drawn back and forth in order to control the light that streamed in. Their cameramen had become experts in the use of lighting. A raised steel walkway accommodated the camera on a trolley that slid along on ball bearings. Of all the studios, this was Helena's favorite.

Lance had gathered them together on this cold November morning. During the ferry ride that morning, both Helena and Ardeen had remained inside in order to get in out of the sleet and icy wind. Standing on the deck was no longer their preference.

Waving his arms to take in the immense studio with all its many sets, Lance explained, "We can do a lot in here. I don't have to tell any of you the many films that we have shot here, but this will never take the place of our splendid outdoor scenes." Looking over at Helena, he said, "In here we'll never be able to hang our star, gagged and tied, from the Palisades cliffs."

This brought laughter from the group and all eyes were on Helena. She had done that. Helena had done that and many more scary stunts. But she had fun with each one. In the edited film, viewers couldn't see that she was hanging from the face of a very small cliff, and that a mattress was positioned beneath her. And also, that there were hidden straps holding her—not just the one visible rope.

Lance continued, "We have to escape these winters. We're losing thousands of dollars every day we can't film. And I have a great idea for a Civil War story. A feature-length drama. I'm ready to produce it now—not next spring."

One lady looked as if she were about to faint at this news. Helena knew her as one of the cooks. One of many employees of the *L&S Artistes Film Company* who lived in Fort Lee and who counted on L&S for their income.

"But California?" This from one of the wranglers who was not a local. "That's a fer piece from here."

His stab at sounding like a cowboy helped to relieve the tension, bringing a bit of laughter.

"Think of this," Lance went on. "What would happen if the Hudson freezes? What kind of a pickle would we be in? A ferry making the trip would be out of the question."

A cameraman spoke up and said, "I've been keeping my eye on the West Coast. I'm in contact with other cameramen and I'm getting firsthand information. It's fast becoming the new mecca for motion picture companies. Acres and acres

of outdoor locations for filming. Can't beat that."

Another voice in the crowd added, "Out there we can forget threats from Mr. Edison for infringing on his film patents."

That remark brought a volley of loud agreements. And Lance added his as well. "We're all mighty tired of ducking his threats."

Helena looked over at her friend to gauge her response. Ardeen was all smiles.

Move all the way across the country? She'd never considered leaving New York. She'd come to love the place. But everything she was hearing in this meeting made perfect sense. She, too, had heard about the town called Hollywood where other studios were thriving. Lance couldn't afford for his company to be left behind. Plus the fact that she'd never been a fan of winter. Icy winds whipping down the street-canyons of Manhattan was sheer torture.

It became obvious that this meeting wasn't called to ask for a vote, rather it was an announcement. Lance made it clear. It was now the first week of November and he said the entire company would be on the West Coast before Thanksgiving.

Most everyone was overjoyed, with the exception of those local employees who would now be out of a job.

That night, Helena and Ardeen talked into the wee hours, making plans and discussing their future as screen stars. The longer they talked, the more excited they grew. They were already living an adventure neither one had ever thought possible. This would be an entirely new adventure.

In the midst of the preparations to move to California, news came that the entire nation had been waiting to hear—the war was over! November 11, 1918. The armistice had been signed. New York City went wild, and the two roommates ventured out into the icy-cold night, into where the raucous, surging mass of humanity had gathered. Shouts, cheers, huzzahs rose from the crowd. Some were weeping openly. Many carried pots and pans, beating them with metal stir-spoons. It was a spontaneous celebration. Like a dream. Too good to be true.

The crowd seemed to be pulled in one direction, all the way down to City Hall where a large platform had been erected. Obviously, the city leaders had been notified that the armistice was imminent. A brass band, now arranged on the platform, played patriotic numbers and the crowd sang along with great gusto. The speeches droned on and on until finally, the girls were too cold to stay any longer. Pushing their way through the crowd toward the subway, they rode it back to their neighborhood.

Later, back in their flat, attempting to thaw out, totally exhausted, as they were getting ready for bed, Ardeen quipped, "Now maybe we'll have some handsome leading men for a change. I'm ready for that."

Helena didn't answer, but realized she had absolutely no interest whatsoever.

Huge shipping crates lined up end-to-end against every wall of every studio at *L&S Artistes*. Every employee pitched in to help pack. It was eerie to experience the sets that only a few days earlier had been overflowing with props and actors, were now silent and empty.

At their flat, Helena and Ardeen attempted to navigate around wardrobe trunks sitting in their midst. Lance was true to his word—Thanksgiving was still a week away and their departure date was being met with ease. Their little apartment was nearly as empty as the studio building.

The Millers insisted on having them come for an early Thanksgiving dinner. Mrs. Miller was visibly saddened by the soon-coming loss of her daughter. Struggling to keep her composure, she periodically turned her head and wiped away the tears with her apron.

"Aw Mama," Ardeen told her. "I'll be sending you train tickets and you can come to California for a fun time. I'll be showing you all the sights."

Mrs. Miller pretended to be comforted by the words, but Helena wondered if she would actually make the trip. New York was all Ardeen's mother had ever known.

Before leaving the city, Helena marched right into Belasco's with her head held high. Her destination was the Wardrobe Department. She wanted to give Deborah and big hug and thank her. But she was surprised as several of the stage hands noticed her and rushed to her side and regaled her with praises, each one out-talking the other, telling her which of her moving pictures they liked the best. Word spread throughout the theater and within minutes a crowd had gathered.

Before she could detach herself from the commotion, she saw Deborah coming toward her with her arms outstretched. Smothering her in a tight hug, Deborah said, "Ah. There's my beautiful Helena. Oh, you showed them, didn't you girl."

Stepping back and taking a good look at Helena, tears glistening, she said, "I knew you would shine. I just didn't know you would outshine them all."

Those in the crowd who knew the story of her being blacklisted, chimed in with their agreement.

Waving them away, Deborah said, "Nothing more for you here, folks. Go back to work. She's all mine." With her arm around Helena's shoulder, she said, "Come on. Let's talk."

It felt like a moment of triumph to return to Deborah's domain in the Wardrobe Department. Helena told her friend about the move to California, and that she'd come to thank her. "You'll never know how you changed my life, Deborah. Your love and caring were precious to me during those days."

As they parted, both in tears, Deborah asked, "Still got the galoshes?"

Helena laughed. "They will be my life-long possession."

Cat's name never came up. Helena had no idea where she was, nor did she care. What a freeing sensation.

Chapter 26

The *L&S Artistes* rode in railway luxury across the country to California. Lance had commissioned private cars which were for *L&S* people exclusively—sleeper cars, parlor cars, lounge, dining. And with their own private staff. The deep forest green of the tapestries, the rich burgundy of the furniture, all accented in gold was reminiscent of the Belasco's interior. Shiny mahogany woodwork reflected the soft gold of inlaid lighting.

They whiled away the hours playing card games, reading books, writing letters, and a great deal of conversation about California. Only one or two among them had ever been there, and they became the center of attention as the others pestered them with questions.

Ardeen was writing letters to her family and seemed to be dropping off a letter or two at every stop. Helena had very few people to write to, but she had promised to keep Deborah updated. She also wrote to Mrs. Miller thanking her for all her many kindnesses.

Lance hadn't told them ahead of time that he'd planned for the private train cars. That had been a nice surprise. Likewise, he'd not told them what awaited them in Hollywood. Offboarding the train, they were ushered into buses which meandered through the town, then north through the wooded hills until they stopped in front of a massive gated entrance bordered by sprawling rock gardens overflowing with rose bushes, chrysanthemums, petunias, carnations, and gardenias, all in bright splashes of colors.

An arching stone façade sported large inlaid scarlet letters that read:

Eleness – Odell

They were leaning out the windows saying *Eleness,* stumbling over the syllables.

Suddenly someone yelled out, "It's *L and S* you dummies. Don't you get it?"

"Our studio? It's our studio?"

It was beyond their ability to grasp what they were seeing.

Lance had ridden in an automobile out ahead, leading the way. As the crew exited the buses, still gaping at the sign, and buzzing in conversation, Lance called out to them. "Okay troupe. Quiet down." Pointing to the sign, he said, "Let me fill you in on what we have here." Taking off his straw boater and stepping closer to the gate, he said, "I'll be quick, then we'll take a tour."

"This is *our* studio?" Again, the question was voiced. Every last one of them was aghast.

Adjusting his glasses, he said. "It is. We are no longer *L&S Artistes.* We are *Eleness – Odell.* New location. New name. New organization. I sent an emissary out here last summer to search out a studio that was on shaky legs. He spent weeks nosing around and asking question and finally found this—*Odell Studios.* Well, it *was* Odell Studios."

Helena had never seen her director so happy. His face was beaming like a kid on Christmas morning.

"It seems the bigger studios had taken all the big-name stars. As a result, Odell had no stars, and had no strong story ideas. We come along with everything they need. And they have everything we need. A fully-equipped, fully-staffed studio complex."

Now the group was buzzing again—with excitement rather than with questions.

Lance yelled over the buzz. "Back to the buses. You'll soon see that this place is much too big to survey on foot."

And he was right. What Helena had thought was a large studio back in Fort Lee was a mere miniature compared to this vast layout. Giant building after giant building housed not only stages, studios, and dressing rooms, but there was a laboratory, carpenter shop, generator plant, prop rooms, wardrobe building, dining hall, garage, and executive offices. The driver kept up a running commentary, pointing from one side of the street to the other.

"Oh, Helena. Look."

Ardeen was pulling her over to the window to see a rambling garden, patterned with winding paths, precise plantings, and a meandering stream overarched by picturesque wooden bridges. Graceful willows seemed to be dipping the tips of their branches in the stream. Inviting white wrought-iron benches were tucked into various shady spots.

"It's a Japanese garden. In the spring we'll see the cherry trees in bloom," Ardeen explained. "The bright reds are azaleas, the variegated green plants are hostas, the bright pinks are camellia and purples are wisteria."

"How do you know all this?"

"New York botanical gardens and greenhouse," she said, then added, "And the straight, tall plants are bamboo."

"Bamboo? Just imagine," Helena said, "none of it will ever freeze. I love that thought." The bus passed by it much too quickly. "I want to be able to walk on those paths and sit on one of those benches."

Ardeen squeezed her arm. "Remember, friend. We'll be spending most of our time here, so you'll surely have the opportunity."

As Lance told them later, he had saved the best until last. The *best* that he referred to was the back lot. Acres of outdoor sets. Facsimiles of city streets, Western towns, medieval castles, Spanish villas, and back alleys of London and much more. It was impossible to see it all. And nearly impossible to comprehend it all.

Of course, each of them had seen many of the epic movies. Now they could grasp how the creation of those pictures had been accomplished.

The last stop on the tour was the dining hall where lunch was served. They ate their fill of cold cuts, cheeses, crackers, and platters full of a vast array of fresh fruit.

It was here that Lance introduced to them the founder of *Odell Studios*, Kenley Odell. Mr. Odell, which he insisted on being called, was a large-jowled man with bulging stomach and ill-fitting clothes. Standing on a raised platform at the far side of the dining hall, he welcomed them, but without much enthusiasm. Not like one would think, coming from a person who just had life infused into his dying studio.

In Helena's mind, he looked nothing like a studio director. Certainly not a stickler for details as his appearance depicted. Perhaps that was part of the reason his studio was failing when Lance came to his rescue.

Mr. Kenley Odell aside, by the time they boarded the buses back to the hotel, they were a happy lot, and still bubbling over with excitement.

Nothing could have prepared Helena for California. After a few weeks, she wondered how she could have ever been content in the stark grayness of New York. Each day greeted her with bright, warm sunshine. Everywhere she looked blooming flowers lent bright cheerful colors to the landscape. Nearly every house sported window boxes overflowing with cascading flowers. Palm trees, waving their fronds in the breeze, fascinated her. But it was the immense ocean that proved to be the most spellbinding.

She'd grown up by the river, and she lived on the showboat that plied the rivers, but it all paled in comparison to the limitlessness of the Pacific Ocean, where one could look out and see forever. Nothing blocked the view of the horizon, except for a few boats and ships here and there. Every free minute she was begging Ardeen to come with her to the beach.

However, there weren't many free minutes. Lance wasted no time in launching into his Civil War picture, *Glory Fields*.

The consistent balmy weather allowed filming with few breaks. Work on creating the location had begun by work crews before the team ever left Jersey. The rugged hills outside the city provided the perfect setting for the battle scenes. Elegant Southern plantation homes—mere shells—had been erected on the back lot, as well as hundreds of white tents depicting military staging arenas. Trees were decked out in Spanish moss, something Helena remembered from her show boat days in the deep South. Streets to depict a small town from that era were located in another area.

Unlike before, where the stories were fabricated each morning, now the cast and crew had the full script, outlining each scene of the story. Hundreds of locals had been brought in as extras—especially for the battle scenes. It was like going backward in time.

Helena and Ardeen starred with equal billing as sisters whose lovers were each one on opposing sides of the conflict. Helena believed the strong story line held great promise. Not an ordinary film like his previous works, Lance Sedgley deemed *The Glory Fields* to be an *epic*. As he worded it—*his epic to top all epics.*

Lance had settled his crew in the splendorous Hotel Hollywood right on Hollywood Boulevard, and fronted by the trolley—an easy ride to the studio. The elaborate edifice boasted tall turrets and delicate gingerbread detailing on the wide wraparound veranda. The rooms were lavish, and surrounding acres of gardens, and groves of lemon and California pepper trees, lent a peaceful calm about the place.

The girls appeared in very few of the battle scenes, which meant their working days were at *Eleness – Odell* studios. Interiors were shot in the closed studios, and exteriors in the back lot.

Early each morning meant showing up at wardrobe for makeup and being outfitted in corsets, hoops, crinolines, pantalets, period dresses, bonnets and all the other minor details for authenticity.

Each day, Lance gathered his crew and impressed upon them that they were on a tight deadline. He'd set his goal of the finished film by early spring. The perfect time for a movie premier. At least that's what he said. And who were they to argue?

By January, great progress had been made on the film. Lance was confident they would finish ahead of his deadline.

Helena could hardly believe it was winter back in New York. Once in a while, the weather turned chilly, but they welcomed those days, because all of their costumes were hot and restrictive.

One morning as she and Ardeen settled into their seats on the trolley, Ardeen said, "I've been thinking."

"Uh oh." Helena never knew what her friend was conjuring up. She was full of plans and ideas.

"I'm beyond weary of living in a hotel. We're going to buy a house."

"Nice thought, but we barely have time to eat. We'd never have time to look for a house."

Helena agreed that she, too, wanted some space. Although Hotel Hollywood was luxurious, with screen stars and movie moguls coming and going in their limousines and town cars, important contractual meetings held forth on the spacious veranda, and lively dances in the ballroom every Thursday night, neither of them were enamored with the glitz and glamor.

"I want to make a pot of stew. *My* stew."

Helena replied, "And I want you to make a pot of your stew. I love your stew."

"I want privacy. Plus, I want to be able to go to my kitchen, open my own icebox, and grab a snack at four in the morning."

"You're never up at four in the morning."

"I know. But you get my point."

Of course, Helena got the point. The two of them were alike in so many ways. It's what had allowed their friendship to strengthen and grow.

"I want to sit in my own living room, listen to my own gramophone, sit on my own patio, and..."

Waving her hands, Helena said, "Okay. I agree. But back to my first response, we have no time to go house hunting."

"Ever heard of a real estate person?"

"No. Never remember having that in Chancey's Bend."

"Someone who deals in selling houses and will know the area. We just tell him what we're looking for."

"What *are* we looking for?"

Ardeen closed her eyes for a minute. "Not a mansion. We don't need a mansion."

"Agreed on that."

"A cottage. A cute little cottage. Tucked up into the hills. With lots of flowers and trees. Maybe even an orange tree."

"And a patio?"

"Definitely a patio."

"A swimming pool?"

Ardeen opened her eyes. "Heavens no. I don't even know how to swim."

Helena laughed. "Growing up by the river, I can swim, but we have no time for such frivolity. And I much prefer the beach."

Plenty of locals worked at the studio. Locals who knew all the business people in the area. From them they got the names of several real estate agents.

Helena gave the task of making the telephone calls over to Ardeen. She disliked the telephone. But she gave her input, which was, "He has to be friendly, and caring," she told Ardeen. "We must make sure that he truly wants our business."

After a few calls, Ardeen soon learned she was being confronted by land development agents who were selling locations in areas where construction was in progress. It took several calls to locate their guy who said he had a cottage that was "precisely what you're looking for." His exact words, per Ardeen.

"I have early call in the morning," Ardeen said after hanging up the telephone in their hotel room. Just one more perk of a luxury hotel—a telephone in every room. "You go on and take a look at it and I'll let you tell me about it."

"Oh no you don't. We go together. No discussion."

"That's not until Sunday. It may be sold by then."

"If it's sold then it wasn't for us."

With a roll of her eyes, Ardeen said, "Oh that Kentucky logic."

Chapter 27

As Lance had done for all his crew back in Jersey, he always gave them Sundays off. No matter how tight the deadline. While other directors might drive their cast seven days a week under deadline, Lance insisted everyone worked better with a breather tucked in.

"Wait and see. He'll be wearing a homburg, a suit coat, a bowtie, and carrying a briefcase," Ardeen quipped as they sat waiting in the hotel lobby for their newly acquired agent to arrive.

"Lay bets," Helena replied. "This isn't New York."

"Yeah, but a pusher is a pusher no matter the geography."

"Twenty."

"Twenty it is."

The young man who strode into the sun-drenched lobby, paused at the door. The moment he spied them sitting together on the sofa, his expression lit up. His tucked-in, printed shirt with open collar and pressed light-wool slacks, meant Helena was twenty dollars richer.

"Told you." She gently poked Ardeen in the ribs. "Not even a hat."

"Miss Miller?" he asked as he approached them.

After introductions, Mason Lynch admitted he was fairly new in the real estate business, but was sure he could help them.

They loaded into his Model T touring car and headed for Beachwood Canyon. Mason chatted about some of the stars he knew and where they lived. He admitted his surprise that they weren't interested in one of the more glamorous mansions. "They love to give big parties," he told them. "Which means they need massive floor space."

"That's not us," Ardeen said.

Driving up a winding road deeper into the hills, through a sparsely populated neighborhood, Mason finally stopped in front of a small white cottage, crowned with a terra cotta roof, and matching terra cotta-tone shutters. Amid thick stands of trees and well-trimmed shrubbery, a curved flagstone walkway led to the wooden front door.

Helena was mesmerized. It was a dreamlike scene and for a moment she felt paralyzed.

Ardeen must have been likewise affected, because as Mason was getting out of the car, he said, "Well ladies? Do you want to see the inside? Or not?"

While seemingly cloistered from the outside, the cottage was all windows and light on the interior. As they stepped down into the sunken living room, Mason said, "I'll leave you two to explore together. I won't bother you."

The far side of the living room led to a long hallway which opened into the two sizeable bedrooms, and the sparkling bathroom fitted with gold fixtures. A curving staircase with wrought iron bannister led to the upstairs which was vast and open, fitted with expansive windows which gave a stunning view for miles out.

But the patio proved to be the winner. Wide and spacious, but walled in, draped in greenery and flowers, plus espaliered fruit trees.

As they sat down together on an upholstered bench Ardeen asked, "What are you thinking?"

Helena couldn't speak.

Ardeen looked over. "Are you crying?" She touched Helena's arm. "What is it? What's the matter?"

"Ardeen, it just hit me that I haven't had a place of my own since I left Chancey's Bend. And even then, I shared the attic with my family."

"And so...?"

Pulling a hanky from her handbag, she dabbed at her cheeks. "I love this house. I absolutely love it."

"Then it's done. You and I—we now have a home."

Mason proved to be a delight to work with. He walked them through every step of the process. It became important to set up the legalities if and when either one of them might want to step out of the agreement.

They were in Mason's office on Hollywood Boulevard going over the paperwork. He looked over his desk at them with a knowing smile. "One or the other of you two beautiful ladies will without a doubt be getting married at some future date. Let's look at options as to how to handle that when it happens."

Since neither of them even had so much as a serious date since they arrived, the statement seemed irrelevant. Of course, the more their publicity grew, the more lovelorn mail they received, but it was handled by the Eleness office. They had secretaries who answered the letters.

"No one knows the future," Mason was saying. "But when handling legal matters, one has to cover all the bases."

It was decided quite simply. The contract stated that when either one was ready to move out, the remaining party would buy out the other.

Because their free time was limited, they hired a designer to decorate and even purchase the furniture—under close supervision of course.

Once the cottage interior pleased both of them, Ardeen came up with yet another idea.

"We need a housekeeper."

As usual, Helena was taken aback. "A housekeeper? Why that's ridiculous."

They were relaxing, drinking coffee on the patio when Ardeen sprung this new one.

"You're only saying that because you never needed a housekeeper before." Helena smiled at the thought. "Or could never afford one before."

"Exactly. Well now you need one. And, my dear fellow movie star, we can certainly afford one." Slowly she took a sip of coffee, pausing to let her idea soak in. "Just imagine it. Coming home from work to a clean house and having a nice supper prepared."

Helena had to agree with the supper part. They tried to cook up a nice dinner on Sundays, but the rest of the week was reduced to snacking. Their wild schedules left no time for cooking.

Ardeen wasted no time asking around the studio and quickly discovered a matronly Mexican lady working as a cook in the dining hall. Her days were free after two. Jacinta Rivera came on board and enhanced their home with her bright personality and joyful nature. A bit on the plump side, her glossy black hair always fastened in neat bun at the nape of her neck, her dark eyes dancing with laughter, Jacinta proved to be a delight. Her experience cooking for cast and crew in the studio dining hall paid off in big dividends—something new greeted them every evening. Eventually, Jacinta also took on the task of grocery shopping, since she knew what was needed for the meals she planned and prepared. All in all, Jacinta changed their lives for the better.

"Now we need a name." This from Ardeen during their early-morning drive to the studio.

Helena never knew what direction Ardeen's mind was headed next. "Name? What exactly are we naming?"

"Our new home, of course. You know, in Britain, they name their palaces, manors, estates, and even cottages."

"Since I've never traveled abroad, I wouldn't know about such things."

"Oh, it's true. Ever heard of Buckingham Palace?"

"Well, of course."

"My point exactly. They don't just call it *the palace,* do they? Now what shall we name our cottage?"

Once again, Ardeen's insight was point on. Helena set to thinking. "It would have to reflect peace and quiet."

"Agreed."

"Peace Cottage?"

Ardeen shook her head. "Not creative enough."

"Serene Cottage?"

"Keep going."

Racking her brain, Helena finally said, "Tranquility? Is that creative enough?"

"Close. But it's too long."

"Well then, how about just tranquil? Tranquil Cottage."

Ardeen took a deep breath. "That's it. Our cottage is now Christened *Tranquil Cottage.*"

"In which we will spend many tranquil hours."

In the ensuing weeks Helena was hard pressed to decide which was more exciting: their epic, feature-length motion picture, or their new house. It was a draw. No matter how late they arrived back at Tranquil Cottage, the delight never faded as they unlocked the front door and entered their own little abode greeted by the aroma of Jacinta's cooking. Late night hours were spent on the patio drinking coffee and discussing the day's shoots.

Realistic battle scenes, strong characterization, believable story line, expert filming techniques all woven together, as Lance repeatedly assured them, was resulting in a wildly successful production. As a surprising plus, they were right on schedule.

Helena played the role of the sister who had moved to the North. She felt deeply immersed into the character, for which she received ongoing praise from the various directors. Lance focused his energies mainly on the exterior scenes, leaving the interiors to his close counterparts, each one of whom was as adept as he.

Because Ardeen's role was set in the South, many of her scenes were exterior and in one instance took her close to the battle scenes, which as she told Helena, "...was realistic enough to be terrifying."

To top it off, Ardeen's role called for riding horseback. She'd never been around horses in her life. "And side saddle," she said, rolling her eyes. "In my voluminous costume!"

"I'm almost jealous. The only time I see a horse is the rear end as I'm riding in the carriage. Sometimes I miss the Westerns."

"Maybe after this?"

"Maybe."

Lance often talked about the *afterward* scenario. *After* meaning when the film reached completion. Premiers. Travel. Promotions. Lots of public appearances. It may have seemed strange to some, but that part appealed to neither Helena nor Ardeen. Neither of them even read their fan mail. They simply loved acting. As Ardeen described it, "It's like playing make-believe every single day."

Lance was standing on the raised platform in the dining hall. Every member of the cast and crew were in attendance seated around the long tables. February was drawing to a close and only a few scenes remained to be filmed. On the platform with him were his several directors. Mr. Odell had joined them as well. He seemed to be in better spirits than when they first arrived last November. Ardeen said it was because he was getting dollar signs in his eyes.

"I just wish he'd spend some of his money on a new wardrobe."

Helena nodded. "Especially a pair of pants that would actually fit over his midriff bulge."

One of those big mansions up in the hills now boasted Lance Sedgley as owner. His wife, Abigail, and their two children had also moved out to the Golden State from Jersey. Everyone associated with *Eleness–Odell* was settling into California life and loving it.

When they had rung in the New Year of 1919, the party was in the Sedgley's massive upstairs ballroom. And now Lance was announcing yet another party. This one to celebrate the completion of *Glory Fields* and to announce the premier and the upcoming promotional plans. Of course, everyone was invited.

"All of us," he indicated those on the platform, "want to show our appreciation to each and every one of you. It's been weeks and months of grueling hard work, and there's not a slouch in the entire group gathered here. I've been fielding questions from newspapers, movie magazines, and radio shows for weeks. Newsreel teams have been on the backlot several times. The anticipation for our premier is explosive. We're the talk of the town. And that's the way we like it."

Being able to actually sit in a theater and view the movie in its entirety would be a wonderful experience, but Helena never wanted the filming to be over. She was already wondering what might come next?

After the meeting, as Ardeen maneuvered their Buick touring car up the hills in Beachwood Canyon toward their cottage, she said, "Helena. I just got an idea."

"Another one?" By now Helena was used to Ardeen having all the great ideas. It had been her idea for them to purchase the cottage. It had been her idea to buy an automobile. Her idea to hire Jacinta. She was always coming up with something new. "Well, let's hear it."

"I'm thinking about our celebration party."

"I was too."

"Were you thinking about what we would wear?"

Helen shook her head. "No. I was thinking about how I don't want to be there."

"Silly. That's why we have a car. We're free and easy. We can leave whenever we want to."

"But you were thinking about what we would wear?"

"I was."

"And you were trying to decide which great and famous designer we would go to."

Ardeen looked over at Helena with laughter in her blue eyes. "Not really. I think I'm looking at our designer."

Helena sat up straighter. "What? What in the world are you talking about?"

"You're a designer. And a seamstress. And now that the shooting is over, you'll have time before the party and the premier to not only design our dresses, but also create them."

"You forget. I have no sewing machine."

"Order one. The whole upstairs can be yours."

"But I'd need a cutting table."

"I think I've seen a few carpenters around. You know, building sets. Building entire houses and..."

"Never mind. I hear you. But even if they build a cutting table, we'd never be able to get it up the stairs."

They were pulling into their drive and Ardeen stopped the car at the front of Tranquil Cottage. Turning to Helena she said, "Perhaps they could bring the lumber and build it right there. Ever think of that?"

"Frankly, I haven't thought of any of this, Ardeen. This is all your idea. Sewing and designing have not been in my little brain for a very long time."

Her friend simply shrugged her shoulders and laughed. "It will never go away. And I'm being selfish. I'd be delighted to have a custom-designed gown for the party. A gown, a copy of which could never be found, no matter if some dame decides to travel all the way to Paris. And," she added, "we can wear them to the premier as well."

Now Helena was laughing. Ardeen—a gift in her life—always a delight.

Chapter 28

The idea was taking shape. Sewing again. Designing. Helena thought back to the excitement and pleasure she experienced when she created the costume for Cat all those months ago. And the pure joy she experienced in the Wardrobe Department at Belasco's with Deborah. Even now, no matter what costume she wore during filming, she found herself inspecting it to see exactly how it was made.

Then, it was the idea of the *idea-person*, to put a notice on the bulletin board in the studio dining hall. The note read:

Need to be built on-site at the home of Ardeen Miller and Helena Heise: A large four-legged table. Nothing fancy, but with a finished surface. Builder furnishes materials—to be reimbursed. Pay negotiable.

Ardeen added their telephone number and their address. As she put it, "One of the set-carpenters will see it and we'll have your cutting table in no time at all."

Meanwhile, Helena went shopping for her sewing machine and found the perfect Singer, encased in a glossy walnut cabinet, complete with several small drawers. The head sported the name *Singer* in swirling gold letters, surrounded by decorative gold curlicues. She was itching to sit down and use it.

The deliverymen had quite a tussle getting it up the stairs, but they managed to accomplish the feat. Once they left, Helena stood there in the room that was awash in the sunshine pouring through the tall windows and felt incredibly satisfied.

The day after the Singer arrived, their dinnertime was interrupted by a knock at the door. They seldom had visitors. For a moment they just looked at one another.

Then shoving back her chair, Ardeen laughed. "I guess we better answer the door."

Ardeen led the way, but Helena was close behind. Looking past Ardeen, Helena saw standing on the flagstone steps, a tall, tanned, broad-shouldered young man dressed in denim pants, an open-collar shirt with rolled-up sleeves, and Western boots. Tall leather boots like Helena remembered the men wearing back in Jersey when they were filming Westerns. His jeans were hitched up with a snakeskin belt and sterling buckle. His straw-colored hair was a curly mass. In one hand he held his hat—also Western—and in the other hand was the note Ardeen had posted.

Ardeen gave a little gasp. "Jonas," she said. "You?"

The cowboy—because that's what he appeared to be from tip to toe—gave a shy grin. "Hi there, Miss Ardeen." He gave the note a little wave. "Saw your note and I'm here to offer my services."

Helena could see her friend was a bit befuddled. Looking back at Helena she cocked her head to bring her friend to the door. "Helena, this is Jonas McCardle."

Helena stepped up and took the outstretched very large, very calloused hand that he extended. "Pleased to meet you Mr. McCardle."

"Aw, it's just Jonas."

"Okay Jonas." Now Helena was befuddled as well.

Ardeen was saying, "Jonas is the wrangler who taught me to ride—sidesaddle."

"And a darn good job she did learning, too," Jonas said, giving a shy grin. "At first she was a mite afraid. But she got over it quick."

"But Jonas, we need a carpenter." Ardeen pointed at the note in his hand. "We weren't expecting..."

"A rough-riding cowhand? Well, here's the gist, ma'am. Any cowhand worth his salt is mighty handy with a hammer and saw as much as he is with a horse and saddle. We can do most everything on the ranch. And that includes building most of whatever is needed. Sometimes even furniture." He gave a low chuckle that made Helena smile. "Even a large table."

Shaking off her disbelief, Ardeen said, "Well, aren't we rude, making you stand out here. Please come in."

"I probably oughta had telephoned first. But I don't have much liking for a telephone."

Helena knew most of her Kentucky family would have said the same thing.

They led him into the sunken living room and offered him the wingback chair while they sat beside one another on the brocade couch.

Propping his hat on his knee, he gave the place an approving look. "Real nice little place you got here, ladies. Seems right cozy."

"Thank you," Ardeen said. "We're quite comfortable here."

"Tell me about this table you're wanting. Don't look much like you're gonna be serving a large company dinner." There was that low chuckle again.

His slow speech amused Helena and reminded her of the folks in Chancey's Bend who seemed never to be in a hurry.

"No," Ardeen was saying. "It's not for entertaining. It's for Helena. A cutting table."

"Cutting? The onliest cutting I know is cutting calves out of the herd during branding time."

"For sewing," Helena added. "Cutting fabric to sew a gown. Or whatever."

Now Jonas nodded. "I got it now. Sure. Just give me the dimensions. I'll get the lumber and have it done in a short shake."

"Don't you want to know how much we planned to pay?" Helena asked.

Jonas was standing up now and seemed to fill the room. It wasn't difficult to imagine him wrangling cows, or riding across the dusty plains with a lariat spinning above his head. Helena had witnessed many actors pretending to be what Jonas happened to be—the genuine article.

"Naw," he said as he headed toward the door. "I know y'all will be fair."

"Well, at least come upstairs so you can get a sense of the space." Helena motioned toward the stairs. "Because I'm not sure about the dimensions."

Jonas nodded. "Yeah. Probably a good idea."

Once they were in the now-to-be-known-as sewing room, Helena said, "It needs to be over here by the windows. And I don't want it to fill the room."

"Like from here?" He walked over to the windows. "To here?"

"Yes. Perfect."

"I'll just step it off." From his pocket he pulled out a small notebook and stub of a pencil. He took good-sized steps one way, then the other way, scribbling down numbers in the notebook. He'd put his hat back on the mussed-up curls.

"What kind of wood?"

"Nothing fancy," Helena told him. "Just no splinters."

"After I sand it down and varnish it, it'll be slick as whistle."

Helena never thought of a whistle as being slick, but she was thrilled that a cutting table would be sitting right there by the tall windows. In a *short shake*.

It became a new saying between her and Ardeen. They began doing everything in a short shake. And laughed every time they said it.

While Jonas dragged lumber in the house and up the stairs to create the cutting table, Helena spent her time at the kitchen table sketching ideas for their gowns, then taking them to Ardeen for her approval. They discussed at length choices of fabrics, colors, and styles. *Understated* was their agreed choice.

"Let others be flamboyant," Ardeen said, "we'll let the fabric and colors make the statement."

Quite often, Ardeen would excuse herself and go upstairs with a glass of ice water, or a cup of coffee for Jonas. Helena could hear the two of them chattering away, and wondered what in the world an Irish lass from the city had to talk about with a ranch hand?

When imagining her cutting table, Helena never pictured anything but straight, squared table legs, but Jonas surprised her.

First of all, he created *five* legs. "One for the center so's it'll always be secure," he explained.

Next, the legs had been worked on a wood lathe creating a delicate, curvy effect. "I visited the carpentry shop at the studio. It ain't very busy right now between productions. And the old boy there give me leave to use the lathe." Each leg had been varnished to a high sheen, perfectly matching the table.

The best part was that Jonah created a metal head on the four corners and middle on the underside of the table, then embedded a bolt into each leg.

"See here, ma'am," he said to Helena. "The legs are removable. That way if and when you ever move from here, you just take them legs off and move it easy-like."

Helena was speechless. She ran her hand over the glossy cherrywood finish. She knelt down to inspect how the legs screwed into the table top. Jonah had definitely delivered the goods. This table would last a lifetime and beyond. She paid him double what she'd originally planned to spend on a cutting table.

She was ready to get to it. Two dress forms stood in the corner waiting patiently for the fancy gowns to draped upon them.

However, the idea-girl had yet another idea.

"Shelves. Built-in shelves," Ardeen said with all the drama of a movie actress. "Look at this." With great aplomb, she waved her hand to take in the room. "You have fabric stacked up everywhere. Are you going to live in a mess? You must have shelves in order to stay organized."

Helena knew her friend was right. Again. And they already had a carpenter in hand. Jonas was called back into action. Once again, the sound of hammering and sawing filled the house. And also, once again, Helena was thrilled with the finished project. Jonas, the cowboy, completed the built-in shelves in a short shake.

Now the room looked as though it were occupied by a professional seamstress.

Helena's sewing room paid off in spades as she and Ardeen were the hit of the celebration party in their custom-designed gowns. Even Lance appeared to be impressed.

"I trust you ladies will be wearing these elegant dresses to the premier." With a wink, he added, "And if you do, we may have to hire armed guards to keep the guys in the crowd from making a full-on attack."

The two offered gracious thanks in return to the barrage of compliments they received during the evening, while being inwardly amused. They knew many of the cast members were dying to ask at what boutique the gowns had been custom-tailored, but none did. Their secret remained safe.

Nearly every movie magazine, every gossip column, every newspaper review, dubbed *Glory Fields* a smash hit. The magnificent premiere at the Orpheum Theater in downtown Los Angeles drew crushing throngs. Lance and Mr. Odell made sure their stars arrived in Rolls Royce limousines. Photographers and sightseers pressed in and policemen held them back. As she and Ardeen made their way to the door of the theater, they heard shouts for them to stop for photographs to be taken. Lance and his wife, a few steps ahead of them, turned back and nodded. Lance held up his first finger, which Helena took to mean—just one time and for just one minute. They complied, then hurried on their way.

Helena heaved a sigh of thanks once she was inside the opulent building and felt a bit safer away from the raucous crowd.

They were guided though white-marbled halls to the mezzanine level, through a door, and ushered to their reserved box seats. From their balcony vantage point they beheld the panoramic view of the vast auditorium replete with scarlet seats, golden arches, gold etched ceiling art, and bronze and crystal chandeliers. The two-thousand-seat theater rivaled anything Helena had seen anywhere. Even Belasco's in New York.

Neither of them had ever watched *Glory Fields* in its entirely. Later, they would become almost weary of watching it as they traveled from city to city. But at the Los Angeles premiere, Helena sat mesmerized at the detailed, wholly authentic, replication of the war that had ripped the country apart. Lance's direction, his plot creativity, and his passion for detail all forged together to create the success of the epic film.

Helena could honestly say that while watching the film, she was so enraptured by the story, and moved almost to tears by the lilting, emotional strains of the Wurlitzer organ, playing music that had been scored expressly for this film, she didn't see the character on the screen as herself. Only as a character who was an integral part of the story.

At the close, the audience, as one, were on their feet roaring their acceptance and approval. Lance stepped out on the stage with his entourage of directors taking bows. He then waved toward the balcony boxes to give tribute to his stars. Helena and Ardeen stood, along with their fellow cast-members, and unsure of what to do, they gave stiff little bows and quickly sat back down.

The musical score had been Lance's clever concept. The score was to accompany the film when distributed to theaters, mainly to be played on the Wurlitzer organ, now a common addition to most big-city theaters. Helena found herself humming the haunting melody as she worked in her sewing studio. Because now, before leaving on tour, the two of them would need several gowns for the various premieres.

Helena experimented with satin, silk, voile, organza, with lace and feather accents. And the choice of colors. Taking into account, Ardeen's red curls, she learned not only which colors complimented her friend's hair and complexion, but also the colors her friend was most comfortable wearing.

One afternoon as Helena was at the sewing machine, Ardeen ventured up the stairs and into the studio. Helena had made it quite clear that she disliked being interrupted while in the heat of creativity. Which was most of the time.

Helena finished the seam and then said, "Hey there Ardeen. I'm not ready for a fitting."

Ardeen paused. The room was quiet. Helena scooted her chair around to see what was up. "Ardeen? Did you need me?"

"Well..."

Helena had never known Ardeen to stammer. Or stall. For the most part, she blurted her words without hesitation. Sometimes without thinking.

Getting up and gathering the half-completed garment in her arms, Helena stepped over to the dress form. "Well? Well, what?"

"Helena, Jonas has invited me to go with him to visit the ranch."

"The ranch? The ranch where he works?" Helena stopped now and looked right at Ardeen. "Now why...?"

Ardeen's laughter bubbled up. "Are you ready for this? He doesn't work on a ranch. No. I take that back. He does work. But it's his ranch. He owns it. The *McCardle Hills Ranch*. It's been in his family since before the Civil War."

Helena stepped back over to the chair which sat in front of the Singer, and sat down. Studying her friend's face, she noticed the sparkle in Ardeen's eyes.

"This is very interesting. He owns a ranch. And he wants you to come for a visit?"

Ardeen nodded. She was blushing. Ardeen, the hardnosed New Yorker, was blushing.

"And where is this ranch located?"

"The Santa Monica Mountains."

"When is this visit to happen?

"The two of us were talking, and since we have no work at the studio before the tour begins. We're sort of free at the present time. And so..." Another long pause. "Probably right away."

"I see."

"Would you be all right with this?"

"Last time I checked, Ardeen, I'm not your mother. I'm not even my sister's keeper. Of course, I'm all right with this. In fact, I'm quite impressed. Here I've been looking at this guy as a ranch hand who's also a handy man who can build things. Time for a mind adjustment."

"I know. Me too."

"And when exactly did you learn all of this?" She put up her hand to silence any reply. "Never mind. Don't tell me. I think I know. It was all those cups of coffee you kept taking up here while he was working. I heard all that chattering. I wondered what you two had to talk about."

Now Ardeen was blushing again. "Plus, he's Irish. His people arrived at Ellis Island just like mine did." Then she quickly added, "Oh, and we'll be chaperoned the whole time. He has a full ranch crew."

Standing and moving back over to the dress form, Helena gave a little shrug. "I'm certainly not concerned about that. So. Go. Get packed. And I'll want to hear all about it. I've never seen a real ranch. Only make believe for a movie."

"Are you sure you're okay with me leaving you with all this work?"

Helena snorted. "Work? You call this work? I'm in heaven. Dressing in hoops, crinolines, tied up in a corset, tripping over a sweeping skirt and acting in front of a camera. Now *that's* work." Pushing one of the dress forms to the center of the room, she added, "Plus, who needs you? I have your stunt double right here."

"Oh Helena. You're such a good friend." Rushing to Helena, she smothered her in a big hug, which was returned.

"We're talking about friends?" Helena countered. "Who rescued who during a New York blizzard and gave the poor little wretch a place to sleep? And then tricked her into signing on with the flickers? Changing the course of her entire life."

"We've had quite a journey, haven't we?"

"That we have."

Ardeen was starting down the stairs when Helena said, "Ardeen?"

Ardeen stopped.

"Tell me. Did you suggest the built-in shelves because I needed them? Or so that Jonas could be around here a little longer?"

With a laugh, she said, "Silly girl. Both!"

Chapter 29

"I think my smile is tired." Ardeen sat slouched in one of the soft, over-stuffed chairs in the lounge car, her head back and her eyes closed. "It seems all Lance can say is, 'Keep smiling, everyone. Keep smiling.'"

Helena knew what her friend meant. She never realized that smiling could be such hard work. Even smiling for the cameras during filming was never this tiring.

Of course, they were all thankful for the luxury of their private custom train cars, nevertheless, the tour was proving to be utterly exhausting.

Omaha, St. Louis, Kansas City, Cincinnati, Chicago. At every stop the crowds nearly overwhelmed them. Lance, and Mr. Odell as well, assured them that, so far, the tour had been a monumental success.

Helena managed to put up with their adoring fans, even when in their exuberance they nearly trampled the stars. But the reporters proved to be rude, pushy, and overbearing, often manufacturing lies and fabrications for their stories. Before the tour began, two different correspondents had discovered where they lived and kept knocking at their cottage door wanting exclusive interviews.

Ardeen finally had had enough. She made a few phone calls and hired a security guard to spend nights near their cottage keeping watch. And to their everlasting delight, Jacinta agreed to move in for the duration of their tour so it wouldn't be empty.

Helena and Ardeen promised to telephone her once a week to check up and see that Tranquil cottage was safe. Both of them sorely missed their cozy home.

Because Lance knew the entertainment business inside out, he realized New York would have their noses out of joint because the city was dead last on the tour. For that reason, from the outset, he dubbed it the *Glory Fields Premier Tour*. In that way every stop was a new premier.

"Just a little play on words," he explained to his crew.

Unlike their journey out west months earlier with the entire cast and crew, the *Premier Tour* entailed only the main stars of the movie. "The ones people are dying to see," Lance said.

"And touch," Ardeen added in a sarcastic tone.

And touched they were. And grabbed. And clutched. The crowd in Kansas City was so raucous, the police escorted them out the back door of the theater after the movie, and quite literally snuck them from the theater to their hotel.

Once safe in their limousine, Helena had said to Ardeen, "Don't they know I'm just a little small-town girl from Kentucky? I'm not the president. I'm not royalty. Who do they think I am? What's gotten into people anyway?"

"It's the movie magazines," Ardeen had replied. "And the gossip columnists."

"And the newsreels." Lance was facing them in the oversized limousine. "Don't forget the newsreels. People not only see you in the moving picture, but also in the news. You've been granted celebrity status."

With a sigh, Helena had said, "I never asked to be a celebrity."

Patting her arm, Ardeen said, "You're just tired. You'll feel better after a good night sleep. And after you take one more look at your bank account."

Ardeen was right. There was more money than either of them had ever seen in their lives. Helena could hardly believe that at a time not too long ago, she was shoving food in her pockets just to have enough to eat.

Even though she despised the crowds, there was something extremely satisfying about her return to New York as a star. Crowds or no.

On the night of the premier, as Lance stood before the crowd on the steps of the Loews Capitol Theater on Broadway, he told New Yorkers that *Eleness-Odell* had designed the tour to save the *best until last*. The crowd roared their approval.

As before, barricades had been erected to keep back the throngs of star-worshipping, movie-goers, in addition to police officers who stood all along the barricades.

Their male counterpart actors dressed in tie and tails, and Ardeen and Helena in their exclusively designed gowns, flanked Lance and Mr. Odell. People pushed and shoved to get a closer look. They seemed to be in a state of disbelief that their favorite screen stars could actually be standing before them. For Helena, the most exciting part was to see hers and Ardeen's names up there in lights on the marquee. On Broadway. She asked Ardeen if she remembered speaking of her dream to see her name in lights. Of course, she remembered quite clearly.

Late that night, following the movie, city officials wined and dined them at Delmonico's. Midway through the meal, Helena was surprised when the *maître d'* came to her and whispered that someone wished to speak to her.

"Me?" Her first thought was an over-zealous fan wanting to spoil her evening. Speaking low, he said, "It's a Mr. Cranston."

Mr. Cranston. This should be interesting. She excused herself and followed the *maître d'* to the front of the restaurant.

There stood the icon of the Broadway theater, Carlyle Cranston, hat in hand. "Hello Helena," he said.

She had no idea what to expect, but his tone was friendly.

Turning to the *maître d'*, he asked, "Is there somewhere Miss Heise and I can talk? Privately?"

"I'm sorry, Mr. Cranston," Helena protested taking a step away from him. She could feel the anger rising up. This man was responsible for her being blacklisted from every theater in New York. "It'd be rude to leave my hosts."

"Please. This will only take a moment." Not waiting for her answer, he turned again to the *maître d'* who gave a respectful nod.

"Of course, Mr. Cranston. Right this way."

He led them down a hallway and into a plush office.

Helena made no effort to walk all the way into the room, but stationed herself near the door which Mr. Cranston had closed.

"Helena, I want you to know that I am thrilled at your success in the flickers."

"Moving pictures," she corrected him, her voice cold. "Flickers went out ever so long ago."

He walked over to a massive desk, laid his hat on it and leaned back against it. "Yes. You're right."

Having starred in dozens of films and now in a major epic production, she knew darn well she was right. "Is that all you wanted to say?"

"No." There was a pause which caused Helena to be even more anxious to return to her party. "Helena, I want to apologize to you."

Now this was a surprise. "For what?"

"For listening to someone like Cat Callahan."

"That was your choice. Wisdom in the situation was not your strong suit."

At this point Mr. Cranston stared at the floor. "Just so you know, a month or so later, she threw me over. Moved to another director without so much as a by-your-leave."

"I'm sorry you had to experience that, Mr. Cranston. But for me, it turned out to be a God blessing. The Bible says that what the enemy means for evil, God turns it for good." She put her hand on the door knob ready to leave.

Then she thought to add, "You also don't know that Cat left me with rent to pay. They changed the lock on my room with all my belongings inside, including the money I had to pay that rent. I was out in the cold. Literally. It was freezing cold that night and I had nowhere to go."

Now he looked up at her. She could see by his expression that he was truly sorry. He started to speak, but she stopped him.

"That's when I connected with my friend, Ardeen. She and her family rescued me. And it was because of Ardeen that I'm a screen star today. So you see, Mr. Cranston, God used all of it."

Turning she opened the door. "And I do accept your apology." With that she walked out.

Later, she realized that was the first time in a very long time that she had given glory to God.

The party at Delmonico's lasted until late. Every one of the *Eleness–Odell* crew slept in. Helena, however, was up and out the door of the hotel. The spring day shone bright, in contrast to that bitter cold day she when she had walked in this direction. Approaching the front of St. Malachy's, she paused and stared up at the imposing structure, crowned with decorative spires. Memories flooded back of that horrific night when she was so alone with nowhere to go. But God had Father Micah ready to help. And then the entire Miller family.

Once inside, she settled into one of the back pews and breathed in the peace. She remained still for a time, resting, and collecting her thoughts.

Presently a prayer came to her heart and into words. "Lord forgive me for leaving you out of my life. I'm inviting you back in. Now. Please guide me. Let me follow Your leading. And thank you for placing people in my life to help when I thought I was completely alone." Taking a deep breath, she added, "In Jesus' name. Amen."

Everything in her wanted to stay right there, experiencing God's presence in the quiet. But the others would be getting up and around, making plans for the day. Plus, Lance said he had a special announcement. She mustn't keep them waiting.

Chapter 30

L ance commandeered a conference room on the top floor of the hotel for their meeting and to give his announcement. Not one person in the group had any idea what was coming.

As Ardeen and Helena rode the elevator to the top floor, Ardeen said, "Remember when Lance announced our move to California?"

"Like it was yesterday."

"And how surprised we were?"

"Shocked is a better word."

"I may be wrong, but I think it's something like that."

Helena shook her head. "I think it has to do with our next production."

"Bet?"

"Twenty."

"You're on."

Before the meeting was over, Helena was pulling a twenty out of her handbag and discreetly handing it over to her friend, who sported a wide smile.

"It's being called a *good-will tour*," Lance was saying. Standing at the end of a long, highly-polished conference table, he waved a sheet of paper. "This is from our Ambassador to England, John W. Davis. He was the one who suggested we make this tour."

They were all caught off guard. All except for Ardeen who suspected that travel was in the works.

Continuing, Lance said, "Our British comrades-in-arms have suffered beyond belief from the war. Especially in the cities where the worst of the bombings wreaked havoc. Even London itself was at the mercy of horrific Zeppelin bombings. Ambassador Davis believes our presence will serve to brighten the place. We've learned that *Glory Field* has already met with rave reviews in London. They'd love to meet the stars."

One of the actresses who'd played a minor role in the movie, spoke up. "I guess that means we head back home to pack."

Mr. Odell usually let Lance do all the talking, but now he said, "I'm afraid not. We leave in two days. It's already been scheduled and tickets purchased. You're already packed for a month-long tour. Surely you don't need anything more."

Ardeen and Helena exchanged glances. Neither of them had much love for Mr. Odell. He never seemed to be able to muster up a friendly tone. Always cold. Or harsh.

Lance, nodding his agreement added, "Whatever you need that you don't have, you can purchase in London." In front of him lay a stack of papers, he picked them up and began handing them out. "This is our itinerary for the tour. Tonight you can call family and friends and let them know the new plans."

It only took a glance to see the tour was scheduled to last three weeks. Counting sailing time, it meant another month away from home. Helena was already homesick for Tranquil Cottage. And was jealous that Jacinta was enjoying it and she was not.

Ardeen, on the other hand, was bubbling over with excitement. "It's the opportunity of a lifetime," she said as they chatted over supper. They'd made the decision to cut away from the others and visit a small eatery near the hotel. "Maybe I'll be able to sneak away and visit my ancestral Ireland home."

Helena hadn't given that a thought. Of course, it would be a blessing for Ardeen to visit her home country.

They telephoned Jacinta that evening and explained the change of plans. She reported that things were fine there. For them not to worry and to enjoy themselves.

Since they were stuck in the city for two more days, they took the subway to visit the Millers. Once their income had increased substantially, Ardeen had been sending money to her family which allowed them to move into a larger flat. It was, however, in the same neighborhood. Mrs. Miller insisted that that was her home and she never wanted to leave it.

Conversation at the kitchen table centered on the Flanagan roots—Mrs. Miller's family name—whom she said hailed from County Roscommon. Digging through old maps, Ardeen and her mother exuded a level of excitement that Helena couldn't seem to match. Mrs. Miller was overjoyed that her daughter might actually walk on the very same soil where their ancestors had walked.

Ever on top of the details, Lance had their luggage sent to their staterooms on board. It was left for them only to climb aboard the RMS Olympic, stand against the railing, and watch passengers waving to the crowds below.

"I so hope I don't get seasick," Ardeen said.

"It's not fatal," Helena replied.

"But it'll ruin the trip. At least you've been on a showboat. I've never been on a boat in my life."

"Ship. This is a ship not a boat."

Ardeen shrugged and laughed. "Well, anything that floats. I've never even been in a canoe."

The girls had requested to share a stateroom because according to Ardeen, "If I'm puking up my socks, I want Helena close by my side."

Thankfully, neither one suffered from seasickness. To their delight, the Atlantic cooperated with smooth sailing and calm weather. And all thoughts of that *other* sickness—homesickness—were forgotten.

Helena's love for the water, and especially for the ocean, gathered her gently into that sensation. Simply standing on the deck watching the gentle waves served as a calming balm. A sweet respite from the swarms of fans and reporters yelling at her, grabbing at her, demanding her attention.

It wasn't until much later she learned that Lance and Mr. Odell had given strict instructions to the captain to order his staff to keep the *Glory Fields* cast safe from even the most innocent autograph hound.

Helena was never sure how that had been accomplished, but they all reveled in the peace and quiet. While others played shuffleboard and deck tennis, she contented herself to snuggle into a deck chair and read a book. She'd been smart to head to a bookstore while they were still in New York, knowing there would be hours to while away.

Every meal was a gourmet feast to the point where Helena began skipping the dinner meal. First of all, dinner demanded formal dress and she was beyond weary of formal gowns—even the most luxurious ones of her own design. And secondly, she was weary of pretention. This was to be her time to rest.

She did take time to make use of the swimming pool early in the morning. It gave her a spark to start her day. She didn't want to become too languid. And she attended the Sunday morning service in the chapel. That was a mistake. She should have stayed in bed. Or taken another stroll around the deck. While she was drawn to the familiar hymns, nothing else spoke to her. Even after the spontaneous prayer in St. Malachy's, which in the moment felt as if it would change everything, failed to do so. God just as well be a million miles away—a miserable sensation.

One morning as she and Ardeen were resting in their deck chairs, soaking up the sunshine, the conversation somehow turned to Jonas and the *McCardle Hills Ranch*. Nothing much had been said after Ardeen had arrived home following her visit to the ranch, and Helena wasn't one to pry. But she was curious.

They'd been talking about California and how they'd come to love it, when Ardeen surprised Helena by saying, "You've never seen California until you've experienced the Santa Monica Mountains."

"Tell me about it." She'd been lying there with her eyes closed. Now she opened her eyes to glance over at her friend. "And was it just the terrain?"

Ardeen smiled. "To say it's beautiful sounds so trite. It's breathtakingly beautiful. Rugged, but yet lush and green."

"And Jonas has a ranch in those mountains?"

"Down in a valley actually." She paused a moment seemingly lost in her reverie. "I've never in my life seen a real ranch. Just make believe for a movie set. This was authentic. A sprawling ranch house, barns, stables, bunkhouse for the ranch hands, corrals. I couldn't take it all in at first."

"Lots of ranch hands?"

"Not just ranch hands, but several Mexican women who work in the house. Domestics I guess we'd call them. Jonas' mother has passed away and his elderly father is ailing, so he manages the whole operation."

"Cows, I suppose?"

Ardeen laughed. "We rode out to where the herds were pastured. Thousands, Helena. Thousands of cattle in his herds."

"You rode?"

"I did."

"Will miracles never cease."

"Now don't make fun of this city girl. I did great. Just a sore rump later."

Helena laughed. "So, you're telling me that it's nothing like a subway ride?"

"Nothing at all."

"But you liked it?"

Ardeen nodded. "I liked it a lot."

"And Jonas?"

"I like him a lot."

"Hmm. And it seems to be mutual, or he wouldn't have invited you."

At that moment the gong sounded for lunch. As they walked down the deck toward the dining room, Helena said, "I find this all to be quite fascinating."

Ardeen tucked her arm into Helena's. "Yeah. Me too."

Chapter 31

The passage to England that Helena had been dreading flew by much too quickly. And if she'd thought the fast pace in the states had been wild, she soon learned she hadn't seen anything yet.

After docking at Southampton, they were guided onto the Pullman boat-train that carried them to Waterloo Station. From there they were destined to travel with their British hosts to their hotel. But nothing could have prepared them for the crowds awaiting their arrival at the station. National officials had told them the people were excited at their coming, but this was beyond belief.

Lance was gazing out the train windows and Helena could tell by the look in his eyes, that he was greatly concerned for their safety. Somehow the arrival time had gotten confused—perhaps they had arrived earlier than expected—so the bobbies were nowhere in sight.

Other disembarking passengers, obviously confused with the mass of humanity crowding the station, were unsure how to proceed. Lance and Mr. Odell could be seen in heated conversations with the boat-train officials, demanding action.

It took more than an hour for the bobbies to push through to the train, set up barricades, and created a path through the crowds.

"I know they simply want to wish us well," Lance could be heard saying, as he nervously puffed on a cigarette, "but dear God, give us some breathing space."

"How about walking space?" Ardeen whispered to Helena. "I'd just like to get to a hotel room."

Helena nodded her agreement. Even though she saw nothing but happy faces, the throng seemed to undulate like a living, breathing creature. Did these people actually want to see movie stars so desperately? Shouldn't they be home? Or at work?

Passengers, quite disgruntled at having to wait to get to where they were going, were finally being allowed to get off. As they dispersed, and the pathway created by the bobbies opened up, a small group of nattily-attired folk stepped from several touring cars and approached the train.

"Get a load of the landed gentry," Ardeen said, throwing all her weight into her seldom-used Irish brogue.

The *Glory Fields cast* had now assembled together, dressed in their best street clothes, complete with hats and gloves, with Lance and Mr. Odell at their head, close to one of the exit doors.

"What are we waiting for?" someone asked.

Everyone was feeling a little jumpy.

"Right there." Lance pointed to the group approaching through the pathway created by the bobbies who were lined up at the barricades, holding back the crowds. "Our host family the Waley-Talbots."

Pushing through the crowds, Helena could see an elderly man with a bit of a limp, arm in arm with a buxom woman adorned in much jewelry and a large flower-bedecked hat, holding forth a great regal bearing. Two young men stepped smartly behind them. The older dressed out in military uniform replete with medals; the younger dressed in classic British tweeds.

Lance waved to his group to back up a bit and allow their hosts space to come aboard. The uniformed man stepped forward and welcomed them. He introduced his father, Erasmus, Earl of Elswick, and his mother, Countess Maude.

"And my younger brother..."

The youngest of the family, who looked to be about fifteen or so, pushed in front, and with a bow announced, "And I'm Clement," which brought laughter. Waving to his brother he added, "And this is our war hero, Lieutenant Rendel Waley-Talbot."

Ardeen elbowed Helena saying, "Would you get a load of the sweater vest?"

"Couldn't miss it."

Clement's sweater, with bold crimson-and-navy argyle pattern beneath his open herringbone jacket, mirrored the brightness of his smile.

The interruption from his younger brother bothered the lieutenant not an iota. Carrying on, he assured them that the American movie stars would be guests at their home, Elswick Manor, and that every effort would be made to ensure they were comfortable and well taken care of.

"Shall we?" Lance prepared to descend the train steps. The moment he appeared, a shout emitted from the crowd. Helena was certain they had no idea who Lance was, but they cheered anyway.

The bobbies were tasked with throwing all their might into restraining the raucous crowd. The people seemed respectful of the Earl and the Countess, no doubt recognizing them.

When they sighted Helena and Ardeen along with Philip and Roger, that's when the shouting rose to a fever pitch. They heard their names being called. People reached out with autograph books extended, begging for an autograph.

Lance attempted to make his voice heard over the melee explaining that they would be giving autographs at the premier that night. But his voice was drowned out by the noisy crowd.

Thankfully, the distance between the train and the touring cars was relatively short. All in the group stepped up their pace. Somehow Helena found herself bringing up the rear. She made a great attempt at smiling and waving—not an easy task. As those ahead of her were escorted into one touring car after another, there were two cars remaining. At that moment, the lines broke free of the restraints and the masses were pressing toward her. In a flash she felt herself being swept up into someone's arms. In her ear came the shout, "Tallyho!" nearly burst her eardrum.

The uniformed driver held the car door open and Helena was very nearly thrown inside with her savior landing awkwardly beside her, his laughter filling the inside of the car. As she straightened her hat and smoothed her skirt, she saw it was the lieutenant who had saved her life. Now she, too, was laughing in spite of herself.

"We're in, Ralph," he said to the driver. "Get on with it."

"Trying, Master Rendel," he said as he waved his hand for the star-seekers to move out of his way. "I'm trying. Go," he was saying to the people. "Move. Get out of the way."

Faces peered into the car windows to catch a glimpse. Helena waved, still trying to control her laughter.

As he straightened his hat, Lieutenant Waley-Talbot, asked, "Are you fit, ma'am?"

"Fit as a fiddle."

Smiling at her, he said, "Ah, a yank expression." Then he added, "I apologize for rough handling you."

Slowly the crowd was left in their wake and the noisy voices faded. "I much prefer your rough handling to their rough handling." She jabbed a thumb back in the direction of the ruckus. Again, she was laughing. Probably more due to relief than from humor.

"Our bobbies weren't too effective, I'm afraid. All British apologies."

"I certainly don't blame them. It's difficult to measure the power of an exuberant mob."

"You do have a way with the masses. They adore you."

"Adoration can often become painful. And a bit scary." She wondered if she looked as mussed as she felt. Luckily, she'd chosen the handbag with the shoulder strap. It was intact. Looking over at him, she said, "I truly thank you for saving me. I'm not sure what would have happened..."

Interrupting her, he said, "No need for thanks. The Yanks came over to give we Brits a helping hand to put down the Huns. It's the least this Brit could do to return the favor."

She paused a moment, letting that comment register. Of course, their dough-boys had helped to win the awful war, but it was nice to hear this military officer extending the compliment.

He sat tall and straight as he turned to take one last look out the rear window, seemingly as thankful as she that they were out of danger. He'd removed his hat now, and his dark hair showed the hint of waves.

Looking at her, he said, "The whole country knows of your arrival, ma'am. Be assured the plans for the Savoy are much more in proper order than the station."

She nodded, unsure what she was supposed to say. Back in New York, she and Ardeen had both witnessed returning veterans whose sad eyes appeared vacant and empty. This officer had none of that. His hazel eyes exhibited gentleness and a measure of caring.

"Is this your first time abroad?" he was asking.

Again, she nodded. She must seem to him like a dummy. This famous starlet who has seemingly lost all ability to converse.

"I can point out the London sights for you as we go if you'd like." Smiling, he added, "I've no intent to bore you. I'm sure you're weary from your travels."

"No. I mean yes. I would very much like for you to point out the sights. And the trip over was restful. I'm not tired a bit."

"A tussle with the overzealous Brits might have been more taxing than an entire ocean voyage."

She smiled. "I agree."

By this time in her film career, she'd seen enough of swooning men all agog at meeting her. Not so with the lieutenant. He was calm as a lullaby. Actually, it was somewhat reversed—she was quite impressed with all this pomp. In an attempt to sound as though she had at least a lick of sense—as Ma used to say—she ventured to ask if he lived in London.

"Our home, Elswick Manor, is situated in the southeast of England. On the Channel. But I know London quite well."

On the Channel. Meaning the coast. Meaning close to water. Things were looking much brighter. She knew from their itinerary that they were scheduled to be in the Savoy for only two nights. Following that, they were to be guests at Elswick Manor. Lance had lined up special interviews and appearances at formal events later on in their stay, but only a few.

By the time their small entourage arrived in London, Helena had learned more about her officer escort. And he about her. He seemed most fascinated with her stories about plying the Mississippi in the *Pleasures A-Plenty* showboat. He'd never heard of such a thing.

At one point, after he'd asked how she came to be in the movies, he said, "I've watched a few of your films." He paused for a moment as though collecting his thoughts. "You come across different from some of the other stars."

"How so?"

"I don't infer that in the negative. Not at all. I'm not sure how to describe it. Wholesome, I guess. More wholesome. You appear to be unpretentious."

That comment made her laugh. "Do you know how tiring it is to be pretentious?"

His laughter joined hers. "As a military officer, and eldest son of a high-ranking earl, I would have to say, yes, I do know a great deal about pretention."

Helena felt her face growing hot. "I didn't mean... I apologize... This is all so new to me."

"Apologies unnecessary. I came to know a number of Yanks during the war, and our peerage rankings quickly became a joke to them. They were not a whit impressed with our titles." He looked over at her. "I found it to be quite refreshing. We Brits can tend to be a bit full of ourselves at times. The war changed a vast number of things."

Chapter 32

Elswick Manor proved to be a dream of living in a storybook setting. The square, many-storied stone house, flanked by two spacious wings, sat in the midst of miles of softly-rolling green hills. The entourage entered though wide wrought-iron gates, and up a winding, graveled drive flanked by towering, stately Italian cypress trees. Sheep grazing in the outlying pastures added to the picturesque setting.

Their private quarters were situated in the north wing, in resplendent rooms that rivaled any upscale hotel they'd ever been in.

In spite of her initial aloof manner, the countess proved to be the consummate hostess, insisting they call her Maude. Showing them their rooms on their arrival, she explained apologetically, that the war had drastically reduced their number of servants. "Hence we're unable to give you the full attention you so deserve.

"Plus," she added as they made their way up the curving marble staircase, "for a short time, at the behest of the military, we opened the house to serve as a war hospital." Then she said, "That quite served to take a bit of the starch out of us.

Decorum became useless as our rooms were filled with wounded young men crying out in pain." She shook her head a bit, as if to erase the awful memories. Then, with a deep sigh, "But, we Brits all did our part."

Entering the upstairs carpeted hallway, lined with ornately-framed works of art, she continued her instructions explaining that breakfast and lunch would be spread in the blue room and they could eat at the time of their choosing. "When it comes to dinner, however," she explained, "we're continuing to strive to hold to a smidgeon of formality. Dinner will be served promptly at eight in the main dining room on the first floor. Please dress accordingly."

The team joked about asking for a map to find their way around, to which Maude gave a smile and reassured them. "It's not as difficult as it first appears. You'll acclimate in no time at all."

Ardeen leaned over to Helena and whispered, "In a short shake."

Helena's room, done in cream and pink, sported a canopy bed, which she immediately sat down on for a little test. Soft as a cloud. In fact, *soft* described the entire room. Gold-framed, pale green botanical prints lined the walls. The French doors off to one side led to a small balcony. Opening the doors and stepping out, she found she was at the rear of the house and could see for miles. Out from the main house sat a cluster of smaller houses which, she later learned, housed the workers—gardeners, grooms, game keepers, footmen, and the like.

Looking off to one side, she could see the stables. But they were nothing like any stable she'd ever seen. Even the vast ones at the *Eleness–Odell* studio back in California were nothing like this. Made of red brick, with white stone accents, it appeared to be two-storied, crowned with elegant dormer windows. Rather than dirt, as she'd been accustomed, the area surrounding the stables was paved. A magnificent bronze statue of a rearing horse graced the area fronting the edifice. In the paddocks on the far side of the stables, she watched grooms putting strikingly beautiful steeds through their paces. Their shiny coats gleamed in the sunshine.

Just the thought of the horses stabled there filled her with excited anticipation.

They were a rather boisterous group at lunch. Even though Maude had noted they could come at any time, they all managed to converge at once. Philip said it was the food aromas drawing them. He was right on cue as it'd been several hours since their breakfast at the hotel that morning.

Talk around the table consisted mainly of the premier, which Lance had deemed an indisputable success in every way. *Glory Fields* had received highest reviews in nearly every newspaper. Before and after the showing of the film, Lance was center stage "playing the crowd" as Mr. Odell put it. No matter the stress or the pressure, Lance was consistently cool and collected, and never tired of talking about his epic film, and never failed to give credit to his cast and crew.

"At least our Imperial Picture Theatre entrance proved to be calmer and safer than our boat-train exit," came a voice from the far end of the lunch table from Helena. The comment brought much laughter and many more remarks. They could laugh and make light now, but not one of them would ever forget the fear created by that unruly mass of well-wishers.

But he was right. Premier night had come off smooth and easy. Crowds yes, but not nearly as forceful as those at the train station. News cameras rolling. Reporters asking sensible questions. Weather perfect. (Not the usual London fog or rain.) The theatre splendorous.

During intermission, as promised, the cast kept busy giving out autographs to the crowd, which, according to the next day's news reports, had endeared them to all Londoners.

And while accommodations at the Savoy hotel were also beyond reproach, it seemed to be unanimous consent among them that they were ready for a break. And Elswick Manor fit the bill perfectly.

The group scattered after lunch. Some planned to walk the formal gardens, others to the library replete with floor-to-ceiling shelves of books, others back to their rooms to rest. Lance had informed them at one point that all he wanted to do was sleep. And sleep. And sleep. They knew their esteemed director and leader was exhausted, and Helena, for one, was thankful that this opportunity to rest had become available to him.

They had learned that the Earl—or the Countess, no one was sure which—was related to the American Ambassador to England, and that connection is how the Waley-Talbots came to be their hosts. Helena cared not how; it was enough for her that she was here.

She, too, wanted to stroll through the gardens, but more than that, she wanted to see the stables. Nothing had been said about any area being off limits, so she made her way to the front house entrance. Surely, there had to be back entrances—probably several, but she took the route most familiar at the moment. Passing the elaborate stone planters set along the pebbled drive, spilling over with purple phlox, she at length came upon a formal, walled garden flush with koi pools, fountains, pruned topiaries, trimmed boxwoods, and sprawling shade trees, all radiant in the afternoon sun. Creeping germander, thick with purple blossoms blanketed one entire area. In the herbal garden she picked a lavender blossom, crushing it between her fingers to inhale the sweet fragrance. Sunshine on the rosemary, dill, chives, sage, and the mint helped bring their distinctive aromas into the air.

Seating herself on a marble bench, she watched birds playing in a nearby splashing fountain and wondered how this precision never made its way to America. She supposed her fellow Yanks, as the Brits loved to call them, were in too much of a hurry to ever fiddle around with formal gardens. She certainly couldn't imagine such a garden set down in the midst of Chancey's Bend.

On the *Eleness–Odell* studio grounds she had often visited the carefully laid-out Japanese garden to relax and unwind. But even as beautiful as it was, it paled in comparison with this. She had no idea the size of this garden because she'd only walked a short way into its secluded interior.

But where she truly wanted to explore was the stables. As she backtracked to the entrance, she heard her name being called. That was Ardeen's voice. Hurrying her step, she saw her friend come tripping down the front steps of the manor house.

"There you are," she called out. "Someone said they saw you coming this way."

Ardeen's ruddy cheeks were flushed, which happened when she got excited.

"Yes," Helena replied with a laugh. "Here I am. Was I lost?"

Ardeen nearly bowled her over, grabbing her by the shoulders, and ignoring the humor. "Helena, you're never going to guess. But guess. Guess anyway. Just guess. Guess where I'm going."

"Back in the house? Out to the garden? Into the pastures to see the sheep? There you go. I'm done guessing. Now I'm fresh out of guesses."

Ardeen's arm was wound tightly around Helena's waist, dragging her back toward the house—the opposite direction in which she wanted to go. She stopped still in order to end the pulling. "You may be going back to the house, but I have other plans," Helena said. "So just tell me what's up."

"I'm sorry. I'm just out of my head with excitement."

"I noticed that."

"Helena, I'm going to Ireland. Ireland. Mama will never believe this. I can hardly believe it myself. My dream come true."

"And how did all this come about? And when are you going? And more importantly, when are you coming back?"

Ardeen sucked in a deep breath. "I'll try to calm down."

"Good idea."

"A sister and brother—both of the household staff—Byrne and Keira, I heard them talking and went to meet them and struck up a conversation. They're from Roscommon, the exact place where our people, the Flanagans, came from. When they sensed my excitement, they offered to take me there. After asking permission, of course. They confided to me that the Waley-Talbots had been given strict instructions by the ambassador to, within reason, grant their American film-star guests every request."

Now Helena could see the tears welling up in her friend's eyes, and realized the depth of this gift that had been handed to her. Helena reached out to enfold Ardeen in a hug. "I'm sorry if I was short with you. What a blessing. And yes, your mama will be thrilled beyond words. You'll take lots of photographs so she'll experience it with you."

"I will. Yes." Pulling a hankie from her pocket she dried her eyes and blew her nose. "Byrne and Keira grew up there, and are thrilled about showing me around."

"When do you leave?"

"Within the hour."

"Oh my."

"Erasmus and Maude are providing a car and driver."

"Oh my, again."

"We'll drive to London, they said. Then take the train from there. We won't be gone long. Just three or four days."

This bit of news surprised Helena. She was sure they'd be returning to the states before that. "But I thought..."

Ardeen seemed to sense her confusion. "Maybe you haven't seen our newest itinerary. We're due to attend several formal receptions in London. And I hope they're scheduled while I'm away. I'm weary of all the folderol." At that, she twirled about in a classic dance step all the while moving toward the house. "I have to pack. Are you coming in?"

Helena shook head. "I'll say bye now. I'm as excited to go to the stables as you are to go to Ireland." She paused and smiled. "Well, almost anyway."

Running back, Ardeen gave another hug. "I'll see you when I get back. Be ready to listen to me for hours."

With a laugh, Helena replied, "And what's new?"

"Aw you." And she was off, pausing at the heavy ornate front door to give a last wave.

The bronze statue of the rearing horse turned out to be much larger and more magnificent up close than when seen from her balcony. Gleaming in the sun it seemed to take on a life of its own. Shading her eyes, she peered up at the proud head, then stepped up to touch one of the hooves admiring the fine detail work.

She noticed the stable doors stood invitingly open. Once inside, it took a bit for her eyes to adjust to the interior, which wasn't in any way dark. There were skylights in the ceiling, plus the sunshine glowing through the dormers. One could scarcely believe this was home for animals as it was sparkling clean. Only that rich equine aroma gave it away. And, of course the heads that were now thrusting through the long row of Dutch door openings checking out who might have entered their domain.

She paused a moment studying each one. Not a wild-eyed maverick in the bunch. Slowly, so as not to make a disturbance, she strolled along, studying their expressions and their attitudes, pausing to touch soft noses. All the horses she'd ridden, both in their Fort Lee studios and later in California, couldn't hold a candle to these mounts, which in every way were a cut above.

As she neared the end of the stalls, she spied a stunning white mare who nickered at her making her smile. Quickening her step, she moved in that direction.

"Yes, I see you," she said aloud. "You are so beautiful. So elegant."

Approaching the animal, she stroked the velvety nose and ran her fingers through the forelock. It was clear from the soft snort that she had been accepted.

"She likes you." The voice from behind her gave her a start making her jump.

Whirling around, she saw Rendel walking toward her. With a kind smile, he said, "Please. I'm so sorry. I had no intention of startling you. I thought you heard my footfalls."

"I guess I was somewhat preoccupied."

He gave a knowing nod. "As I was saying, she likes you, and I can say of a truth, that doesn't happen often."

The military officer, without his military uniform, came off like a totally different person. He didn't even have on the familiar British riding habit that she might have expected, but informal flannel trousers and a patterned, open-collared shirt.

"Are you enjoying your stay? Are you being treated well?" he asked. "Everyone comfortable?"

"Yes, yes, and yes. Comfortable and well-fed."

He was standing closer now, which gave her an odd, nervous sensation. She turned away and went back to stroking the horse to alleviate the feeling. She had an easy time with all those googly-eyed, hangers-on types. They were simple to dismiss. But Rendel demonstrated none of that. Casual and sincere proved to be quite different.

"Good," He said. "I'm sure it's not what you're accustomed to."

"At this point, with so much travel and bouncing around, I'm not sure if we're accustomed to much of anything. But I will say it's restful here."

Moving even closer, he reached out to stroke the horse's neck. "I'm sure you're wondering. Her name is Amari."

"Amari," she repeated. "Beautiful."

"It means *miracle*. She gave us a bit of a fright at her foaling, hence the name."

"Even more fitting."

Pausing, he then asked, "Would you like to ride her?"

She had to bite her tongue to keep from scoffing right out loud. It was such a preposterous question. First of all, the answer would seem to be obvious. But secondly, she was quite sure this family didn't allow just anyone to ride their expensive, high-bred mounts.

"You do ride, am I correct? That is actually you riding in your moving pictures."

Now she had to laugh. "Yes, that's actually me. I do have wranglers who help some, giving me insights on handling horses and riding."

"Well then?"

She started to protest, using that thing about not allowing just anyone to ride their horses, but then put the thought away. How could she pass this up this opportunity?

"I would love to ride Amari. Do I need jodhpurs, tall black boots, a top hat?"

Once again, she heard that infectious laughter from Rendel that she remembered from their time together in the touring car after he'd rescued her from the crowd. "Of course, in some instances the full-out habit might be necessary, but for this event, we'll choose to forego the formalities. How about a casual ride around the grounds?"

"I accept."

Chapter 33

"We'll only go about an hour out," Rendel explained after they were saddled up and were leaving the grounds near the house. He led out in the direction she'd viewed that morning from the balcony. "That way it'll give you a chance to become accustomed to the different saddle."

The smaller English saddle did indeed feel different, but she rather liked it. Rendel showed her how to bit-rein as opposed to neck-reining. Amari behaved like a perfect lady. It was as if she sensed this greenhorn rider had no idea what she was doing.

As they rode farther, the landscape changed dramatically from rolling pastures to hedgerow-lined, tree-studded high hills and deep valleys dotted with blankets of blue and yellow wildflowers, cut through by narrow streams that reflected diamond sparkles in the sunlight. Several areas were defined by ancient moss-covered stone walls surrounding rustic farms. It was rather like riding into a painting in a nursery tale. Each scene offered too much to take in. Helena could only hope her memory bank would serve her well, to never forget this lush beauty.

They rode in companionable silence, broken only by Rendel pointing out a few landmarks now and then.

"How far to the Channel?" she asked at one point. She knew their approximate location, having studied the map, and by that knew the English Channel lay in this general direction.

"Too far to go on horseback."

She gave a nod. "But it's in this direction."

"Correct. Could it be you're keen to see it?"

Anything that had to do with vast bodies of water, she was all in. But she gave only a simple yes.

"We'll go tomorrow. Pack a lunch and motor over first thing after breakfast. We can spend the day. How's that for a plan?"

For a split second at the mention of *pack a lunch,* she was hit with an instance of flashback, remembering how Brett had packed their lunch in the saddlebags. The two of them walking and talking together in the lilac bower. Sitting on the decrepit front porch of the ramshackle house, eating together, vowing their love to one another among the fragrance of lilacs in bloom. She could almost smell the blossoms now. Had it all been a silly, childish dream?

Misunderstanding her quiet pause, he spoke into her reverie. "If you have other plans, I understand completely. We don't want to monopolize your time with our plans."

She hadn't thought about Brett for many long weeks. Why now? And so vivid. Snapping back to the present, she realized what he just said. "Me have plans? Heaven's sake, no. And yes, I like your idea. Let's do it."

The formal dinners, which Helena had initially dreaded, proved to be not at all stuffy or demanding. Because the *Eleness–Odell* crew had scant knowledge of which utensil to use when, or how to spoon their soup correctly, it turned to gaiety, and the Waley-Talbots joined in the laughter.

Clement, quick to be their tutor, enjoyed showing off his knowledge, instilled into him from birth. It was easy to see, he relished being the center of attention. His personality was that of outgoing and fun loving, reminding Helena of her cousin, LeRoi.

At one point he broke into their ongoing chatter to say, "Jolly good it was that you blokes won the war."

The remark came as a surprise as they hadn't been talking about the war at all. And to the last one of them, thought he was referring to the Great War.

Lance answered by saying, "Well Clement, we blokes didn't win the war alone. We only came in at the last minute to give a helping hand."

Clement shook his head. "Not that war, sir. I'm talking about when America gave King Charles the flip and won your independence."

Someone laughed then and said, "He's talking about the Revolutionary War."

"Of course. That war. I'm awfully glad you won it. Yanks are so much more fun than we stuffy Brits."

The Earl spoke up then. "Clement here spent untold hours with the wounded in our makeshift hospital."

Helena said, "I'm sure you were a comfort and consolation for those men."

At the compliment, Clement blushed a bit. "I'm not sure about that, but I learned a lot about your country."

"Add to that the fact that we turned the North Wing sitting room into a theater," Rendel explained. "The government made sure we had the projector, the screen, and motion picture films to show to the men." Turning to look directly at Helena, he added, "That's how we came to know about the *Eleness–Odell* studios."

"And," Clement went on, "when I saw the cowboy pictures."

"Our Clement was quite taken with the rough and tumble cowboys." This from his mother. "We thought for a while we might have to exchange our English saddles for the Western ones."

With a shake of his head, Clement said, "One cannot rope a cow when one cannot keep the lariat on the saddle horn. Because there is no saddle horn." A strong emphasis on the last words.

"And I might add," the Earl put in, "there are no cows on Elswick Manor that need roping."

Clement had tuned a deaf ear to his parents' remarks. "I know moving pictures are all make believe and pretend, but are there real cowboys where you are? Real ranches where they ride bucking broncos and rope the cows?"

Helena spoke up. "Ardeen visited a real ranch, Clement. When she returns from Ireland, you'll have to ask her to tell you all about it."

The boy's attention was captivated. "Is that a true fact? She saw real cowboys? Was the ranch big? Were there Indians to fight off?"

Members of the crew were tying not to snicker.

"She said nothing about fighting Indians, but yes, it is a big place." Thinking a moment, she added, "Probably similar in size to your manor here, only in rugged country with craggy mountains, deep valleys, and replete with pine trees."

"And cows?"

"Yes. Ardeen told me the cattle numbered in the thousands."

"I'm going to go to America one day," Clement announced with great aplomb, "and I'll work on a ranch and be a real cowboy. Not just a make-believe like in a moving picture."

Lance spoke up and said, "Clement, you just let us know when you're on your way and we'll show you around." Glancing over at the Earl and Countess, he added, "And we'll take as good care of you as you have our little motley crew."

Helena could tell by their expressions that this kind remark touched Clement's parents.

It was later that they learned that Clement had suffered from horrendous nightmares after Rendel left for the front—dreaming that Rendel had died in the fighting. It wasn't until they began caring for the wounded men that the nightmares ceased. Helena was certain that theirs was only one of a million stories of how people had suffered during the war years.

The next morning, as Helena readied herself for the day, a knock sounded on her door.

"Yes? Who is it?"

"Me Mum. Glynis."

Glynis, the elder parlor maid, had become known to all the crew, as she was always at hand to help in any way she could to make them feel at home.

Opening the door, Helena saw Glynis standing there with a moss-green Shetland sweater spread across her forearm. "For you, Mum," She said extending the sweater toward her. "Master Rendel thought it might be chilly at the channel and wanted me to bring this to you."

Helena was taken aback. How do you receive, or refuse, a gift that's not given in person? With a sigh, she realized there was nothing to do but to take it. It was soft as a downy cloud. "Please give him my thanks."

"You'll be doing that your own self in a short while, Mum. Master Rendel has pulled the car around front. He's in the kitchen now, letting the cooks know precisely what goes into your picnic." With that she gave a little wink and was gone.

Perfect fit. Admiring herself in the mirror she wondered how he could have known her size. Most men have no knowledge of such details. The sweater's shade of green definitely brought out the color of her eyes.

The only automobiles Helena had seen belonging to the Waley-Talbots were the touring cars which had transported the crew from the train station to the hotel in London. Then from London to Elswick Manor. Now here she was riding in a red roadster convertible with the wind blowing her hair.

Later, Helena attempted to remember what all they talked about as they motored through the countryside, but was at a loss. Conversation continued nonstop jumping from one subject to another. She knew nothing about England, and Rendel's knowledge of the states had been formed mostly from the doughboys he'd met during the war. And, like Clement, he could add in the moving pictures he'd seen. She was quick to clear up a few misconceptions.

"Nothing in any part of America is the same as the other parts," she told him. "The immensity of the country isn't simply geographical, but different cultures, and different attitudes."

She tried to describe the difference of the lackadaisical lifestyle in California where men seldom wore a necktie, and women went without gloves. Unheard of in the city of New York.

"Similar to England," he rejoined. "Except it tends to do more with rank than with geography."

He talked some about the history of his family, how land ownership dating back hundreds of years set them in a position of peerage. Helena couldn't imagine such a situation, thinking of how land was bought and sold on a daily basis back home. But for all his having lived in a favored station in life, Rendel's personality spoke nothing of entitlement. Instead, he was quite humble and genuine in his mannerisms and conversation.

"It's not much farther," he told her a few hours into their journey. "It's a bay area I discovered during the war. I traveled extensively around the country helping to discover locations for possible defenses. It's called Kingsgate."

"Kingsgate? Does that mean it belongs to the king?"

Rendel shook his head. "If I remember right, it had to do with a king whose ship landed on the site during a bad storm."

Kingsgate bay turned out to be more like a cove, protected by high white rock walls, which allowed for only the gentlest waves.

"You forgot to tell me about the castle," she said as they drove up and parked.

How could such a massive edifice have been built to such scale so many centuries past? Poised high on the bluff, the gray imposing castle bristled with turrets fit to repel any approaching enemy.

He turned to look at her, studying her face which he seemed to do quite often. "Something told me you'd prefer the beach over touring through an ancient castle."

"And that *something* was absolutely correct."Pulling the picnic basket from the back, he said, "Would you mind bringing the blanket?"

The blanket was red-and-navy plaid wool, soft to the touch. "We're not putting this down on the sand, are we?"

Smiling, he answered, "We most certainly are." He held out his free hand. "Watch your step. Steep stairs ahead."

She accepted his hand, thinking to herself, that the Waley-Talbots probably had dozens of blankets as beautiful as this one. Her mother would have had an old raggedy quilt worn to threads to spread out for a picnic. Even Brett had brought along an old blanket when they picnicked on the porch of the deserted house. Shaking away the thought, she had to remind herself where she was and whom she was with.

After maneuvering the stone steps, they came to stand together on the sandy beach. As with the Pacific, this view of the vastness of the Channel affected her deep within her soul. Streaks of blue, turquoise, and purple, all intermingled with moving lines of white surf, and far out lay the knife-sharp line of horizon. Swooping gulls wheeled overhead, breaking the silence with their calls. Rock pools shone like small jewels. Such beauty was almost more than she could take in.

Leaving the basket and blanket near the rock wall, they walked hand-in-hand out to the where the water lapped the sandy beach, which seemed to go on for miles in both directions. A few other visitors also strolled the beach, but for the most part it was nearly deserted.

"May we wade?" she asked.

Rendel gave an easy laugh. "Nothing to stop us." With that he leaned down and pulled off one of his shoes and waved it in the air.

Such a delightful invitation. Leaving shoes and socks behind they ventured out into the water, leaving prints in the sand as they went. Soft waves lapping at her ankles made her wish for a bathing suit to allow her to jump in and swim out into deeper waters.

The beach was spangled with myriads of seashells, and it took all her resistance not to scoop them up by the handfuls. Back home she had cluttered their cottage with her collection of shells discovered on the beach. Now she simply selected a few of the most unique that caught her eye, and tucked them into her pocket. They would be mementoes of this magical day.

They strolled aimlessly, with Helena especially feeling free and unencumbered from deadlines and schedules. It was only their appetite that turned them back toward the basket of food.

Quite different from an American picnic, their fare consisted of sandwiches of pastry filled with eggs, meat, and cheese, a container of fresh strawberries, light buttery scones, and small cupcakes, of which Rendel downed four in short order. All washed down with thermoses of strong, dark tea, for which Helena still had not quite acquired the taste. Brits and their tea—a tight bond.

As with the drive over, their conversation seemed to never wane. She marveled at how she relished hearing his laugh and watching his gentle expression change from amusement, to pensive, to deeply serious. No masking of emotions, he was open and transparent.

He spoke some of the war saying how utterly useless it had all turned out to be, with the loss of so many thousands of fine young men.

"The glory of fighting for our homeland is ingrained in us almost from infancy," he said. "But when you see war firsthand, all the glory fades away. The glory is only gore."

His description, short on detail, gave enough information to realize he was at the front only as a liaison officer, and carried a measure of guilt that so many suffered in the trenches, and he had not.

As the sun moved over the cliffs, the air quickly cooled, and Helena realized she never wanted this day to end. How could she have such a passion for the ocean when she grew up being familiar only with a small, nondescript river? A baffling mystery.

Before leaving Kingsgate, Rendel put up the top on the roadster. "Might have a chill," he said. "Don't want you to catch a nasty cold."

She didn't think that was a worry, but she appreciated his concern.

Earlier she'd commented to Rendel regarding the abundance of flocks of sheep in England. Back home, she rarely saw sheep, at least not in large flocks, but here it seemed no matter where they traveled, sheep filled the landscape.

"Wool and mutton is of great importance to Britishers," he told her.

"I gathered that." She waved her hand to indicate his gift of the lovely Shetland sweater, which had indeed protected her from the chilly breeze off the water.

As they drove home in the evening twilight, the grazing sheep almost seemed to glow. Looking out across the expanse a scripture came to mind.

"The Lord is my Shepherd; I shall not want..." she said, almost without thinking.

Then she heard Rendel saying softly,

He maketh me to lie down in green pastures: he leadeth me beside the still waters.

"That's the twenty-third Psalm isn't it."

"It is," she said. "Watching the sheep brings it to my mind."

Rendel continued,

He restoreth my soul: he leadeth me in the paths of righteousness for his name's sake.

In unison, they recited the remainder...

Yea, though I walk through the valley of the shadow of death, I will fear no evil: for thou art with me; thy rod and thy staff they comfort me.

Thou preparest a table before me in the presence of mine enemies: thou anointest my head with oil; my cup runneth over.

Surely goodness and mercy shall follow me all the days of my life: and I will dwell in the house of the LORD for ever.

Rendel was silent for a few minutes, then said, "I found that in the despair and ugliness of war, those in desperation either cursed God, or embraced Him. The latter included embracing the Holy Scriptures. That particular Psalm is one we—meaning my family and I—spoke often over the wounded soldiers who temporarily came under our care." He paused, then added, "You're correct that our Good Shepherd watches over us, and cares for us, we who are the sheep of His pasture."

Helena wondered if she truly believed that.

Chapter 34

For the remaining few social gatherings on their itinerary, Rendel had remained close by her side as her escort. Had this been planned? Or was it just happenstance? She never could sort it out.

Interspersed amongst the formal events were sunny afternoons of horseback riding, strolls through the gardens, and Rendel showing her the workings of the estate, of which it was quite clear, he was justifiably proud.

Ardeen's return from her Ireland foray exploded into Helena's quiet routine. She'd stayed away longer than expected, and she fairly bubbled over with stories and accounts of her visit to her "mother country" as she called it.

Had Ardeen's hair turned a more vibrant hue of red, or was it Helena's imagination? Were those clear blue eyes a brighter blue and her cheeks rosier? Whatever had transpired, Ardeen held forth at dinner by regaling them with non-stop chattering.

In Roscommon she'd actually been able to locate the village of her Flanagan ancestors, and then with the help of Byrne and Keira, they tracked down a distant cousin and his family.

Later on, the evening of Ardeen's return, the two friends were hidden away in Helena's room talking into the late hours.

"Never have you ever seen such beauty," she told Helena. "I simply cannot describe how the green the countryside is, and it goes on for miles and miles. No wonder it's called the Emerald Isle. Castles and ancient ruins galore. And the warmth of the people. Everyone wanting to help me discover my roots."

"Your brogue is heavier than ever," Helena teased. "You'll be no good for any future roles in the upcoming pictures produced by the studio." With a smile, she added, "Think of the waste of all that money you spent on acting school."

At that, Ardeen's expression changed.

"What? What did I say?" Helena tried to read Ardeen's face. "What are you not telling me?"

"The Irish flavor of my speech might not matter, Helena. My movie star days may be coming to a close."

The words hit Helena like ice water in the face. "Ardeen. No. That can't be. I need you. Did Lance fire you?"

Ardeen shook her head. "It's nothing like that."

Helena felt she was going to be sick. She stepped over to sit down on the bed close by Ardeen's side.

"It's Jonas."

"Jonas? Why he's thousands of miles away."

"I received a cablegram from him. It took a while to catch up with me, but Lance made sure I received it."

"He said nothing about you receiving a cablegram."

"Well, I guess I can thank him for that, can't I."

The remark stung Helena to the quick. Of course, it was none of her business, but the two of them had shared so much together. She quickly realized that Ardeen meant nothing by it so she had to let it pass.

"In the cablegram, Jonas wanted to know when I was leaving to come home, what ship I would be on, and our arrival date. He plans to meet me. I sent my reply giving all the details."

"Oh my. Coming all the way from the west coast to meet you. This is serious."

"That may be the understatement of the century." Taking a deep breath, she said, "He's going to ask me to marry him, Helena. I'm sure of it."

This unexpected bit of news left Helena's head reeling. It seemed so sudden. A million questions rose up, but she wanted to tread softly. This certainly explained why Ardeen was absolutely glowing.

"And if and when the question is asked, do I have to guess what your answer will be?"

"No guessing at all. He's been in my thoughts almost constantly since I left home. I just..." Ardeen paused and Helena saw this faraway look in her eyes.

"Just?"

"I just want to be by his side."

"Even if it means living out in the Santa Monica Mountains on a ranch?"

At that Ardeen grabbed Helena's hands, squeezing tightly. "Most especially if it means living on a ranch. That place stole my heart. I'm ready to learn everything about the ranch and how I can be the best ranch wife ever."

"A New Yorker gal becomes a rancher's wife. Hey, wouldn't that make a great movie plot?"

"Wouldn't it though. But this isn't a movie. This is real life."

"And you're ready to step away from moving pictures? Away from being a star?"

"I never was cut out for it. Not really."

"But I thought it was what you always wanted."

Ardeen nodded. "I did too. But I was wrong." She was on her feet again pacing across Helena's palatial room. "Oh Helena, I'll never been the actress that you are. You were always so much better that I could ever be. Even without the acting lessons."

"But you never said..."

"I'm not a whiny baby. I had made my nest, and I was bound and determined to sit in it to the best of my abilities." She stopped in her tracks. "Now I don't have to pretend anymore. I can be the real me."

Forcing herself to be happy for Ardeen, Helena couldn't even begin to imagine life at the studio without her dear friend. Then her mind raced forward in time and she wondered about what they would do about Tranquil Cottage.

"But let's wait till we dock in New York," Ardeen said. "There'll be no more suppositions then. I'll know for sure."

Helena was willing to bet even now, that no suppositions were needed. Why else would Jonas travel all the way across the country to greet Ardeen on her homecoming? Just to say a polite hello? Not a chance.

The reception held in a manor house a few miles outside London would be the final social obligation for the *Eleness-Odell* crew. The days at Elswick had been a welcome break. Rendel, once again in uniform, brass buttons and medals shining, invited Helena to ride with him in the roadster. The others were loaded into the several touring cars.

When Ardeen learned of this, she elbowed Helena and raised her eyebrows. Lance had gathered them into the main grand hallway to await their transportation.

"What?"

"A little birdie told me you and the lieutenant have been in one another's company a great deal while I was away."

"And what little birdie might have even noticed my activities? Could his name start with a C?"

On a few occasions, they'd caught Clement following them, doing his best to remain undetected, but doing a poor job of it. It gave her and Rendel a good laugh. She knew for a fact that no one else cared about her comings and goings. She also knew, first of all, that Clement was quite taken with the fact that real live moving picture stars were under their roof. But secondly, and this was a bit more serious, it had occurred to Helena that Clement might have been a bit jealous of losing his brother's attention. Both might have prompted him to follow them.

"That would be correct."

"And what all did this C-person tell you?"

"Not much really. But I find it fascinating information."

Just then, the cars arrived and Rendel was quite suddenly by her side. "Shall we?" Stretching out his hand, he nodded toward the side door where he'd parked the roadster.

To Ardeen she said, "See you at the shindig."

Helena had long ago ceased trying to remember names of the various estates, or names of their hosts. Each one more immense and magnificent than the previous, and all began to blur together in her mind. As Ardeen had said at one point, "If you've seen one, you've seen all." It was easy for her to be flippant, since she'd missed out on several formal events while visiting Ireland.

The crowds of people at these social gatherings, overly anxious to meet the stars and making dull, mundane conversation, served to drain Helena's energy more than an entire day of shooting scenes on location. She was secretly thankful that this one—which she learned was Bolewood Manor—was the final *demand performance*. That's what Lance called them, but not within earshot of their kind hosts. This was, in essence, a goodwill tour, and a massive public relations boost for their pictures and the studio.

Only the dances with Rendel made the ordeal bearable. His skill on the dancefloor surpassed any guy she'd ever danced with back home. She assumed dance lessons would be a requirement for a young lad growing up in a privileged position. Add to that, the orchestra seemed to be familiar with every current popular American song, which added to the gaiety. They conquered the jazz steps as well as the waltzes. As he held her close, she realized she'd grown rather comfortable in their closeness. And liked it.

At one point he had to leave her side, saying that his senior officer was in attendance, which, as she understood it, meant he needed to speak to the gentleman in private. He apologized profusely, encouraging her feel free to explore the place. She accepted that invitation as the enormous manor seemed to sprawl out for acres. Perhaps other rooms wouldn't be quite as crowded. She knew the location of the ballroom, and the room where food and drinks were freely dispersed. Each room she entered rivaled the one previous in elegance and rich furnishings. And she still remained on the first story, knowing from her first glimpse that two more stories above held dozens more rooms.

As she ventured down a long hall, she heard music. She was headed in the direction from which she'd first come, so naturally she assumed it was the orchestra, but it wasn't. She paused for a moment to listen. She was hearing the piano score to *Glory Fields*. Someone must be playing gramophone record. The score, she knew, had become available on records which added to the studio revenue. Lance was the ultimate marketer.

The room, as she approached wide double doors, appeared to be yet another immense ballroom. No dancers filled the floor, but rather it seemed be a gathering place. People milled about chatting, grabbing drinks from silver trays being offered by staff in starched uniforms. A few overstuffed velvet chairs and sofas were set about on which the drinking guests lounged.

As she entered, it was immediately evident there was no gramophone but a shiny grand piano off to the side.

The pianist looked up and their eyes met. A sensation of dizziness swept over her.

"Brett." A mere whisper was all she could manage. Her eyes were surely deceiving her. This was impossible. She'd not fully entered the room which allowed her to reach out for the door frame, or she most certainly would have collapsed in a heap.

Making a few trills and ending the number Brett stood and walked toward her. She noted his limp was negligible. "Hello Helen."

She'd not been called Helen for ever so long.

"I was told you would be here, but I never thought you'd come to the very room where I was playing."

Finding her voice over the lump in her throat, she managed to say, "The *Glory Fields* score drew me."

He nodded and smiled. "A masterful composition. A joy to play."

In answer to her unspoken question he said, "I'm touring Britain and Europe with Evangelist Ian Buchanan as his pianist. But I'm free to take on other engagements. Like this one."

Helena recalled the evangelist's name. The one whose rally she attended in the Bronx with Ardeen and her mother. That seemed eons ago. In another life.

Looking at his sweet face, his gentle demeanor, his kind eyes, she was overpowered by a rush of memories. She knew he was uncomfortable, but she was helpless to ease it.

Filling the silence, he said, "You're an excellent actress, Helen. I greatly admire your talent." Pausing, he added, "I've not seen all your pictures, but I've seen *Glory Fields* several times as I've played the score in several theaters." Then he added with a smile, "I've conquered the Wurlitzer."

This bit of information released yet another series of questions that screamed inside her to be answered. Someone calling her name shut it all down.

"Helena, there you are." It was Rendel, cutting a fine figure in his uniform, rushing toward her. "I've been looking all over for you. I guess you took me seriously when I suggested you go explore the place."

Placing his hand on her waist in a familiar gesture, turning her around to look into her face, he said, "People are waiting to meet you. Namely my commanding officer, as well as our hosts."

Stopping for a moment, he glanced at Brett and intuitively realized he'd interrupted something. "Apology, old chap. Did I barge in on a conversation?"

Helena hurried to explain. "I heard someone playing the *Glory Fields* score and stopped to investigate." For a split-second she thought to introduce the two, but as she turned to look, Brett was already moving away, returning to the piano. He sat down and began to play and never looked her way again.

Someone had told him she'd be there, he said. Did that mean he was there just to seek her out? Or was it a coincidence? And he's just a pianist making extra money on the side while traveling with Evangelist Buchanan. But how was it that she just happened to be wandering around, and just happened to be drawn to that room? Too strange to be believed.

Hadn't Brett made it clear he was to become a pastor in Chancey's Bend? What changed? And other than shock, what had she felt at seeing him? Were there still feelings in her heart toward him? She hadn't even had time to glance at his ring finger.

She wished a million times that she'd never stopped reading his letters. That had been selfish and cruel on her part. She agonized under the weight of the guilt. When would she ever know the truth?

The storm of confusing thoughts kept her silent during their return drive to Elswick Manor in the wee hours of the morning. Rendel kindly did not intrude or attempt to make small talk.

As they entered through the wide gates, the pea gravel crunched beneath the tires. She was exhausted, but tried to rouse herself to at least show Rendel her appreciation.

They had cruised far ahead of the touring cars driven by the staff members. As he pulled into the side drive, and stopped the roadster, he turned to her.

"He wasn't a stranger, was he?"

She knew what he meant. She shook her head.

"An old beau from your past?"

"You could say that. Far, far past."

"Was he looking for you?"

"I'm.... I'm not sure."

"Forgive me if I blundered..."

"No Rendel. Not at all. It was nothing. Just a bit of a surprise seeing him there."

Getting out of the roadster, he came around and helped her out as he always had, ever since they first traveled to the Channel that day for their picnic.

Entering the front hall, she turned toward the stairs, so ready to sleep and forget. Tomorrow the crew would leave for London, and then home.

"There're not enough words in my vocabulary to express how grateful I am for all your kindnesses to me these past few weeks," she told him

"Entirely my pleasure. You succeeded in bringing light and life into my life at a time when I was struggling to find my way in my world."

He stepped toward her, took her hand and gently kissed it. She was frightened that he intended to make an advance, but of course, gentleman that he was, he did not.

Without another word, she hurried up the winding marble staircase to her room. But sleep was a long time coming. All she could see was a lilac bower. All she could hear were verses they'd shared.

In the dooryard fronting an old farm-house near the white-wash'd palings,
Stands the lilac-bush tall-growing with heart-shaped leaves of rich green,
With many a pointed blossom rising delicate, with the perfume strong I love...

Chapter 35

It would have been impossible to leave Elswick without saying good-bye to Amari. In spite of little sleep, Helena arose before daylight the next morning and made her way to the stable. By this time, she knew every hallway, and every entrance and exit. She went out through the downstairs kitchen, where the cooks were already busy preparing breakfast for all the crew.

She gave them a smile and a nod and hurried out the door. Although the sun hadn't made its way over the distant horizon, the stable lights shone bright. In a moment, she was in the door and down the long line of stalls to where Amari showed her proud head over the Dutch door. It was almost as if the mare had expected this visit.

Helena wondered if ever in her life would she again ride such a magnificent, regal animal. Laying her head against Amari's soft face, feeling the warm breath on her hand, she expressed her deep thanks for being such a patient, understanding horse. "I will forever remember you, and all the wonderful times we had together. You are a dear friend. Good-bye Amari."

One more hug and a light kiss on the velvety nose, she turned to go and stopped short. Down the way she could see Rendel standing in the shadows of the front doorway. "I thought I would find you here."

"How discerning of you." And she meant it.

"I knew you wouldn't leave without telling her good-bye. And it's quite evident she appreciated it."

As she approached him, Rendel stepped toward her and reached out to take her hand. "Helena, if there were any way in which I could prolong your visit, I would do so in a heartbeat."

Gently he put his arms around her and drew her in his embrace. In all their times together, he had never held her. Offering no resistance, she felt his soft kiss on the top of her head and felt comforted.

"I've grown quite fond of you," he said, "and I long to know you better. To continue our amazing friendship."

"It seems providential that the two of us both needed this time. This space. This closeness. But only for a season. Whatever the reason, we may never know. We'll always hold these memories close, with full hearts."

"Yes. With full hearts."

He released her then as hand-in-hand they walked together back to the house.

The crew's departure turned out to be a tearful affair. Who would have imagined that total strangers could have become so close in a few short weeks? Even the staff were wiping their eyes. The cooks with the tail of their aprons; Maude with a lace kerchief. Had they been in America, warm hugs would have been the order of the day. Brits, however, were good with handshakes and light kisses on each cheek.

Rendel, Helena noted, remained a step or two away from the group. But when they made eye contact, he gave a nod and a smile.

The Earl made a bit of a stuffy, but heartfelt, speech letting them know that from the "shadows of darkness of a dastardly war, you have brought to our home a bright, shining light. And we are forever in your debt."

Lance responded by thanking them for the kind hospitality. The crew learned much later that Lance, by way of the Ambassador, made sure the Waley-Talbots were financially rewarded for their kindness. It was no secret that all of Britain suffered lack after the ravages of war.

As uniformed footmen loaded luggage in the touring cars, Helena made certain she and Ardeen were side-by-side for the drive to London. Ahead of them lay many days in which they could talk non-stop.

Their arrival in New York harbor was eventful to say the least. Jonas, the only person in the crowd on the dock waving a cowboy hat, grabbed hold of Ardeen in an embrace to rival any movie screen love scene. Within seconds he'd popped the question—with a ring in hand, no less. And she happily accepted.

All the guys in the crew were slapping Jonas on the back; the gals, in turn gave Ardeen hugs, admiring her engagement ring.

Not wanting to waste a minute, Jonas had arrived with train tickets for the two of them.

Realizing that their train was scheduled for late in the day, Ardeen let Jonas know they'd be taking a side trip to meet her family. That announcement brought laughter from the group.

"Ain't even hitched yet," came one comment, "and he's already hen-pecked."

"Woah there, Jonas," said another, "you gotcha a lively one there. She'll rule the roost."

Yet another had to add, "It's that flaming red hair. That'll do it every time."

Ardeen gave them all a hard stare. "Will you stop feeding ideas into this man's head?"

But it was all show. She knew they were all happy for her. Having traveled together for the past few months, the give-and-take kidding had at times been nonstop.

Lance made it clear to Ardeen that he was going to dearly miss one of his brightest stars. Mr. Odell made a few cursory remarks in parting, but Helena never saw him as a genuine personality. She was never able to figure that man out.

Helena was the last in line to hug, cry, and express how she was going to miss Ardeen. Of course, they'd be together at the cottage until the wedding, but both recognized that nothing would ever be the same.

"Start designing my wedding dress," Ardeen said over her shoulder as she and Jonas walked arm-in-arm toward a waiting taxi. "You know my style."

If that had been the only earth-shattering event upon arriving home, Helena might have been okay. But even before they docked, Lance had received news that his mother was gravely ill. She and Lance's father were long-time residents of New Jersey where Lance had grown up. He was the only living offspring to take care of the aging couple. This meant he would stay in Jersey and not return with them to Hollywood. It put a damper on the entire crew.

He gathered them together in his hotel suite that night to discuss future plans. Yet one more night in a hotel as their train would not leave until the next morning. Helena wasn't quite sure which she missed most, her homey little cottage in California, or the exquisite Elswick Manor where she'd spent so many utterly glorious, restful days.

"Nothing will slow down, or even create a little hiccup in the studio." Lance stood in their midst, sometimes pacing around the room, addressing each one. "Mr. Odell and I have not been entirely idle the past few weeks. We've been reading and reviewing scripts and making selections as to which will be the best followup to our epic."

A question then came up. "Will we create another epic?"

"You can count on it," Lance answered. "But not too soon. We don't want our fans expecting epics every few months. I have several in mind, and they're in the works. For now, we'll continue making audience-pleasing, high-quality motion pictures and continue to build on our solid reputation."

He went on to thank them for their commitment to the many premier showings, the endless hotel rooms, the constant interaction with the public, and how they had impressed all the right people at all the right times.

That prompted jokes about the dangers they'd experienced at the London train station. The laughter helped relieve the tension they all felt at the moment.

"I will never be out of touch," Lance went on. "Telegrams and telephones mean there will be no real distance. However, you will now be answerable to Mr. Odell. I turn you over to his capable hands."

Helena so wished Ardeen were by her side. They would be exchanging glances and probably elbowing one another. She was certain not one crew member felt any real respect toward Mr. Odell. Nor did they think his hands were *capable* hands. Ever since they first arrived in Hollywood, all those months ago, Mr. Odell had remained a nonentity. He was someone they simply put up with, never paying much attention to him at all. For his part, he'd never made any attempt to warm up to any one of them, nor to really get to know them as Lance had.

As a gifted director, Lance knew his people and knew how to bring out their best possible artistic abilities.

Helena wanted to ask the question of how long they would be without him, but of course she knew the answer. His parents needed him, and he was not about to abandon his responsibility. She knew he would stay as long as needed.

Chapter 36

Never would Helena be able to thank Jacinta enough for how she had cared for Tranquil Cottage during their absence. Jacinta sent her elder son, Cedro, to meet Helena's train—which arrived in early evening—and to drive her home. Heavenly food aromas greeted her as she walked in the door, and rainbows of cut flowers were set about in strategically-placed vases.

The table was spread for just her, and Jacinta after giving warm hugs, telling her about the pot of chili on the stove, politely left her.

Jonas and Ardeen weren't scheduled to arrive until the next day as they had taken a few side trips on their journey across the country.

Jacinta had laid Helena's dressing gown across her bed. Slippers nearby on the floor. So many small kindnesses nearly brought Helena to tears. It was her weariness that brought emotions to the surface.

After devouring the scrumptious supper, she went straight to bed. The luggage, taken to her room by Cedro, remained in the same spot until the next day. Home at long last. Back in her own bedroom. Sleep overtook her almost the moment her head hit the pillow, and she didn't awaken until nearly noon the next day.

Helena spent the ensuing days designing the wedding dress, which Ardeen insisted be quite informal.

"I want a dress that won't be packed away for a lifetime," she told Helena. "Of course, it'll be white, but designed so that color accents and highlights can be added later."

It was an easy request to fulfill.

The rest of Helena's time was spent reading the scripts that Lance had handed off to her before she left New York. He insisted she be one of the first to review and let him know her thoughts. It pleased her that he respected her opinion. He not only respected her opinion, but also respected her stance to refrain from any on-screen love scenes.

Evenings she and Ardeen spent on the patio soaking in the California atmosphere and floral fragrances, both admitting how much they'd missed it. And of course, Helena spent hours walking the beaches, watching golden-crimson sunrises, and searching for unique, pristine shells.

Off and on, Ardeen devoted days to the ranch spending time with Jonas and learning her way around. Jonas always came to fetch her in order to leave the Buick for Helena. Helena quickly realized she must learn to deal with the ensuing emptiness after the wedding. Perhaps she'd get a dog.

The wedding location, the engaged pair finally decided, would be the dining hall at the studio. That way everyone even remotely connected with the *Eleness–Odell* studios could attend. Helena agreed it would be perfect. It wasn't the most attractive building around. In fact, it was more like a vast warehouse with a raised platform at one end, the kitchen taking up the far side, and long lines of tables and chairs. Nothing glamorous.

Ardeen said she didn't care how it looked. "We'll just cover it with flowers and it'll do fine."

After much discussion, it was decided the wedding ceremony could take place at the end where the raised platform was located. The tables would be moved out of the way and chairs set up in auditorium fashion.

The reception, then, would be held in the other end of the hall, still within easy reach of the kitchen and with all the tables moved to that area.

Much of the planning landed in Helena's lap, which she minded not at all. The tasks meant a drive to the studio several times a week. Since there was no filming as yet, no new picture scheduled, she welcomed being busy.

One particular day she was in the dining hall talking with Dan, the head of the kitchen staff, comparing notes and discussing what items needed to be ordered and dates for delivery, when she saw that one of the wranglers had come in.

"Thanks Dan, for all your help," she said, scooting back her chair. "Did we cover everything?"

"Yep. I think we got everything under control. Me and Jonas go back a long way. I'm more than happy to be a part of the happy event."

Leaving him, she walked over to where the wrangler was sitting sipping a mug of coffee and munching on a donut.

"Hi Birch."

"Well looky here who's come back from the nether lands." Stretching out his calloused hand he took hers and gave a strong shake. "You still on a long vacation?"

"I'm helping with the wedding."

Pushing back his Stetson with his thumb, he said, "Oh yeah. I heard about old Jonas tying the knot. It's Ardeen. That right?"

"He's stealing away my closest friend." She pulled up a chair and sat down beside him.

He took a gulp of coffee. Shaking his head, he said, "Unforgivable. Cupid can mess up a bunch of things."

"I'm only kidding. I'm thrilled for both of them. This time cupid did a good thing."

"So, no filming happening right now. What're you doing out here today?"

She explained that the dining hall was the wedding location, and mentioned her tasks in the wedding preparations—which, she surmised correctly, would be of little interest to him. But then she went on to tell him about her time at Elswick Manor and the horses there. Most particularly about Amari, and about learning to ride English style.

"I've heard tell of those horses back there in Europe. Fine stock. And I've seen a few Arabians here. But not many. Mostly we just got our quarter horses, appaloosies, and cow ponies."

Presently, she got around to the point of wanting to talk to him. "Birch, you know all the animal trainers connected with the studio. I'm interested in finding a dog."

"Ah. Need a new companion, huh?"

She nodded with a smile. "For the time being a dog will have to do."

The comment made him laugh. "I know several in the dog business. What're you looking for? Big? Little?"

"I don't need a Saint Bernard, but I sure don't want a little lap dog either."

Nodding, he said, "I hear you. I got some ideas. Let me get back with you. Are you here every day?"

"Not every day. It just seems like every day. I'll be back on Friday."

Reaching out to shake her hand again, he said, "Okie doke, ma'am. See you Friday then."

"I'm going to get a dog," she told Ardeen that evening. They were in the upstairs sewing studio conducting another fitting session. The wedding dress, styled with a drop waist, cascading tiers of delicate lace in the skirt which was ankle-length, and covered with seed-pearls, fit Ardeen perfectly. She'd decided to opt out of wearing a veil. "Just a crown of flower blossoms," she said. And since the wedding wasn't formal, Helena agreed with that decision.

"A dog? Oh, Helena, that's a wonderful plan."

For some reason, she thought Ardeen might laugh at the idea. "You think so?"

"You should see the dogs at the ranch. Such loving companions. I've already made friends with them. I never had a dog growing up. Pets didn't fit with New York City."

"I asked Birch to make the contact for me. I trust his knowledge of animal personalities."

"He certainly knows horses."

"I saw him today when I was in the dining hall. Perfect timing."

From that point, the conversation, as usual, turned to wedding plans. By Friday, Helena had nearly forgotten about any dog. Her schedule was jam-packed from dawn till dusk.

"Golden? I never in my life heard of a golden dog."

But there she was standing peacefully beside her trainer, plumed tail waving in friendly fashion.

Helena had had in her mind, if the dog were female, she would name her Amari, because of the sweet memories of the miracle back at Elswick Manor. But when she laid eyes on this golden beauty, she knew that name would be all wrong.

She had just pulled into the gravel drive outside the dining hall and stepped out of her car. Birch was standing outside the building. He called out, "Looky here little lady, what we rounded up for you."

Walking toward them, she couldn't take her eyes off that golden dog. The trainer, whose name was Warren, stepped forward, the dog promptly following. Helena saw no leash.

"Will she come to me?"

"She already likes you," Warren said. "See that tail? See those eyes?"

"How can she know?"

It was a silly question. She thought back to how Amari nickered the moment she approached.

She knelt down and held out her hand. The golden animal came right up and nuzzled her hand. Laying her face on the dog's silky head she stroked the fur which seemed to glow in the sunshine.

"Her coat is so soft."

"That's because we just came from a special beauty shop appointment. Shampoo and trim to get ready for this special meeting."

"I never knew a dog could be so stunningly beautiful."

Warren, in his soft voice—just like an animal trainer—said, "A beautiful animal for a beautiful actress. It just seemed to fit."

"What kind of breed is this?" Helena wanted to know.

"It's called a golden retriever."

She nodded, as the dog was now pressing into her side nearly knocking her over.

Now Birch spoke up. "Sorta looks like a match made in heaven, Warren. You done good."

Helena felt suspended in an air of disbelief. "Can she be mine?"

"Do you want her?" Warren asked.

Helena felt unbidden tears welling up in her eyes that she couldn't explain. "Oh yes. I feel we're already connected. Our spirits are joined." She stood to her feet then, but the dog continued to press into her leg, making her laugh. "But with wedding just two days away, I have no time..."

"My plan, now that I see it's a fit," Warren interrupted her, "would be to bring the two of you together as soon as you get the wedding out of the way."

At that point Helena leaned down once again to stroke that golden fur.

"Whatcha gonna call her?" Birch wanted to know. "A beauty like that gotta have a good solid name."

"Glory," Helena blurted out almost without thinking. "Actually, Golden Glory, but Glory for short."

Birch nodded. "For *Glory Fields*?"

"Exactly. *Glory Fields* has been more than good to me."

"And for the whole lot of us," Birch agreed. "Made you a star. Made you a whole bunch of money."

"Correct on both counts."

"I'll have her papers when we meet again," Warren explained.

"I didn't ask her price. Shall I give you a check now?"

Warren shook his head. "Now that I know for sure it's a go, I'll see to it that no else takes her. We'll settle up next week."

Helena was reluctant to release Glory. Tilting up the dog's chin she looked her right in the eyes. "You hear that girl? You and I belong together. And your name is Golden Glory. Glory you'll be to me."

Dan had told Helena not to worry about decorating the dining hall for the wedding. "Our ladies in the kitchen are excited about taking care of that part. They all love Ardeen. And Jonas too. And what woman doesn't get all giddy for a wedding?"

Helena happily complied with Dan's *don't worry* admonition. It was her pleasure to strike that off her long to-do list as maid-of-honor, dress designer, and general flunky. But when she stepped foot into the dining hall early on the day of the wedding, she was nearly bowled over with disbelief. Never could she have imagined the place could have been so transformed. The tables were covered with white linen cloths, glass vases of multi-colored flowers on each one. Blue willow China place settings were flanked by silverware laid out on neatly folded navy-blue napkins.

Pedestaled Grecian urns, props no doubt pilfered from one of the studio sets, lined against one wall overflowed with glossy ferns and draping moss. Navy blue and crimson streamers draped from the rafters perfectly disguised the warehouse effect. On the platform stood a regal, white wrought-iron arch, surrounded with more flower-filled urns. Helena could hardly take it all in.

Cedro was slated to drive Ardeen from the cottage a few minutes prior to the time of the wedding. Helena debated whether she needed to be on site, or by Ardeen's side. But since they had her dressed early on in the day, Ardeen urged her to go and make sure all details were in order, which she did.

Helena had never before served as a maid-of-honor, nor had she even attended many weddings. But this wasn't just any wedding. This was her dearest and closest friend who would now be living a life far away from her. She was able to hold back the tears until the ceremony was over and the couple had left.

The wedding itself was flawless. Jonas, wildly handsome, decked out in his best tailored Western suit, sans his Stetson, Helena could see why Ardeen fell for him so quickly. The hall, filled with nearly anyone and everyone connected with the studio, turned into standing-room-only, the crowd which then proceeded to consume mountains of food during the reception. They'd all become one big family.

Ardeen hadn't too keen about allowing reporters on site—her wedding had become big news for the movie magazines—but she agreed to allow a few she had personally selected. She definitely didn't want to be interviewed, nor did she want photographers telling her to look here, or look there, or stand here or stand there.

This wedding, unlike others, was attended not by guests who left to go home once the newly-married couple drove away, these guests felt they were already at home. They amazed Helena by pitching in to clean up and then return the room to its normal setup. It warmed her heart when she saw several men loading the heavy urns into the back of trucks to return them to their respective prop storage areas.

By the time she felt confident everything was in tiptop shape, and was walking out to the Buick with the last armload of flowers—which the ladies in the kitchen insist she take home—she wasn't sure she had the strength to drive home.

Opening the rear door and laying the flowers on the backseat she heard her name called out. Turning around she saw Warren standing nearby. By his side stood Glory, and as before waving her plume of a tail. The dog was fairly quivering and appeared ready to burst.

"Hello there, Helena. Glory and I thought you might welcome company tonight."

Closing the car door, she leaned back against it. "Oh my. I can't believe this. I almost forgot."

"Just tell her to come."

"Glory. Here girl. Come."

The dog dashed to her. Helena knelt down and embraced her new friend.

Chapter 37

The ensuing session with Warren was, at her request, on the beach. Aside from Tranquil Cottage, it was her favorite place in the world. The expert trainer taught her how to work with Glory and how to issue the commands and what responses to expect. He told her he'd seldom seen a dog take to a new owner like Glory had taken to Helena. His words made her wonderfully happy.

"Use the leash out in public," he told her, "not because Glory will need it, but out of respect to people who distrust an unleashed dog."

Helena paid close attention to all Warren's instructions. She trusted his guidance.

Helena and Glory became inseparable. No matter where she went—to the grocer, to the studio, to the hair solon, to the filling station, and the beach—Glory went with her. The dog loved riding in the car, sitting up in the front seat like it had been her spot for all her young life. As soon as she heard Helena rattling the car keys, she was by the door flying her flag of a tail in eager anticipation.

By now, two weeks after the wedding, Helena began to wonder when Mr. Odell would call her in to talk about their next film production. In her mind, they needed to get busy. In order for a studio to maintain their position in this mushrooming industry there should never be too big a lag between pictures. Competition heated up with each passing day. Surely Mr. Odell knew that.

It was close to dark one evening when a courier arrived at her door with a package. "From the studio," he said, and was gone.

She could tell by the size and shape that it was a script. She assumed it was a reworked, edited version of one that Lance had handed off to her the day they parted in Jersey.

But it wasn't.

Sitting on her couch in the brightly-lit living room, with Glory snug by her side, she began reading. And received the shock of her life.

Picking up the telephone from the table beside her, she called Mr. Odell's number at his home.

"Odell here."

"What in the world have you given me, Mr. Odell? This is not what Lance had scheduled for our next film."

"Hello to you, too, Miss Helena. What seems to be your problem?"

"I think you know full well. This is not Lance's script, and nothing in here would meet with his approval."

Over the line, she heard Mr. Odell loudly clear his throat. "In case you've been asleep, or brain dead, my dear, your beloved Lance left us high and dry."

"That's not true. He's within reach. A quick phone call or telegram…"

"Now now. Calm yourself. We all know that Lance is going through a very trying time in his life, what with his mother so ill and his father to care for. We want to respect his time and not bother him. In fact, it's my strong recommendation that no one on salary at Eleness-Odell studios contact Lance just now."

In this heavy pause, she recognized the thinly veiled threat. *Strong recommendation?* In an attempt to quell her rising anger, she said nothing.

"Don't you remember Lance's exact words? He said he was leaving the running of the studio in my *capable hands.*"

Helena remembered all too well. And she knew in Lance's best judgement at the time, he genuinely felt he could trust his partner.

"Come to my office in the morning and we'll talk." With that, the line went dead.

It seemed clear there'd be nothing to talk about. The risqué scenes presented in the script that lay in her lap were ones Lance would never ask her to play. From the outset, he had always respected her request for no full-on screen kiss or overt love scenes. Nor would she appear in any state of undress. And all of these, and more, were in this script. It caused her to recoil at the very thought.

Stroking Glory's soft fur, she said, "What do you think girl? This doesn't bode well at all."

Glory's soft brown eyes looked up at her. She then laid her head on Helena's lap, directly over the script and gave a soft throaty whine.

"I agree."

Because Mr. Odell had been owner and director at the studio prior to Lance coming on board, he held forth with the larger office. Helena knew such petty matters never bothered Lance. Actually, he'd never spent much time in his office. Especially during days of filming.

With Glory securely on her leash, Helena walked into the central office building and took the elevator to the third floor. Betsy, the receptionist, greeted her with a welcoming smile.

The vast outer office reminded Helena of the opulence she'd seen in the many theaters she'd visited in her travels. Heavy furniture, dark floral-patterned, oriental carpets, paneling on the walls. The tall windows were covered in cascading draperies. The walls filled with framed newspaper clippings, photos of stars, glass cases lined with trophies of one sort or another. Who knew what. Before Lance came on the scene and created *Glory Fields,* the old studio was dying on the vine.

"Hello Helena," Betsy said. "I've missed seeing you around here. You're looking more beautiful than ever. Did you enjoy your overseas travels?"

Helena had barely ever been inside this particular office, so she was unsure how to answer. With a nod, she said she loved traveling out of the county.

Noticing Glory, Betsy said, "And who's this? I love dogs."

"I call her Glory."

In the short time she'd had Glory, Helena quickly learned that the dog had a keen sense of people. At Betsy's voice, which Glory knew was directed at her, the plumed tail began its friendly wagging.

"She's gorgeous. May I pet her?"

"Of course. She loves attention." Helena led Glory around the desk to allow Betsy to stroke the luxurious golden coat, and let her marvel over such beauty. At that moment, the intercom crackled. Mr. Odell's voice sounded. "Betsy, did I hear Miss Helena come in."

"You did, sir."

"Well, send her in. I'm waiting for her."

Clicking it off, Betsy gave a little smirk of a smile. Waving her hand toward the double doors, she said, "Mustn't keep boss man waiting."

As Helena stepped through the double wooden doors, Mr. Odell, all smiles, got up from his desk. In all these months, standing in the role as part owner of a famous studio, the man had never learned how to dress professionally. No matter what he wore, nothing ever seemed to fit correctly, nor did anything match.

"Ah Helena, my dear. Haven't seen you since the wedding. How are you? And how's Ardeen? Is she adjusting well to ranch life?"

Never since she'd met this man months ago had he said so many words to her at one time. She wasn't sure what to answer first. Beside her Glory emitted a soft low growl. Over his jabbering, Mr. Odell probably didn't even notice.

"Ardeen's fine. Now why am I here?"

Mr. Odell was now close enough to give Helena a little pat on the shoulder. A patronizing pat. "Always the no-nonsense Helena."

"No-nonsense is exactly what I'm requesting. And nonsense is exactly what's in this script." She pulled it from the bag that was slung on her shoulder. "Where did this come from? Not from Lance." She reached out to hand it to him, but he ignored the gesture.

"Times in the moving picture industry are changing," he said. "It's time for our studio to keep up with the changes."

"By lowering our standards? You know full well Lance's position has been to keep our movies decent."

Another low soft growl. *Thank you, Glory.*

"*Glory Fields* won countless thousands of fans all over the world," she continued. "Are you willing to throw that away?" She wanted to add the fact of her own star-status, but resisted the temptation.

Mr. Odell's feigned friendliness had drained away. He had yet to invite her to sit down. Or offer a cup of coffee. Nothing.

"Perhaps in your naiveté, Helena, you are unaware that Broadway stars are flocking to Hollywood. These are professionals in the world of entertainment, not just a few upstarts. Names that are recognized."

What Mr. Odell was getting at, she wasn't sure. Was he insinuating she was an upstart? At what point she'd stopped counting the number of films she'd starred in, she couldn't say. Early on, it added up to several pictures each and every week for months on end. Did that make her an upstart? Her photos in magazines, glowing reviews worldwide, and reporters dogging her heels. Did that make her an upstart?

"What I need from you now, Helena," he said, "is a true showing of loyalty, and a higher level of professionalism."

That's not what she saw in the script he'd delivered to her. She countered his remark with a shake of her head. "No Mr. Odell. What you want is a showing of leg and a lower level of morality."

His voice growing cold, he said, "You are an impudent young lady, and full of self-importance." Stepping away from her, he waved to another set of double doors and said, "Let's retire to the conference room. There's someone I want you to meet."

He pushed open the door and held it for her. There sitting on the edge of a settee, with her legs crossed, her skirt hiked, and a cigarette stuck in a silver holder was Cat Callahan—more strikingly gorgeous than Helena ever remembered her.

"Well, if it isn't the backwoods seamstress girl. Our own little Helen. How are you, my dear?"

The demeaning tone raised Helena's ire almost to the boiling point. Glory agreed with a throaty growl.

"Oh, that's right. I nearly forgot. You two know one another," came Mr. Odell's fake innocent remark. It was obvious he was lying. Of course, he knew of their history.

It took only a few seconds for Helena to size up the situation. Since she would not acquiesce to Mr. Odell's demands, he would bring in someone who would.

Mr. Odell was talking faster now, in an evident attempt to fill the awkward silence. "We feel it's time for the moving picture industry to rise up to higher professional standards. Hence, we are looking to bring in experienced stars."

Helena turned to look Mr. Odell straight in the eye. "What you seem to be looking for, sir, is not higher professional standards, but lower moral standards. Isn't that right?"

Unable to hold her gaze, he stepped over to the conference table and opened a gold box drew out a cigarette and lit it with the matching lighter.

"I've tried to explain to you before, Helena, the industry is changing, and we must keep up with the times."

She wondered who he referred to when he said *we.*

"I've never heard this outlook from Lance. Is he not part owner?"

As before, Lance's name seemed to spark his visible anger. "You keep forgetting. Lance Sedgley is not here. I'm running the studio."

"As the one who's running the studio are you giving me the freedom to say no to the scenes in that script?"

"Well of course you can say no. And you can also be cast in the many supporting roles we have available in all our films."

To be demoted from a main star to a supporting role? The audacity of this man.

Now Cat stood to her feet. She was taller than Helena remembered. In a dramatic wave of her hand, a gesture fit for center stage, she said, "Oh little Helen. You always were such a rube. You were always good for a few laughs at Belasco."

"Oh really? Is that why Mr. Cranston came to me with an apology and told me how you double-crossed him, leaving the show high and dry? He didn't seem to view that as humorous."

Now Mr. Odell broke in with surprise in his voice. "High and dry? A famous Broadway director? Did you do that?"

Cat acted as though she hadn't heard a word. With an hollow laugh, she said, "You never learn do you, little Helen? One must do what one must do to make it in this world. We can't just roll over and play dead like you do."

If the great Cat Callahan thought the moniker of *little Helen* bothered Helena, she couldn't have been more mistaken. Actually, it revealed the insecurity of the so-called Broadway star.

Glory was clearly rankled. Helena reached down and touched the dog's head to calm her. "Okay, girl. It's okay."

Seemingly recovered from the shock of learning more about his Broadway star, Mr. Odell blew a cloud of blue smoke into the air and said, "You don't have to decide this minute, Helena. But I will say Cat is simply wild about the script and is ready to jump into rehearsals this week."

Joining her cloud of smoke with his, Cat added, "Or tomorrow. I'm that eager to get started."

Helena had witnessed many other Broadway actors make an attempt to adjust to moving picture cameras, and she was well aware of their intense frustrations. Being surrounded by cameras was nothing like being on stage. It could be that Cat was jumping right into disaster. But no matter. At this point Helena felt no need to grovel.

In the past few weeks, talking to God had returned to her life in a big way. Which no doubt accounted for the comforting presence she experienced now, in spite of the seriousness of this situation.

The bound script was still in her hand. Stepping over to the table, she threw it down causing it to slide a few feet on the polished surface.

Turning toward the door, she said, "Have fun together you two. I must say, you're a perfect match."

As she opened the door, Glory's growl, louder now, exposed bared teeth.

"You're right, Glory. I agree wholeheartedly."

Chapter 38

J acinta pushed the stack of accounting books to the center of the table, took the top one, placed it in front of Helena, and opened to the current month.

Nothing had surprised Helena more than learning that her cook and housekeeper had a penchant for numbers. Numbers—as in bookkeeping.

Finding a new housekeeper took no time at all, which meant Jacinta was free to step into her role as office manager and bookkeeper at the shop.

Pointing to the entries, Jacinta explained how each new moving-picture premier had caused a surge in business. Helena already knew this, of course, but she loved going over the figures which equated to a successful venture.

Once the stars got wind of *Helena's Custom Designs,* the shop became a central gathering place whenever the need for a new gown presented itself.

Throughout her film career, she and Ardeen were often quizzed about their unique evening gowns. Reporters wanted to know what boutique they used. Was it in Chicago? New York? Paris?

They managed to keep it private between the two of them. Now the secret had been released. All of Hollywood knew Helena Heise had been the creator of the exclusive gowns.

The stars raved about how Helena seemed to have a sixth sense as to how to design creations reflecting the personality of each individual. Each could be guaranteed there'd never be a replica of their outfit on premier night.

Helena's Custom Designs housed not only the shop proper, but a large store-room lined with shelves holding bolts of every type of cloth, a workroom (where several employees spent hours at the cutting tables), the dress forms and sewing machines, several private fitting rooms, and then Helena's office where Jacinta held court as to who was and was not allowed to come in and see the owner.

"You're too busy to waste time on just anyone who walks in that door," Jacinta would say.

"Now I have two guards—you and Glory," Helena said, petting Glory's silky head.

Glory did have an amazing accuracy in her judge of character. It was evident who she accepted by her frantic tail-wagging, tongue lolling, and open approach. Then there were a few who never earned this greeting. For those particular individuals, Glory simply stayed on her cushion in the corner of the shop, her head on her paws peeking out with great suspicion.

Lillian Gish was a special favorite, who was due to come for a fitting that evening. It was getting late and the workroom girls were gone for the day.

Closing the accounting books and returning them to the file cabinet and locking it, Helena told Jacinta to go on home.

"You need time with your family. You've done enough today." Shooing her hand at Jacinta, she added, "Now get on out of here. It's only Lillian and she's never a bother. And she's not due for another half hour or so."

"She is one of the easier ones," Jacinta said. Leaning down to take Glory's face in her hand, she added, "I'm leaving now, Glory. You keep watch over our girl here."

After hearing the front door close, Helena stepped into the workroom where Lillian's pink lace-and-chiffon gown graced one of the dress forms. Helena felt it was one of her finest creations so far. Slowly, she stepped around the form checking the dress over from top to bottom, making her final inspection.

Just then, the front door opened and closed. Glory jumped up and almost went wild with joy.

"Well, I know you like Lillian, but my goodness. Not that much. Come on let's show her your welcome. Lillian? You're early," she called out.

She stepped out of the workroom and into the shop and stopped cold. It couldn't be. This was impossible. But there he stood right inside her shop, as real as life.

"I'm not Lillian, but your dog seems to like me anyway."

Glory was beside herself with joy. The whole tail-wagging, tongue-lolling, turning-in-circles performance, and even licking Brett's free hand. The one that wasn't holding a very large bouquet of lilacs. In all her time with Glory, Helena had never seen her display such an open show of emotion.

"She's a great judge of character." Her voice was barely a whisper. Then, "How did you find me?"

"Believe me when I say, it was not an easy task. I'd almost given up."

"You've been trying?" Her mind struggled to take this in.

She couldn't stop staring at him with a silent joy. He looked great. More handsome than she'd ever remembered. Even that night when she saw him at Bolewood Manor. Stepping across the room toward her, he held out the lilacs. "In honor of our lilac hideaway."

Hot tears burned her eyes as she accepted the bouquet and inhaled the sweet fragrance. "Thank you so much. They'll always be my favorite flower."

Glory had quieted, but remained resolutely at Brett's side.

"After England, there were no more pictures with you as the star," he said. "I assumed you decided to stay there. With the uniformed officer."

"That was Lieutenant Rendel Waley-Talbot. He came through the war as well."

Brett paused for a moment. "I saw the look in his eyes when he approached you. He was quite smitten."

"Yes, I think he was. But that same look was not in my eyes. He was very kind, and he did want me to stay, but I declined." She gave a light laugh. "As you can see."

Glancing around the shop, he said, "This is such a reflection of you, Helen. Of who you are. Creative. Talented. Caring. With close attention to detail."

The phone on the counter gave its shrill ring, breaking the spell. Still holding the bouquet, Helena hurried to answer. It was Lillian on the line. She needed to change her fitting to another day. Such interesting timing.

Hanging the receiver on the hook, she said, "I have a vase in the workroom. I'll be right back."

As she located the large vase on a shelf, it gave her a moment to pull her emotions into check. She took a hanky from her pocket to press against her eyes to stop the threatening tears. Surely, her heart was going to burst. Taking her time, she filled vase at the sink and arranged the lilacs. As she did so, she once again inhaled the nostalgic aroma that never failed to whisk her back to those long-ago days... But why was he here? And why had he been looking for her? Curiosity? Just a social call to remember old times? A simple connection recalling their young fling? Conflicting thoughts swirled in her head.

Back in the shop, she found that Brett had made himself comfortable in one of the overstuffed chairs. Glory had planted her head on his knee.

She placed the vase right in the middle of the front counter, thanking him once again for his thoughtfulness.

In a few minutes, Helena was sure she'd wake up and this would all have been a dream.

Gently pushing Glory's head from his knee, he stood up. "Can we talk? Is there someplace...?"

"Do you like the beach?"

"I love the beach."

"Let me lock up and we'll go."

With their shoes and socks in hand, and Glory running wildly ahead, they strolled in the purple twilight along the wet sand. A pleasant breeze blew in just enough to ruffle their hair.

Helena's belief system still had not fully come alive. That Brett was now by her side seemed dreamlike.

"I have to ask you, Helen," Brett said as they walked. "Is there anyone in your life now? A special someone?"

Now she was beginning to feel a bit giddy. With laughter in her voice, she said, "Only Glory." Then waving her hand to indicate her shop, she added, "Oh and my fashion-design business. I seem to be quite married to it."

She thought he might react to this news, but instead he began to make a confession.

"The stupidest mistake of my life," he was saying, "was when I asked you to return to Chancey's Bend to live. Even back then I knew that small town could never contain all that you were destined to do. And to be."

Contenting herself to listen to his thoughts and feelings, she offered no comment.

"The second stupidest mistake was thinking I had any calling to be a pastor. I guess it was the desperation born of escaping the war with my life intact. That, plus thinking that being a preacher was the only way to serve God."

He stopped and looked at her. "Helen. Helena—I need to get used to your new name. I can't begin to tell you what a clunk I was in that pulpit."

He laughed and the sound of it warmed her heart.

"Not too good?"

"I had no more talent to write a sermon than a two-year-old." Laughing again, he added, "And the delivery was worse. If anything could have been worse."

"And the turning point?" She thought about his appearance with Evangelist Buchanan in the Bronx.

"It was when Ian Buchanan came to Chancey's Bend for a revival. When he heard me play, he took me aside after the service and told me I was missing my calling."

"Did you agree?"

"Not at first. Everyone in town knew I was a lousy preacher, but they were quite forgiving. Just being polite I suppose. I kept telling myself I'd get better with time."

Wooden stairs that descended from the street above down to the beach appeared ahead of them. As he guided her toward them, they sat down beside one another on the steps.

When Glory realized they were no longer following her, she raced back and lay down at Brett's feet. Her paws were dripping from running through the shallow waves.

"Once I had time to digest his words, and accept the truth that I was missing my calling, I agreed to travel and serve with him in his crusades."

"I saw you."

He turned to look at her, puzzled. "You saw me? Where?"

"The Coliseum in the Bronx."

"You were there." He was quiet for a moment.

"Sort of there. When I saw it was you, I stayed out in the lobby."

Making a stab at humor, he quipped, "My playing was that bad?"

"You were in New York and didn't try to find me. I was hurt I guess."

"But my letters... I tried to apologize. To explain my crazy mistake. When no replies came, the silence let me know you were traveling a different path."

"My turn to apologize, Brett. Not only did you ask me to return home, my family made it clear they saw it as my bound duty to do so." Taking up a handful of sand, she let it trickle from her fingers. "I couldn't bear their judging me, so I stopped reading the letters. I knew that was wrong, and I was filled with guilt. Your letters that explained your change of mind were never even opened." Shaking her head, she added, "I know it was wrong."

"Wrong? Perhaps. But definitely understandable."

"Even when I was all alone out on the streets of New York on a freezing, snowy night with nowhere to go, it was suggested to me that I contact my family and go home. I could not. I knew deep in my heart that that was not the direction I should take."

"You continue to amaze me, Helena." She realized he was trying out the new name, getting used to it. "But one thing I don't understand. I never knew you wanted to star in moving pictures."

"Oh, I never did." She brightened as her thoughts turned away from the awful memory of that winter night in New York. "I never sought it out. The whole thing found me. That I was good at it was the biggest surprise of all."

Briefly, she told about working in the sewing factory and how Ardeen convinced her to try out the *flickers*. About Lance and the studio in Jersey, and the subsequent move to Hollywood. Of course, he then wanted to know why she quit, adding that she was not only a great actress, but beloved by all her fans.

She explained about Lance having to stay back east and Mr. Odell taking the reins and how quality and excellence were being sacrificed for turning out quick lackluster films.

"When I refused to compromise my morals, I was shown the door, so to speak. I could have stayed and played bit parts, but I found that to be an insult."

She left out the part about Cat Callahan. That particular incident was still too raw.

Standing up and shaking sand from her skirt, she changed the subject and asked, "Would you like to see my cottage?"

"Very much."

The abundance of flowers surrounding her patio filled the night air with sweet fragrances. As they sat in her upholstered patio chairs sipping coffee, she said, "You seem to know more about me than I do about you. Where have you been,

Brett—besides Bolewood Manor in England—and what's God doing in your life?"

Feigning being insulted he said, "I'm crushed. You've not heard my radio programs, or bought and played my gramophone records?"

"You're joking me, aren't you?"

"I'm not. It's evident that California has been good to both of us. I live in Los Angeles, just a few miles from here."

Helena felt she couldn't breathe. He'd been here. All this time. So close.

"I've recorded two records now and they're selling well. My agent believes the American public wants to hear on their gramophones what they would hear in a concert hall. It's a whole new frontier."

"Classical? Hymns? Jazz?"

"Mainly classical since so many households, especially the children, rarely have the opportunity to hear classical compositions." After taking a sip of coffee, he added softly, "And a few original compositions."

"Original? Whose?"

Even in the dim glow of a few outside lights she saw his face light up as he answered, "Mine."

Original compositions. Brett Lochlann had become a composer. Before she could comment on this startling revelation, he said, "I was somewhat joking about the radio program, because it's still on paper. We're signing contracts in a few days."

"We?" It was the first time he'd used that plural pronoun. She waited.

"My agent, Vernon Barrett. Vern is a master at negotiations."

She could only hope he hadn't detected her sigh of relief.

"The program may involve several orchestras. Hopefully offering variety for our listeners. Plus, we have a sponsor."

"A sponsor. Would it be soap?"

He laughed. "I know. They seem to be the ones at the front of the line, aren't they. No, actually it's toothpaste."

"A sort of a soap. For the teeth."

Now they were both laughing. But Helena felt a bit overwhelmed at Brett's successes.

They were still talking and it was nearing midnight. So much to catch up on. As Brett rose to excuse himself, Helena felt a pang. She didn't want him to leave. And she still had no idea why he was sitting here on her patio, chatting and drinking coffee.

"I'm sorry to have kept you up so late. I really need to go. I have early morning meetings with our potential sponsors, and more contracts to sign. And I'm sure you have much to do in your shop."

Glory got up from her spot by Brett's feet, stretched and gave a throaty whine. She didn't want him to leave either.

They walked back through the cottage where Brett retrieved his hat. As she opened the front door to let him out, he turned to her, reached out and took her hand but said nothing.

She could stand it no longer.

"Brett, why are you here? Why were you looking for me?"

Now he threw back his head and let out a hearty laugh. "Well, silly me. I guess I was trying to give you a quick course on mindreading. I haven't made it clear, have I?"

She shook her head, fearful if she spoke the unbidden tears would flow.

Placing his hat back down on the entryway table, he took both her hands.

"I can learn to use your present name of Helena, but my darling, I can never learn to live without you. I will never be complete until you agree to be by my side. For the rest of our lives. I want you for my wife."

At that, he enfolded her in his arms and held her tight. Like the day when he left on the train to go to war—all those years ago—the same emotions arose within her.

Lifting her chin, and looking into her eyes, he said, "I've prayed that God would allow me to find you, and prayed that it wouldn't be too late." Then he added, "We've both made mistakes, Helena. But not fatal ones. You forgive me for mistakenly asking you to be a small-town preacher's wife. And I forgive you for not reading the letters. Can we start all over again?"

Now the tears came. She could only nod. And sniff.

Suddenly, Glory was there pushing against them, demanding attention.

"Glory says yes," Helena managed to say. "And I do too."

And their declarations were sealed with a soft kiss.

Vernon Barrett's reaction to the news that his client was planning to marry was quite humorous.

"Not only do you fail to inform me you have a secret sweetheart, you shock me down to my shoes to learn it's the most famous fashion designer in the country."

Brett had invited her to meet Vern in his Los Angeles office. "You two will have to connect," he had told her.

She'd offered to meet him at Vern's office since he was already in the city, but he politely refused.

"I will come and fetch you. Now that I have you back, I don't want to let another moment slip by without you by my side."

She had to make sure Brett was agreeable to have dog paws on the upholstery of his cream-colored roadster. He assured her that he'd even let Glory drive if that's what the situation required.

Glory's initial reaction to his entrance in the shop had become a much-repeated subject of conversation. Helena continually assured Brett that Glory had never displayed such immediate open affection. Even to her. And he'd thanked Glory many times for the vote of confidence.

Vern's low-key, modest office located in a high-rise on Wilshire indicated his success, but also his modesty. His list of clientele would impress anyone who knew anyone in Southern California. Helena liked him immediately. He had Glory's vote as well.

"I wasn't keeping Helena a secret," Brett said in defense. "I had to track her down and make sure she was still mine."

Vern's brightly-colored bow tie and matching suspenders reminded her of Coop. They were sitting in his office, the walls of which were plastered with photographs of his successful clients. Brett and Helena had accepted his offer of coffee, but after one taste wished they hadn't. It was pretty awful.

He worked with only one stenographer, which meant he did all the legwork solo, which Helena found impressive. She didn't know all that much about agents, but knew their days were filled with making contacts—finding clients, then promoting those clients to make a buck.

He suggested lunch at a nearby restaurant which meant they could leave behind the mugs of half-drunk coffee. Brett caught her eye and winked.

Over lunch Vern was quite candid with them. Now that he knew their wedding plans were in the works, he offered a few suggestions.

"I'm an agent, not a nursemaid." He was speaking directly to Helena which surprised her. "Meaning I don't try to run Brett's life, but I have to tell you that I see a powerful opportunity here."

She looked at Brett. He shrugged. This seemed to be news to him.

"Let me be clear. You don't have to do anything I suggest. If you say no, everything will proceed the same as before."

Brett appeared to be getting a bit flustered. "Vern, for heaven's sake. Will you get to the point."

"Sure. Sure. Just want everything to be clear." He was busy cutting into his steak. "I think we have a colossal event here. A concert-pianist, radio-star weds the most famous fashion designer in Southern California, who just so happened to have had a starring role in the epic film, *Glory Fields.* The press will eat it up. And it could give the both of you a big boost."

"I'm not sure we want to make our wedding into a newsreel feature." This from Brett.

Helena was quiet. She wasn't sure. For the past several months, she'd enjoyed the time away from all the flair and attention. But Vern was right. Not for herself so much as for Brett. He was still on the cusp of his career.

"Would you handle most of the details?" Helena wanted to know.

She and Brett had already decided on the church in Hollywood where she'd been attending, as their venue.

She could feel Brett looking at her. Probably wondering if she'd lost her mind. "When do you need our answer?" she asked Vern.

"Oh, yesterday would be fine." Taking another bite of steak and talking around a mouthful, he said, "Seriously, this would require some insightful crafting. Meaning I need time. Get it?"

"Brett and I will need to talk, and think, and pray."

Vern gave a little laugh. "I don't have many praying clients, Miss Heise. But that sounds perfectly agreeable to me."

"The past few years has presented me with a college degree in dealing with reporters and the news," Helena explained as they were driving back to Hollywood. "They can be friendly one moment, and ravenous wolves the next."

She was sitting closely snuggled against Brett's side. It was obvious he was listening.

She continued. "Vern has probably had the same education. And he knows the game. He's right, you know. About us. Like it or not, we're in the limelight."

"You maybe," he replied. "But not me."

"Not now perhaps. But once you become a radio personality, it will happen."

"I just want to share music. With everyone. I'm not looking to be some kind of celebrity."

"I wasn't either. Even now. But when God promotes, we embrace it. Lance believed that wholeheartedly. He constantly admonished his crew to present ourselves as God's Ambassadors."

He looked over at her. "I knew I needed you in my life. For many reasons. Thank you for the explanation. I'd never thought of my calling in that light."

"But you knew it was a calling. It had to have been a thrill to fill a coliseum with melodious praises to the Lord, and then see hundreds of souls being saved. You were certainly in the spotlight at that moment."

And it was settled. The wedding was scheduled. Vern wrote up press releases and the press had a heyday. And as fate would have it—or as God designed it, because they neither one believed in fate—Brett's debut radio show aired the very week before the wedding.

Helena was now making weekly telephone calls to her family. At the same time every Friday night, they were all gathered around so Helena could speak to each one. On this day, she called to give them the time and station in order for them to listen to Brett's radio program.

She and her mother had both asked for, and extended, forgiveness to one another, much as she and Brett had done. Forgiveness and forgiving surely had to be the most healing of experiences.

Helena invited Jonas and Ardeen to come to Tranquil Cottage to spend the evening so they could all listen together. They had yet to meet Brett, but of course Helena had written letter after letter sharing all the wonderful details.

"A few things make more sense now that I know the details," Ardeen was saying as they settled in the living room close by the Carlson radio. "Your leaving the service at the coliseum pretending to be sick. The incident with the lilacs during the filming." She stopped for a minute as she remembered. "I'd never seen Lance get so upset with you."

"Well, I did ruin the scene."

"And never wanting to go home, even for a visit."

Helena grimaced. "Please. Don't remind me."

"Well, dear friend, in spite of it all, you can be thankful that your Brett never gave up trying to find you."

"Beyond thankful."

They'd all heard the story of Glory's amazing reaction the moment the door opened and Brett entered. "It'll be the story you'll tell your children one day," Ardeen said.

At that moment, Helena jumped up and knelt in front of the radio. "That's his theme song." Turning the knobs, she brought the station in a bit clearer and turned up the volume.

After the announcer stated that this was the "Brett Lochlann Show brought to you by Minty-Paste toothpaste..."

"A high-paying sponsor," she said as she returned to the couch.

Then came Brett's voice over the airwaves. Helena felt she was near to bursting. This was her love. Her husband-to-be.

At that moment, Glory came bounding in from the kitchen looking everywhere for Brett, which set them all to laughing.

"Come here, girl," Helena said patting the couch. "You can listen from here."

Hello everyone and welcome to the debut of the Brett Lochlann Show where we plan to offer beautiful music to bring joy to your heart, and peace and rest to your soul.

After a few more comments, he began to play Brahms' piano concerto #2.

"I hear orchestra accompanying," Ardeen said. "He has an orchestra in the studio?"

Helena nodded and with unconcealed pride answered, "That he does."

With each selection, Brett told a few facts about the composer which made it almost like an ongoing lesson in classical music. Only Helena knew the countless hours he'd spent planning the program and rehearsing every segment.

The half hour was drawing to a close, when they heard Brett saying:

My final selection for the very first Brett Lochlann Show was composed by a lesser known composer. Which just happens to be yours truly. This is a special work that is near and dear to my heart. It's been years in the making.

I am dedicating it to someone many of you know as the celebrated fashion designer, Helena Heise. But to me, she is the love of my life, and my bride-to-be.

As Brett was speaking, listeners could hear him softly playing a haunting melody as the background to his words. Violins joined in.

The reason this music is so very special is because at first, I was composing it out of heartache. I thought I had lost my love. Now, after a few revisions, it has become my sonnet of pure joy and thanksgiving. God, in His infinite mercy, led me to her.

The sound of Helena's sobs filled the living room. Ardeen moved to sit beside her, put her arm around her friend, and handed her a handkerchief.

"Years," came Helena's voice muffled through the handkerchief. "He's been writing a song for me for years."

But Brett wasn't finished. Now as he played, he began reciting:

In the dooryard fronting an old farm-house near the white-wash'd palings,
Stands the lilac-bush tall-growing with heart-shaped leaves of rich green,
With many a pointed blossom rising delicate, with the perfume strong I love...

At each break, each pause, the powerful music rose in crescendo. It wasn't that Brett had put Walt Whitman's poem to music, he simply created a brilliant canvas accompaniment on which to paint the melodic words.

With every leaf a miracle—and from this bush in the dooryard,
With delicate-color'd blossoms and heart-shaped leaves of rich green,
A sprig with its flower I break.

At the most poignant intervals, the entire orchestra lent their voices to fill the entire atmosphere. Had Brett been performing in a vast concert hall, Helena was certain there would have been a standing ovation. But now after the harmonies of the finale faded away, and only a few soft trills on the keyboard could be heard, Brett was thanking his audience for tuning in. Then almost as an afterthought he said,

Oh, before I sign off, I bet all of you out there are wondering about the name of that piece that I and the orchestra just performed. It will be featured on my newest gramophone record album. You'll need to know what to look for.

I call it Time of Our Lilac Love.

Epilogue

A s the lights dimmed, the curtains flew open, and the opening credits lit up on the screen, Helena smiled to herself as she saw the logo for *Eleness Studios* at the top of the screen. When the title, *Kindred Spirits of Glengarry* showed, the audience gave instant applause. The film had been a hit since the Hollywood premier two weeks earlier. She'd not watched the film the night of the premier as she was too busy fitting out the stars in their unique *Helena Heise Custom Designs* gowns.

She was proud of her former film director who'd taught her so much during her days as a starlet. But she was even more proud of the pianist who'd been commissioned by Lance Sedgley to compose the film's accompanying theme music. Sitting close to the front, in the second row, she was so enchanted watching her husband, she could scarcely watch the film.

Moving around a bit to find a comfortable spot as the little one abiding within her tummy had decided it was time to get active. Or perhaps he (or she) knew that his famous father was at the keyboard playing the powerful theme music.

It had taken many months of courtroom battles for Lance to win his lawsuit against Kenley Odell for breach of contract. But win he did.

While still in Jersey, Lance was shocked to see the two films bearing the moniker of *Eleness–Odell*. Even his anger-filled telephone calls, telegrams, and letters could not get the attention of Mr. Odell who was having the time of his life being in control of the entire studio.

It wasn't until the passing of both of his parents that Lance could return to Hollywood and begin legal action to remove his name, and claim his share of the business. So many details were wrapped up in their joint venture, it took a whiz of an attorney to not only sort it all out, but make sure Lance walked away with what was legally his. Which in the end wasn't all that much.

He did finally win the case, and *Eleness Studio* started again from the ground up. Lance's reputation saved the day as many of his former staff and crew quickly departed Odell and flocked to *Eleness*.

Lance had no trouble finding land to purchase for his studio in the hills outside Hollywood, but for a time he was forced to rent studio back lots from the more established entities. He was armed with the scripts he'd shown his players when they parted company following their return from Britain. They were scripts that Helena had loved.

Within a year of Odell working once again in his solo position, his studio began hemorrhaging money. As Lance put it, "No good can come from a lack of integrity."

When the day of the foreclosure auction arrived, many studio executives were on hand to scoop up the bargains that Odell left behind.

When asked why he wasn't at the front of the line, Lance was quoted as saying he had no desire to cash in on the misfortune of another. That statement reminded Helena why she held Lance in such high regard. She knew he was destined for greatness.

On another note—and it wasn't as though Helena were watching or keeping tabs—the name of Cat Callahan, after starring in two poorly received films, faded into oblivion.

To Helena's everlasting delight, her highly-talented husband, his clever and successful agent, Vern, and Helena's beloved director, Lance—who had believed in her and taught her so much—all became fast friends, as well as business associates. The threesome became a force to be reckoned with in Hollywood.

Lance desperately needed a seasoned agent to begin building his crew, and Vern jumped at the opportunity. Meanwhile, Vern was crafting Brett's career with great precision—such as their *lilac wedding* as the news people came to call it. (Yes, the church overflowed with lilacs, so much so, the entire place smelled of the extravagant aroma.) The public loved it.

What made a very good situation even better is when Lance commissioned Brett to compose theme music for his films. Those scores traveled with the films, all bearing the name of the composer, Brett Lochlann.

Helena knew the story line of this particular film because she'd been one of the first ones to read the script. But the moment she became engrossed in the action, the baby started moving again and she had to keep twisting a bit in her seat to get comfortable.

Seth, sitting beside her looked over at her. Probably wondering why his sister couldn't sit still.

"Baby keeps moving," she whispered. To which he smiled and nodded.

When her family had traveled to Hollywood for her wedding, Seth fell in love with the place and asked to stay. He now lived in the apartment above the garage next to their two-story home. (They had decided early on to forego the mansion-mania which seemed to affect every star in the area. They settled for simplicity.)

Seth worked for Lance doing whatever Lance told him to do. Her brother had made it clear at the outset that he wanted no favors just because of being related to Helena Heise-Lochlann. He wanted to learn all about filmmaking. Lance took him at his word and kept the boy busy.

When *The End* finally appeared on the screen and the lights came up in the theater, someone called out, "*Lilac Love. Play Lilac Love.*"

These were Hollywood folk and they all knew Brett. Others in the crowd quickly picked up the chant.

Brett turned around from where he sat at the piano, caught her eye and smiled. It was their story. It was their music, but they shared it with the world. He stood up, gave a bow and sat back down. As he began playing the captivating, haunting melody that had taken the world by storm, applause exploded.

Time of Our Lilac Love was now the theme song for the *Brett Lochlann Show* and remained so for many years. It eventually became known as Brett's signature song.

But for Helena, *Time of Our Lilac Love* would be her very own theme song for the rest of her life.

Norma Jean Lutz Bio

Norma Jean Lutz's writing career began professionally in 1977 when she enrolled in a writing correspondence course. Since then, she has had over 250 short stories and articles published in both secular and Christian publications. The full-time writer is also the author of over 50 published books under her own name and many ghostwritten books. Her books have been favorably reviewed in *Affair de Coeur, Coffee Time Romance, Romance Reader at Heart, and The Romance Studio* magazines, and her short fiction has garnered a number of first prizes in local writing contests.

Norma Jean is the founder of the Professionalism In Writing School, which was held annually in Tulsa for fourteen years. This writers' conference, which closed its doors in 1996, gave many writers their start in the publishing world.

A gifted teacher, Norma Jean has taught a variety of writing courses at local colleges and community schools, and is a frequent speaker at writers' seminars around the country. For eight years, she taught on staff for the Institute of Children's Literature. She has served as artist-in-residence at grade schools, and for two years taught a staff development workshop for language arts teachers in schools in Northeastern Oklahoma.

This is your invitation to become a VIP Reader of the **_Norma Jean's Notations_** newsletter. Lots of fun stuff about books, reading, stories, libraries, and of course, insights into my releases and re-releases. (Lots of freebies and perks as well!) Come join the fun.

https://norma-jean-lutz.kit.com/7473d1145b

Also by

Other Titles by Norma Jean Lutz

Titles Featured HERE https://njnotations.shopify.com
The Tulsa Series
#1 Tulsa Tempest (Christian historical romance)

#2 Tulsa Turning (Christian historical romance)

#3 Tulsa Trespass (Christian historical romance)

#4 Return to Tulsa (Christian historical romance)
The Tulsa Series Sequel
Red Fork Roots
The Norma Jean Lutz Classic Collection
Flower in the Hills (a sweet teen romance)

Tiger Beetle at Kendallwood (a sweet teen romance)

Rockin' into Romance (a sweet teen romance)

Oklahoma Exile (a sweet teen romance)

Forever is Over (a pre-teen novel about friendship)

Lingering Dreams (a sweet teen romance)

Teen Coming-of-Age Action Adventure Novels

Brought To You By The Color Drab

A Noble Cause: An Honorable Man Will Uphold a Noble Cause

20th Century Inspirational Historical Romance

Cater to a Whim

The Winning Heart

Fields of Sweet Content

REVIEWS

If you love any (or all) of my titles, please take a minute and leave a review. Reviews can be shared on Amazon or GoodReads. Authors were not the inventors of "algorithms" but we have to live with them. And reviews help to bring higher rankings on these sites. Thank you SO much! I appreciate all my readers!

www.ingramcontent.com/pod-product-compliance
Lightning Source LLC
Chambersburg PA
CBHW070650180626
46817CB00006B/2303